I0831974

SWISCOCK

SWISCOCK

L. GRAYSON
J. YOBER

Leviathan Grayson & Josey Yober
2020

This is a work of fiction. Names, characters, places, and incidents are either the product of the authors' imaginations or are used fictitiously. Any resemblance to actual characters, living or dead, events, or locales, is entirely coincidental.

Second hardback edition published Winter 2020
ISBN 978-0-578-52549-5

Published by Leviathan Grayson & Josey Yober
fb.me/swiscock

je suis mon propre pére

contents

ABOUT THE AUTHORS

Leviathan Grayson – (1972 - present)

Once upon a time in Virginia, U.S.A.: a small baby boy, wrapped in layers of an old Norwegian wool, was left to die. The boy, no more than two years of age, cried out into the starless night like a frightened wolf pup, defying the hoards of nocturnal creatures that surely descended upon him. Unfortunately for the predators, however, these woods belonged to Man.

To put it more accurately, they belonged to one woman– the world -renowned pastel caricature artist, Lilian Grayson. It was common knowledge to the public that she, by night, stalked the quiet leafy mountainscape of her own backyard in search of beauty. Finding instead the boy, she took him in and then took to him, finally giving him the name Leviathan after her own late father.

Young Leviathan Grayson crashed into his youth with a head full of steam and an affection for the written word. The day he learned to draw letters with a pencil he was already penning stories. He kept a journal of his adventures with his friends, and he embellished their journeys across the quiet countryside with his quiet style of whimsy and wonder. He wrote every day. The boy, then the man, never was without his journal. His writing became crafted, vivid, electrifying, and then sombre– suddenly his words were leaping up from the page with the ugly spasms of nihilism. The boy headed off to the university, wondering if it was there he would confront the newfound darkness in his soul.

Leviathan fell into dangerous cycles of binge-writing and binge-drinking. Life was an unhealthy series of gushing ecstasies to sullen depressions. Each time he returned to his home from the university, his childhood friends recognized him less and less. His hair was thinning and the skin on his face had become cracked. His eyes, once bright and pure with certainty, now seemed to look everywhere and nowhere at once, like he had gone blind within the cage of his own skull. His stories, even, had lost their lustre. To Lilian Grayson, the sharp decline of Levi's grades was the final straw. She recommended he make a change– and not to bother coming back home until he did.

Levi's memories of his own abandonment as a child came back to haunt him and he was heartbroken, though he understood this time was different; his adoptive mother had given him an ultimatum, not given him up. He left his friends and left his formal studies incomplete and headed across the Atlantic, promising her he would find what he needed so that he could come back home.

Thus the sandaled feet of the lone traveler struck across the continents of Africa and then Europe. Levi found he could apply his knack for writing to the forgery of expensive documents, and he found he was very good at it. For seven years nigh, he ate expensive foods, drank expensive bourbon, and slept with expensive women, yet he hadn't written a single sentence that was truly worth a damn. The hundred-so empty pages and half-hearted chicken-scratch on his journal taunted him so much that he tossed the thing into a creek. It was then, to his surprise, that his consciousness began to ease.

One bright fall morning as he was passing through a French meadow, he discovered a solitary car that had wrecked on a gravel road. The hood of the car had crumpled in the effect of what had had to have been a head-on collision with another vehicle. He looked around. Where was this other vehicle? Where were all the occupants of the crash? Grayson, against his better judgement, peered into the car's interior and found what appeared to be a manuscript for a novel, sitting plainly in the open glove box.

As he flipped through the pages, day turned into night. Without realizing it he was suddenly reading the manuscript by lamplight. Then it became day again and he put the lamp away. Then it became night and he brought the lamp back out. He'd become captive to the story in his hands. Love, lust, pain, and true heartfelt sentiment were conveyed here in ways he never thought possible. To Levi's understanding, this manuscript was possibly the greatest example of the written word since Shakespeare's *Othello,* even more poignant, and possibly more tactful in its open handling of racism.

There was not a doubt in his mind that this manuscript was the work of Josey Yober, his most favorite author of all time, and that this was, without a doubt, Josey Yober's greatest work. Levi knew that his life was about to change forever. And he was more right than he knew.

The next day, as Levi was relieving himself behind a tree near the crashed vehicle, a pair of pale, featureless men in black suits seemingly appeared from nowhere to poke around. Levi, remaining unseen, watched as the two men discussed the wreck with one another. They spoke in a language that was incomprehensible to him yet somehow, unquestionably— vile. It sent chills up his spine. One of the black-suited men then made a black cacophonous noise at the vacant glove-box. Levi clutched the manuscript and ran.

He sat on the first flight back home, his eyes flickering nervously over every man wearing a black suit. A day later, when the news broke out on the television of Yober's death, Grayson didn't believe it. He knew, intrinsically, that the manuscript he held was proof of the author's survival, and that there was more to the story than met the eye. He would prove to the world that Yober was alive. Even if it meant the men in suits would kill him. Levi had awakened to a higher purpose, and when Lilian Grayson answered her front door in mountainous rural Virginia, she found her son the way she always remembered him– a magical boy who penned stories full of whimsy and wonder.

He worked tirelessly to stitch the unfinished work together, to refine it, and to do it the justice it deserved, as it would become no doubt, Yober's single finest contribution to American Literature.

With the help of a few of Yober's seedier relatives, Grayson was able to fast track the polished manuscript, bringing it to light while landing a few royalty deals of his own. Now, as he sits at a desk by a window that overlooks a shaded creek, he indulges himself with a glass of chilled Kentucky bourbon. Grayson grins, for he has won this battle and he knows that the next chapter will be a doozy.

Josey Yober – (1950 - ???)

Little is known of the famed author Josey Yober beyond the rumors and hushed whisperings of his sudden, mysterious death in Versailles, in 1993. The death sent a shock wave across America. School days were canceled, church functions, postponed. Government workers took a holiday. Riots erupted in New York, California, and Pennsylvania. The despair was so horrible that even Punxsutawney Phil refused to emerge from his den in Gobbler's Knob. The gentle groundhog feared to see his own shadow, knowing fully that if he did, the winter would gain another six months in yet another blow to the Greater American Psyche. Yet, as it turned out, Phil's inaction had some sour ramifications of its own. The American people were left in limbo. How long would winter last, exactly, without Phil to observe his own shadow? They craved an appearance, craved an answer from the universe, even demanded it outright, with one extremist group threatening Phil's den with artillery fire– but to no avail. Punxsutawney Phil never showed his whiskers, so the history books gave that winter a name: Schrödinger's Winter. It lasted about four extra weeks.

After the dust settled, so to speak, the American people began to think clearly again. They saw that the clouded tragedy in Versailles was not without a ray of conspiracy. Circumstances provoked investigation. An autopsy of Yober's '81 Rolls Royce suggested that the car had suffered a head-on collision with another vehicle, yet this other vehicle was never found. Neither had any bodies been found. Was Yober really dead?

Bits of torn, bloody fabrics clung to the broken glass in the windshield. The pieces were positively identified as belonging to both Josey Yober and Ms. Abigail Yussef, his mistress at the time. It seemed that the two had been hurled from the front seats of the vehicle and through the windshield. (Josey had recently made public his distaste for wearing seat belts and perhaps had swayed Ms. Yussef to his tragic philosophy.)

Nothing was ever discovered about the other vehicle, though it was hypothesized to have a green color, as there were unknown green markings on the mangled hood of Yober's otherwise pristine, cream-colored Rolls Royce.

With each passing year, time cloaks myth in darker shades of gray. Real answers retreat to the fringes of the imagination. Where was Yober? Or Ms. Yussef? Where were the bodies? Where was the other vehicle? Was this a murder, an accident, or a charade? Did Yober and Yussef organize the whole spectacle in order to live the rest of their lives together in perfect secrecy? Well, ever since their disappearance, there was in existence one clue, one hard piece of evidence that had never been disclosed to the public. That is, until now: a single manuscript for a work of fiction somehow survived the fate of Yober, and has made its way into the States.

Under the careful supervision of the industrious Leviathan Grayson, self-proclaimed Yober-scholar, and by all the good graces of the esteemed Yober Estate, Yober's final manuscript has been clipped, cleaned, edited, and then completely rewritten. The result is, assuredly, a masterpiece.

ACT I: SUMMERFALL

1 Party Time

"Doesn't it ever get boring to you?" she asked as he loaded the clip of his gun. He was Peter Swiscock and she was Autumn Summerfall. Together they had made a name for themselves in the closely interwoven circles of justice and criminality. Autumn, who believed the fame was well-earned, worried that it was consuming her. She was more than a hot piece of ass that could shoot a gun and pilot any machine known to man, that's for sure. She also liked to knit and do the Sunday crosswords.

And now, at the end of another rigorous morning of building criminal profiles and another one of Pete's overly thorough debriefings, Autumn was trying to steer the conversation toward her qualms before she exited Pete's 1971 Ford Maverick and returned to her own life, possibly forever. He spoke first. "I don't do this work for my own entertainment," he said. His voice was gruff, mere decibels above a whisper.

"My point exactly. It's got to get tedious," she said. She shook her head in a pained way. Autumn could never break through the cold, gloomy exterior of the man who sat across from her in the driver's seat. Swiscock rarely looked at her when they spoke. Those noble eyes of his were always scanning for danger. They sat now looking out into the largely empty parking lot of Pete's private headquarters, the car idling quietly.

"I've lost every person I've ever loved to criminals, Honeycakes," he said. It was a dramatic twist of truth that would have made Obi-Wan Kenobi proud. "Justice is all I have now." He took a long drag from his Parliament cigarette and a quick sip from his coffee and then another long drag from his Parliament, followed by an even quicker sip of his coffee.

Autumn knew Pete tended to speak hyperbolically in order to close himself off to her, though she knew they both knew that he was only closing himself off to himself. She closed her eyes. It was time. "Pete. Listen. I don't think I can keep–"

"This morning there was a message on my answering machine," he said, his train of thought bearing down its own track. "I don't know. It could be nothing. I debated all day whether I should answer the message."

"What was the message?"

"It would mean nothing to you."

"I see," she said. Another layer of secrecy. Autumn had gone to open the door handle to get out of the car; her fingers held lightly the silver bar that would release the door's lock, yet she paused. He pulled once again at the cigarette. She knew by his stoic silence he was asking her to stay with him. "Where are we headed?" she asked, feeling her fingers slip off of the door handle. Maybe she was intrigued.

"Buena Vista," he said with a voice like wet gravel. "Maryland. The most beautiful state of them all."

A harsh rain rattled on the roof of the car as the clouds above had finally given up. Pete didn't roll up the window though, instead let the rain sting the left side of his face and soak his arm, which hung coolly out the window, holding the lit cigarette. While this kind of behavior might have surprised some, it didn't surprise Autumn. She knew him. This didn't mean she was keen to get soaked herself, however.

"I didn't know Peter Swiscock could appreciate beauty," she said, half truthfully, half toying with him as she rolled up her window. "I thought it was all *crime, crime, crime, justice, justice, justice, Honeycakes,"* she said, giving her best Swiscock impression.

But Pete was not in the mood for banter. He put the cigarette in his lips, and threw the stick into first gear. "Thanks," he said.

They left the desolate parking lot.

Autumn flipped on the car radio and Kurtis Blow sang out sweet nothings through static. Windshield wipers slapped out of rhythm with the music.

Eventually they left the interstate and turned onto a quiet country road. The road turned from asphalt to gravel to dirt to a solid bed of chirping crickets back to dirt as they progressed deeper into the woods and farther from the reaches of society. Arching withered trees enclosed them on either side. The woods beyond the trees seemed devoid of life, as though nothing dared tread there. Maybe it was just the rain, thought Autumn hopefully, and all the creatures had taken refuge.

After many turns down the muddy road, the trees eventually parted and they found themselves parked before a house. It was a two-story monstrosity with dust-caked windows and weathered blue siding, and its complete eerie stillness was enough to give Autumn a shiver.

"So this is where your friend lives?" she asked.

Pete said nothing and parked them some distance from the front of the property. They had trudged halfway across an unkempt yard when a sudden loud wind pressed against them. Autumn, clutching the collar of her coat, leaned into it, and then stopped walking altogether. Then it passed. The house had exhaled, thought Autumn. Pete had merely pushed forward, turning his face away from the hostile gust.

At last they had reached the creaky steps that led to the porch, and Pete knocked on the familiar green door with lines of cracked paint. With a low whine it crept ajar. He and Autumn exchanged a look. They drew their sidearms and Pete entered the darkness.

The air was damp and stale and the overbearing scent of decay turned his stomach, almost giving last night's *turkey bolognese* an encore appearance all over the entryway of his friend's home. Pete gritted his teeth in agitation; he'd hate to waste good food.

"Jesus H, Pete, what is this?" Autumn asked, though not so much from the smell but from the sight. Arranged concentrically around the foyer was a dozen, maybe more, large, vicious birds, each one different from the last, frozen in fury. Here the wings extended threateningly, there the eyes, sharp and defiant, gave challenge.

She leaned around the corner. The assemblage of avian taxidermy extended down the hallway, and then spread its wings throughout the house. Everywhere there were birds. Some of them were colorful, some drab, some big, others tiny. All of them, entirely still. *So Pete's friend was a collector. Probably a lonesome man too.*

"Stay quiet, Honeycakes– we may not be alone," he whispered, ducking a stork.

Autumn followed him past the giant bird, following the stench, and stopped next to Pete at a sight neither was prepared for.

At the head of an expensive, solid oak table sat slumped backward a massive tree-trunk of a man, Swiscock's most trusted friend, Barnaby Weatherspoon. Weatherspoon had his head thrown over the back of the chair, baring the neck in its shameless slumber. The dead man was as fat as Pete remembered him. The poor, fat fuck. An enormous black crow stood high on a fixture behind Barnaby as if to keep a watchful eye over its master. Had the crow failed or succeeded?

"No-no-no-no-no-no-no-no," Pete cried. Beneath him, his legs had suddenly felt like wobbly wooden spoons.

It looked as if Barnaby had been shot from behind while he ate his dinner; a single can of cold chicken noodle soup sat plainly before him on the table. He was still dressed in an expensive black two-piece and red tie. It was red cause he didn't trust liberals.

It was red because of the blood that had run down his neck and dried.

"No!" Pete gasped. He propped himself weakly against the kitchen counter.

"What the hell is this?" Autumn said.

Pete took a bar stool and sat down. "This man here, I told you he was my friend."

Autumn nodded.

"Well, he was not just my friend. He was my best friend."

In that moment, Autumn understood completely.

"Pete–"

"Don't."

"I'm so sorry, Pete."

"I'm going to find out whoever did this and... stick them feet first into a meat grinder. *Burger time,"* he added.

A sound from above, a heavy thump, alerted them to a presence upstairs. This time it was Autumn who led. She thumbed the safety off of her .22. Having trained extensively with Swiscock, she was just as deft in the field, and thus she took her next footsteps carefully.

They rotated from the kitchen into a hallway that led to a staircase to the second floor. Pete grimaced; beneath his feet, a wooden floorboard protested loudly like a baby crying at 3 A.M. Stealth was out of the question. He was angry, angry at himself, at Barnaby. Whatever the big fella had gotten himself into was bad, dang bad. Pete could tell that all hell was about to break loose. He felt it in his loins. Pete trusted his loins.

He aimed the sight of his pistol over the top of the staircase and waited for movement. Nothing. He crept ahead of Autumn, who was tense as a coiled spring.

Autumn followed her partner up the stairs, slowly. "Pete," she whispered, and then her eyes went wide in a look of horror and surprise.

Suddenly, gunfire erupted from all sides at once and Pete spun. He felt the bullets shred through him like creamy milk, and he crashed backward through the railing, his last glimpse of Autumn eclipsed by darkness.

Nine months later...

"Vitals check out. Patient appears to be waking up. Somebody get C.L.U. on the line."

"No, not C.L.U., get Autumn. Get Autumn," Pete moaned, discombobulated. He tossed and turned, trapped at the tail end of a nine month nightmare. "Autumn," he said. "Look out." Autumn was standing at the rail again, and a dark cloud was swelling up between them. Somewhere behind the dream, a woman's voice spoke with the devoid quality of a seasoned medical practitioner: *"Patient tense, wriggling uncontrollably."* Autumn was staring past him to where Barnaby had been, and there was something frightening about her. Her pupils had grown wide as portals.

It was too much. With full consciousness and clarity, Pete's eyelids burst open. The figure of a semi-attractive blonde nurse looming over him became readily apparent. He lunged towards her, pulling the whole bed with him. Ultimately a set of beige nylon straps bound to his wrists and forearms restrained him, but his face was mere inches from hers.

"Where's Autumn?!" he shouted, spitting up the hot cum the doctors had filled him with to lubricate his vocal cords. "What the hell?"

Whumpf! He'd fallen back into the bed.

"Please rest, Mr. Swiscock," said the nurse. "C.L.U. is on the way to pick you up."

“Fucking Gibson,” Pete whimpered, and she left.

“Maybe the hot cum was a bit much,” he heard someone say just outside the room.

Paranoia set in; how could he trust Gibson or C.L.U. to protect him when someone had so easily gotten to Barnaby? Furthermore, Barnaby’s house had been a trap. Our hero looked for an escape.

Thick IV needles had been embedded into his forearms and abdomen by the doctors, whom Pete didn’t trust either. Summoning strength unnatural to a man freshly waking from a nine-month coma, he raised his arms as high as he could, straining the restrictive straps until they gave way. Each tore thinly, haggardly, anticlimactically. He pulled out the IVs, relishing the vague pain that made him feel alive. He ripped the heart monitor off his chest, to which the machine responded with a solid *BEEEEEEE!,* and scooted to the edge of the bed. Dark red blood leaked from where the needles had just been, but Pete didn’t care. He was alive. He couldn’t say the same for— he had to find Autumn. Somewhere in this hospital?

The door flung open and the semi-attractive blonde nurse and a male nurse came in, their expressions changing from surprise to panic, as Peter Swiscock greeted them with one of his legendary Swiscock fighting maneuvers, a move that remains to this day impossible to replicate in words.

He grabbed the dazed male nurse by the front of his black scrub and lifted him from the floor.

“Where’s Autumn?” he shouted.

“Who?” The nurse was dizzy.

“My partner. Autumn Summerfall. She has to be here.”

“Sir,” stammered the poor boy. “There’s no one by that name.”

And just like that he let him drop back to the floor next to the other nurse.

Swiscock went to the window and shoved it upward. Cold wind whipped into the sweat-matted tendrils of his blonde hair. The pores of his face awakened to the thin mist that hung about outside. God, it was good to inhale that fresh air.

He searched down past the rows of windows beneath him, counting. His room was on the ninth floor. It would be a long drop, but he had made that jump before. He gave the two nurses a curt smile over his shoulder and then, without further ado, sprung out into the damp air. To his favor, he fell into an open dumpster, big bags of trash cushioning his landing. The sudden smell caused him to reel, and this time he could not hold it in. He spewed a liter of the hot cum, nearly all of it, onto a black garbage bag. Swiscock was just wiping his mouth off with the sleeve of his light blue, checkered hospital gown, when a car pulled up to the curb next to him. It was a bright red Ford Mustang. The engine purred expectantly. Pete did not move, at first. He crawled forward out of the dumpster and approached the car.

The window rolled down and Pete could swear it was Autumn sitting in the driver's seat. His eyes were still adjusting.

"Get in," said a woman's voice deeper and more sultry than the one he'd expected to hear. Pete glanced about his shoulder. C.L.U. would be there any minute now, and Pete had no better option in mind. He climbed in.

"Nine months ago," she began as she took them away from the hospital, "You were admitted to Scooberdoo. Your body had been riddled with bullets, your insides looking something like Swiss cheese. You were barely alive. And still you were taken in, and cared for, without any questions, despite leaving behind you a gruesome crime-scene in an old house off of Buena Vista Road."

So it had all been real. "What about Autumn?"

The driver said nothing.

Icy clouds loomed above. Promises of a heavy blizzard– four inches– someone was saying on the radio. Pete didn't doubt the forecast, though the blizzard he had in mind was more in the metaphysical sense. "Who are you?" he asked, shaking the dark thoughts.

"The name's May Swallows," she said.

Her voice was rich, like a drop of honey on the tongue. Her straight, chestnut hair which fell like curtains around a slender face, was cropped neatly just below her jaw. A pair of teal-rimmed sunglasses concealed her eyes. Pete was confused, yet aroused.

"May Swallows," said Pete, gesturing to himself in the pathetic gown, "meet Peter Swiscock."

May responded with a slight curl of the lips, though not the ones on her face.

2 Gibson

The sound of the hospital room was of a general murmur: the forensics team taking pictures of the window and the bed, the beeping and whining of machinery, a standby police officer making passes at the semi-attractive blonde nurse, the male nurse animatedly recreating his encounter with Swiscock.

– Enter, Garrison Cross, a young detective in blue jeans and a neat, navy blue suit jacket. In his hand a cup of coffee and his heart on his sleeve:

"What do you mean he escaped?" he demanded of the male nurse. Cross was good at demanding things.

"All I'm saying is that we walked into the room, and he was standing right there, and the next thing I knew I was on the floor." The semi-attractive blonde nurse had been nodding her head along to the story.

"Is that it?" asked Cross.

"He asked me about a name, Autumn Summerfall. I told him we didn't have any patients by that name."

"Interesting. And then what happened?"

"And then he leapt," said the male nurse pointing with a wag of his nose at the window.

"You mean to tell me he jumped out of a ninth-story window?"

Garrison Cross, age 26, had just recently divorced for the second time, and he knew Swiscock's disappearance would add even more stress to his life on top of the child support payments. He rubbed his temples and said to the officer standing by, "You better call Gibson." The officer danced out of the room and, almost immediately, in strode the big guns.

Patrick Gibson was a tower. Even though he had reached his peak athleticism in college and had since rounded out and gone nearly bald on top, his size still offered him a formidable appearance. In the summer, he'd visit Maine where he grew up and he'd spend his time playing Frisbee with this best friend, his dog, Buddy, while his other dog watched. His parents died when he was twelve, in a freak water skiing accident. This made him resent water. The rain frankly pissed him off.

"Gibson!"

He awoke from his reverie to a now-empty hospital room except for Cross, who must have been expecting him to say something. He shook his head. "I know Pete. Hell, I know him better than most... But there's no way he could have survived the fall from this window." The Northeastern boy had spoken with his grown-up, adult Northeastern certainty. *Swiscock lives that so may I,* whispered a disquieting voice in his head. *Bring the bomb, McTavish!* A sharp tingle skittered down the length of his spine, and the foreign voice laughed mightily as it faded into silence and from his memory.

Cross had stuck his head out the window and then pulled it back in. He shrugged. "Well then where is he?" he said.

Gibson grumbled and then turned away. "God damn it Pete. First Barnaby's and now this; you've really given me a mess. Alright," he shouted into his walkie, "Close down this hospital under the authority of C.L.U. I want a complete lockdown. No one leaves until we find Pete Swiscock! And Cross–"

Cross stopped mid-sip of coffee.

"Take the rest of the day off. You look like shit."

3 Jarvan Manor

"Where are you taking me?" Swiscock demanded. He cursed himself once he realized he'd nodded off for some time now.

"To the beginning," May had answered, visibly struggling to find her most enigmatic tone. "In the glove box," she said. "Open it."

Pete reached forward feebly and clicked the latch open. A small light on the inside, some papers, and a little black box.

"What's in the box?" he asked, picking it up. It was not too heavy.

"My mascara. You're my date tonight."

"Tonight," Pete repeated unintentionally. The sky was growing dark already. Street lamps that flanked the highway passed by, each carrying a dull glow to match the clouded sunset.

"I don't think in my current state I'll make the impression you think I'll make, Ms. Swallows," he said. "I look and smell like shit."

May said she agreed.

"You know you remind me of someone I used to know." Pete wracked his brain. Dreams flushed over. Old times, good and bad. Friends, landmarks, smiles, tears, laughter, kisses with cute girls down by the docks. Where had he seen her before? Or someone like her? He could vaguely make out the image of someone beautiful, as if viewing a portrait through a murky window. He had blocked the memory, locked it in his own vault of Things Willfully Forgotten, and thrown away the key. When he had been just a teenager, Swiscock had been trained to forget things in case of capture, and had succeeded in keeping such secrets from the most skilled of hypnotists. It was a powerful ability, but its application would occasionally leave him feeling hollow and confused. And other times a strong air of nostalgia would strike, but he wouldn't be able to place its origin. His training, he wondered— had he ever really completed his training?

"Mr. Swiscock."

Her voice shook him from his past.

"We're here."

Pete stepped out of the car onto solid ground and felt tiny bits of gravel bite into his bare feet, which were soft after nine months of non -use. He looked up.

The acclaimed three-storied Jarvan Manor stood before them both, high up on a hill. Its fearsome size spoke eons of wealth and power.

"The man who had this structure built was the man who owned the men who owned the plantations in Virginia before the war," May informed him. "And then years ago, Jarvan moved in. When you were lost in thought about some woman or other, I had you showered and fitted for a tux." She moved to the trunk of her car and lifted it. "Now quick, change into this."

Cars passed them on the long walk up the hill to the impending party. For brief moments light would appear in the doorway and a silhouette; someone ushered guests inside. "Come on," urged May, as cackles of laughter bounded down toward them from the property on the top of the hill. Someone was playing a jazz rendition of the Spiderman Theme Song on the piano. Pete was getting excited, as Jarvan's parties were reputed to be straight up out-of-this-world.

Giant oak doors swung open like when Kramer has something important to tell Jerry, and the music swelled up to a crescendo. May and Swiscock were greeted with a smile and a glass of champagne from their impossibly ancient-looking host, Kendall Jarvan the Fourth.

"May, darling, it's wonderful to see you're still breathing."

"Ken, you don't look a day over a hundred."

"Ha! I'll get there." Jarvan smiled genially. "I don't believe we've met. Kendall Jarvan the Fourth."

"Swiscock," said Pete shaking the host's hand firmly. "Peter Swiscock. I must say you have a remarkable home."

"This is just the outside! Come in, come see my dragon!"

They stepped into the entrance after Jarvan and Jarvan spun around slowly, as if admiring his own residence for the first time. Indeed, the staircase that spiraled away from the edge of the foyer was made to look like a dragon; the thick red-colored railing shimmered like scales with an impressive rainbow sheen. At the top of the spiraling staircase lay open the sharp-fanged mouth of the dragon and directly above them hung a massive chandelier like a luminous gem, a treasure fitting for a dragon's protection. Wealth needed protection which, Pete mused, was a kind of weakness. A pair of giggling party goers, both wearing masks, rushed past the trio, farting loudly and laughing as they escaped around the corner.

"Mr. Swiscock, have one of my maids fix you a drink," said Jarvan, covering his nose. His eyes glistened a little and Pete immediately felt sorry for the guy, for he must have gotten a direct blast. "May– oh God." Abruptly, Jarvan hurried off.

"Come on," said May, taking Pete's arm. "I know what you need." She led him down a hall and through the dining room, past the music, madness, laughter, and debauchery that assailed them on every front. Jarvan's friends were wild and Pete wondered what the hurry was for.

May turned on the light in the liquor shed behind Jarvan's home. It was just the two of them, some liquor, and a plain wooden table.

May poured each of them a small glass of tequila, and then she placed the bottle between them at the table. The two studied one another without drinking, nor saying anything.

He realized now that she looked nothing like Autumn Summerfall at all. He was thinking back to when he first climbed into the car with May: his strong desire to see Autumn had interlaced with the ethereal tendrils of his dream about her and superimposed itself onto his waking reality. No, the woman across from him was not Autumn Summerfall.

"Where is she?" He demanded, glad to be thinking clearly at last. "Autumn."

"I don't know who you're talking about," said May.

"Autumn Summerfall. She was with me in Buena Vista. You knew where I'd be. You must know where she *is.*"

"I'm sorry, Pete," she said, bringing her glass closer to her so that she was almost huddling over it. "I was only told about you. You and you, alone."

Pete eyed the silver drink in his hand and then said, "Ms. Swallows, I appreciate you rescuing me."

"No, you're not leaving so soon. You're a wanted man, Peter Swiscock. The state wants you. The feds want you. Even C.L.U. wants you."

"It's okay. I know the boss," he said, referring to Gibson, who was C.L.U.'s director. The two, Pete and Gibson, shared a secret history that extended over two decades into the past. That history had culminated in flames and horror, thus they had consequentially broken off their connection, save for a few Christmas cards, birthday cards and candy grams. Pete knew how to avoid the feds and he knew he could dodge Gibson when it came down to it.

"Stay, Pete," she said. She had placed her hand over his. "You don't know what's out there."

"Autumn's out there," he said, curtly.

Pete watched her as she took back her hand. Who was she? CIA? He figured he should entertain his savior for a little while longer, if only to find out more about her before he dispatched her. "So what's in it for you?" Pete asked. "A promotion? Some sort of revenge? Plenty of people want me dead. Lots of people. Now that I consider it, I probably should have stayed dead and just saved everyone the hassle—"

"Money," she said. "I'm in it for the money."

"Maybe," Pete admitted. He'd raised an eyebrow. He sipped from his glass. "But money is not your singular motivator. No, you are motivated by something deep within yourself. It's why you and I are alone in this quiet place so soon after arriving. The tequila is welcome, by the way." Pete took another drink of it. It was very smooth. Relaxing, even. The silver liquid in the glass expanded and contracted in a steady rhythm. He shook his head.

At the other end of the table, May seemed very far away.

"Damn, I've talked too much," said Pete. He stood up and knocked into his chair. "Too quickly," he muttered. "Too... quickly."

He felt the glass slip from his fingers but he never heard it land. As Pete slipped into blackness, a memory of Autumn Summerfall stabbed him with a black knife. *Forget me, Pete,* she whispered. A sick, unnatural slumber crept over him, and he wondered if it would be another nine months before he woke up, and then—

4 C.L.U.

BREAKING NEWS:
INTERNATIONAL
SUPER-SPY
PETER SWISCOCK
ON THE LOOSE!

According to the staff at Scooberdoo Hospital in Buena Vista, Maryland, ("the most beautiful state of them all") legendary playboy super-spy Peter Swiscock simply "up and left" yesterday afternoon after waking from a nine-month coma. And he did it by leaping out of the building from his room on the ninth story.

"*And* he didn't ever take no physical therapy or nothin'," stated one of the hospital employees. "Like he just straight up woke up and dipped out the window."

The hospital has since drawn intense criticism for letting the famed anti-hero escape but it has shifted the blame over to local government for not giving fair warning as to Swiscock's capabilities, or even supplying the hospital with a single armed guard to monitor the sleeping lethal weapon. "You expect us to learn *karate*?" said head nurse Kathrine Meyers, who can only be described as a semi-attractive blonde. Indeed she was one of two hospital staff incapacitated by Swiscock during his escape. "Besides, his moves were so *deft*, so *indescribable.* I could never fight a man like that. I would make love to him instead."

So far any information as to what put the legendary crime-fighter in a hospital bed in Buena Vista has been kept tightly under wrap. The local police force is collaborating with Swiscock's own former employer, C.L.U. to bring him back in. The current head of C.L.U., Patrick Gibson...

...was feeling incredibly tired. His head was spinning. What the hell had happened at Barnaby's? It had looked like a massacre had taken place. And then finally Pete wakes up and *both of my God-damned hands are empty.* Two birds, no stones, no birds. His outrage at being eluded by his old friend was magnified by a certain pang of jealousy, for it seemed like Swiscock and Barnaby were still involved in some crazy shit, despite the cabalistic oath the three had sworn. Was this proof the oath had been broken? *Or had someone stirred the pot?*

"Gibson!" came a voice.

Gibson looked up from the article like a boy who had gotten caught rifling through his grandfather's dirty magazines.

"Cross," he said. "What are you still doing here at this hour?"

"It's three in the afternoon, sir. I came to tell you there's a phone call for you on line six."

"I'm very busy, Cross. I can't stop to answer every phone call that comes through this place. Too many reporters asking about Swiscock, and I've got no more left of my soul to give."

"You might want to take this one, sir. I think it's a lead."

If Gibson's head could have shot up again, it would have, although this would be an exercise in the impossible, as his head was already looking up.

"Put 'er on," he said.

"No, you," said Cross. "Line six." He left the doorway.

Remind me to fire that man, Gibson thought to himself, placing the corded landline to his ear. He pressed the button next to the only green blinking light, and waited.

"I have the whereabouts of Peter Gerald Swiscock," said a voice, suddenly. The voice was a rough-synthetic, its original, human timbre masked beneath countless layers of digital modulations. It had the effect of getting a blast of cheap perfume right up the nostrils. Gibson had to squint.

"Who is this?" he demanded.

"Jarvan Manor."

"Who?"

The line went dead. Gibson set the phone on the receiver and called out the doorway for Cross, who was already standing in it. *Damn, that man's fast.*

"What do you know about a Jarvan Manor?" Gibson asked. "Who is that?"

"Not a who, sir," said Cross, severely, "a what." He paused before entering Gibson's office and then stood on the other side of Gibson's desk, handing down photographs and documents to his superior as he spoke. "Last night Kendall Jarvan the Fourth held a charity ball at his estate, commonly known as 'Jarvan Manor.' They are lavish and fun and chock-full of celebrities. I could not go last night because I had prior engagements." Cross did not, in fact, have prior engagements, nor was he invited, but he had been struck by an impulsive desire for Gibson to view him as a man of culture and sophistication. "I wouldn't put it past Swiscock to have ended up on the guest list, however," he concluded.

This man needs a promotion, thought Gibson. He stood up. "Get your detective shoes on, Garry. We're going to a one Jarvan Manor."

The organization provided state-issued cars for all employees, but Cross hated them. "I look like a fucking cop. I didn't go through three years of training to be mistaken for a fucking cop," his co-workers would often hear him say. The two men got into Cross's old F-150 and made for Jarvan Manor. George Strait sang to them timeless classics of his time and bright sunlight sent shadows down the mountains that flanked them on either side. Cross pretended his hand was a dolphin out the window, and then Gibson did it too and suddenly they had become a dolphin squad. They laughed about it later. Together Cross and Gibson would exchange stories of the past and jokes that only the two of them could find funny. "You had to be there," was a phrase they were both tired of saying. Although Gibson was his superior, Cross was mostly treated as an equal. They'd go out to bars, casinos, theaters, hitting on anything with a pulse. Perhaps that's why Cross couldn't have a successful marriage. He loved women.

As the vehicle climbed, the trees along the side of the highway became more barren of leaves, and it was Cross that pointed out the elusive Jarvan Manor hiding off in the distance behind them, even higher still on the mountain. "I'd always wondered who lived there," Gibson said.

"Jarvan does," Cross responded.

Before long they'd ascended the same winding road as Peter Swiscock and May Swallows the night before, and came face-to-face with the same impressive sight.

Gibson rapped his knuckles on the giant oak door.

"Hello there," said the voice of a kind old man. The massive door cracked open and out poked a kind old man's face. It was Kendall J! Because the man was half concealed behind the door, Cross could only guess what he was wearing. He guessed it was probably a robe, silken, primarily red with golden oriental inlays.

"Mr. Jarvan," Gibson stated.

"Kendall Jarvan the Fourth, yes," he said with a kind old smirk. "My friends call me Kenny."

“My name is Patrick Gibson, and this is Garrison Cross. We’re from C.L.U.”

“Ah yes, tell me what that acronym stands for again.”

“It’s Crime League United,” interjected Cross, eager to impress. “It’s kind of confusing because we fight crime, but the name makes it sound like we commit crime. I didn’t come up with it.”

Gibson shot him a look.

“Very good,” said the wealthy man, opening the door fully. Cross was dead on about the outfit, by the way. “I expected a visit what with the commotion last night.”

How behind are we? wondered Gibson.

“Don’t just stand there, come in! But do remove your shoes,” he added, splitting hairs.

Aw, my detective shoes, thought Cross.

Shoes in hand, the two C.L.U. officers entered the estate. Cross’s eyes were drawn to the spiral staircase that was made to look like a dragon. Colorful light shined down through a large, circular stained glass window on the front of the house and gave the dragon’s scales myriad pretty colors. The effect was striking.

“Do you like the dragon? The dragon is just the beginning,” said their host. “But before I show you the rest of the home, let us have lunch.”

Jarvan led them to a dining room straight out of the 18th century. Where the dragon had been an addition to the home, this room was surely true to its original construction. A white cloth covered the long table at which they took seats, with Jarvan at the head, then Gibson to this left, then Cross. Between the various paintings of whom Gibson presumed were Jarvan’s ancestors, the walls were turquoise.

“This looks like a great place to host a charity ball,” Gibson said, cutting to the chase.

“I should hope so,” said Kendall, ahead of the chase, “considering I tend to host those.”

“I bet you get a lot of celebrities.”

“You’d win that bet. Last night we had a great party. I’m sorry you missed it.”

“I’m sorry I wasn’t invited,” Cross snapped. Truthfully, his feelings had been hurt, but he wasn’t about to admit it. He crossed his arms and frowned out the window.

“Garrison Cross, was it?” said Jarvan, jotting the name down on a pad of paper. “I’ll add you to the invite list for next weekend. It’s gonna be huge. Madonna will be here, and possibly Kurt Russell.”

"I don't care."

Gibson shifted suddenly in his seat. "Damn it, this is about Swiscock!" he said, *actually* cutting to the chase this time

"Ah, the fatal name," said the old man. "Few survive its utterance and none are out of its reach."

Cross and Gibson shared a glance. The way Kendall Jarvan the Fourth had just spoken gave Cross the chills as though an icy shadow had passed over him. An icy foreshadow.

"Fatal?" the young detective inquired.

"Fatal."

One of the maids brought out hot tea on a tray.

"Please, enjoy," said Jarvan with a gesture of his hand. "This tea is from the Isles of Mozambique. Very potent stuff."

Oh boy, thought Cross, taking a quick sip. It burned the roof of his mouth badly and also his tongue. He would not be able to taste anything for a few days, if anyone cared to know. As a young boy, Cross was always quick to eat food, especially meats and fruits. Nowadays, conscious of his weight, he displaced his ravenous hunger for food with a ravenous hunger for solving crimes. Yet he found himself thinking "old habits die hard–"

The tea sprayed from his mouth; Gibson had smacked him on the back between the shoulder blades.

"Don't drink the tea," he cautioned. "It's obviously poisoned."

"Nonsense," said Kenny J.. He took several loud gulps of the hot tea straight from the pitcher. "I wouldn't waste poison on a pair of the law's finest."

"How will you be able to taste anything?" Cross wondered aloud.

"My boy," Kendall said gravely, "in my business, you learn quick it's best not to taste anything at all."

Gibson had had enough of Jarvan's shtick. "Enough of your shtick, Jarvan." He slammed his fist upon the table, startling one of the help. "Where's Swiscock?"

"I don't know."

"Damn it, old man!"

Gibson reached across the table and pulled Jarvan toward himself by the collar of his robe. He held Jarvan's face inches from his snarling own. "You need to start talking." A big bloody vein had emerged from beneath the surface of Gibson's right temple, indicating a sharp spike in blood pressure. Jarvan, on the other hand, appeared calm. Gently he placed his hands on Gibson's wrists and the senior detective began to relax. He let go of the Jarvan's collar, softly, and dropped backward into his chair, feeling confused and ashamed.

"The truth is I can't tell you where Swiscock is, or where he is headed. But I am glad to be rid of him. And you should be too—Swiscock has enemies. People you'd turn and run from if you knew what was good for you. And some things that aren't people..." Jarvan trailed off, hinting at stuff later in this book.

Cross's imagination immediately tried to conjure things that weren't people but he kept drawing up a blank. Dogs? Cats? Spoons? No good, he couldn't remember what anything looked like except for people and their faces, going about their ordinary lives. He frowned quietly.

"You said you were glad to be rid of him?" asked Gibson. This had come as a relief, for part of him had suspected Jarvan of treachery. The news about enemies wasn't news, however. Gibson had worked closely with Pete in the past, more than Cross knew, more so than most anyone knew, and they had had their fair share of run-ins with high-rollers.

"Yes. He draws too much attention, and it worries people. Last night his presence alone here cost me five investors. Nice, expensive folks whom I'd invited to my home for a couple hours of music and senseless fun..." He stopped. Gibson's cold eyes disturbed him. "Well, I think this concludes the tour," he said abruptly. "I think it's time you went your separate way."

"We'll be in touch," said Cross, and they departed, but not before putting their detective shoes back on.

Kendall Jarvan the Fourth watched from the doorway to the concrete patio as the F-150 pulled away. The sun was getting ready to go down and the whisper of a cool breeze played gently with the fine white tuft of hair on his head. Silently, he closed the door to the outside world.

"Be glad. It's out of your hands now," said someone behind him. He whipped around angrily. "May," he said. "I feel the walls closing in already. You should never have brought him here. What were you thinking? A spy, in my home! And Swiscock at that! He's gone?"

She appeared under the colored light coming down through the stained glass window. "Yes, he's gone."

"Damn it! I don't like it."

"Don't be dramatic, Ken," she said. "You're giving this whole thing an air of conspiracy."

“Well this is Swiscock,” he countered. He paced. “The man reeks of conspiracy.” He suddenly added with an eye-glint of menace: “And so do you, May. It clings to you like a cigarette.”

Her heart flickered– what did he know? To which conspiracy was Jarvan referring? Jarvan sighed and then fell into a wicker chair. The vile went out of his voice: “I’m sorry, May. I’m getting too old for this, all this pretending and politics. And you couldn’t have known what Swiscock represents to my friends. They hate him. The odds that he’d show up here are unfathomable, but what’s done is done. Tell me,” he said, “how did you two meet?” Jarvan’s voice betrayed no suspicion, only curiosity.

She closed her eyes and thought furiously for only a second. She knew that it was just a matter of time before Jarvan would learn of the details of Swiscock’s escape from Scooberdoo Hospital and then the chances of the spy appearing at his manor would become even more ‘unfathomable.’ Instead of going with the long story Sturkwise Pendleton, aka Sturkey, her partner in espionage, had fabricated for her, she decided to take a chance because part of her loved the old man and trusted him in his weak state, sitting in that chair.

She told Jarvan everything. Pacing, she confessed she was a spy, herself, and that she knew about the funds Jarvan was sending to a bank account in Africa, and that the basics of her mission included siphoning off some of those funds. Then, she recounted the night she’d received an anonymous telegraph with the assignment to sweep up the legendary super-spy from the hospital, and how everything had been planned to a ‘T’ and then how, miraculously, it had all played out according to the plan. She revealed that some of the investors at Jarvan’s party weren’t really investors at all, but agents of some powerful organization she’d never heard of. How they had slipped away with Swiscock in the trunk of a car with bright headlights, and how that had been the end of it. How exhausting it had all been, everything leading up to now, even the telling of the story; (throughout the telling she had been careful not to say anything that would incriminate her partner.) After an intense yawn, she opened her eyes.

Jarvan was asleep.

5 Justice With a J

"Gibson!"

"Fuck! What?" said Gibson, irritated. He removed his ear buds and turned to face his real bud, Garrison Cross, who was munching down some chili cheese fries in the hurried way one does when they have something to say but don't want to talk with their mouth full.

Gibson had parked them behind the Sonic just up the highway from Jarvan Manor.

"I think I've got it," Cross said. "I think Jarvan was hiding something from us. As we were leaving I think I saw a woman standing there in the back, plain as day!"

Gibson balked. "Why... did you wait all this time to say something?"

"Well getting food was your idea, sir, and I went along with it because I was hungry too."

First chance I get, I'm having this man transferred to Langley.

"We have to go back," said Cross.

"And just waltz on in? No. But you're right. But we can't just waltz on in." Gibson looked suddenly serious. "We need to have finesse, Cross– *finesse.*"

They ate in silence for a few chewy minutes, observing the comings and goings from their parking spot. Without pretense, Cross became aware of a sound coming from the pair of ear buds that lay in Gibson's lap. It was a beautiful sound, though small. It was as if a tiny insect had harnessed the soul of Beyoncé, and was belting its heartfelt audition to the judges on American Singing Competition, the TV show that everybody was sick of. Without being too obvious, he took a glance towards Gibson's crotch region to double-check that it was not, in fact, a tiny insect with serious pipes. *Nope, just ear buds.*

Cross sighed with relief, then stiffened up. Jesus, what was wrong with him?

"I've got it!" said Gibson, happily, and slapped Cross on the shoulder. Cross spat out his food.

Twenty minutes later the two were back on Jarvan's enormous driveway, this time donning a pair of matching white chef's hats and aprons. Side-by-side they casually raised their pistols to the air: in Cross's hand a .22 Smith & Wesson and in Gibson's, a custom-made bright blue Desert Eagle (blue was his favorite color). As long-time partners in the pursuit of Justice and easy women, they had become synchronized in many ways; they ate-out together, ate-in together, and, unbeknownst to either of them, often had their bowel movements at the same time. Today they cocked their pistols together, and the sunset blazed gloriously behind them like a big fuckin' American flag.

They climbed the steps to the front door and made noise.

"Knock knock, mother fucker," said Gibson.

"Who's there?" said a feminine voice from inside.

"Catering!" answered Cross in a dopey Italian accent.

"Catering 'who?'" said the voice as the door opened.

Gibson burst in, knocking the oak door fully aside and the woman jumped back, apparently startled. It was one of the maids who had provided the hot tea from the Isles of Mozambique earlier in the day. She appeared to recover from the surprise and her face set hard like the edge of a kitana. She took a stance.

Like a karate stance, thought Cross, entering quietly behind Gibson. His heart gave a flutter at the sight of the beautiful housemaid who looked ready to do battle. Her angry brown eyes glowed like the lightly dusted surface of a mahogany end table with a fresh lacquer caught in the morning sun. Her jet black hair was bound up in a pair of tight little buns like sun-blocking curtains that had been tucked behind the finials. Her black eyebrows were narrow but just as neat and gave definition to her smooth, healthy brow, the way a well-placed hanging wall shelf can lend character and passion to an interior.

His finger hovered over the cold trigger of the .22. In college, he'd put plenty of holes in the drywall. This, he had to remind himself, would be no different.

Appearing at either side of the detectives were two more equally stunning maids. (Worth noting: the word 'equally' is used in its literal fashion here, as the three maids bore an uncanny resemblance to one another.)

"Looks like you are outnumbered," said the first maid.

"Well at C.L.U. we strive for quality over quantity," answered Gibson, tucking the pistol into his belt behind his back. "Now, let's make this fair."

Cross, holstering his gun, said, "I'll take the one on the left."

"Then I'll take the other two," said Gibson.

They went shoulder-to-shoulder, then back-to-back, as the trio of maids circled slyly around them. Above, the staircase-dragon coiled and spectated. The gems in its greedy eyes glinted in approval of the impending fight. "I guess left or right doesn't matter anymore," said Cross.

"I guess not."

The first maid dashed in. Cross ducked a fist thrown and countered with a roundhouse kick, regretting the violence against a pretty face. The maid took the kick in stride, so to speak, and spun, sweeping Cross's leg out from under him. He crashed painfully to the floor.

Gibson leapt over Cross and smashed the heel of his foot sideways against her cheekbone, this time knocking her out cold. The other two maids were stunned as the big Caucasian man helped his partner get to his feet.

"Good play," said Cross, brushing his lip. He turned back to the fight, which resumed with all of the rhythm and spunk of an uptown jazz-ensemble. The girls used some kind of karate-judo on the men, but the men had their superior male-instincts and natural strength. In the end it was the latter that won the fight. "I'll say it once again," said Cross, panting heavily. "I'm glad I have a Y-chromosome."

Gibson clasped his shoulder in a supremely masculine way and they laughed together like men do.

In the hallway entrance, a recently refreshed Jarvan had joined in the laughter and was clapping, slowly.

They froze.

"What?" said the old man. "Can I not stand here and clap ominously? You put on a good show!"

Abruptly the guns were out again, now leveled at the chest of the red and gold silken robe.

"Where's Swiscock?" demanded Gibson, angrily. "And where's the girl, you old *fuck*?" And then he had it. "The basement. Show me the basement!"

"I'm terribly sorry," Cross began, referring to Gibson. "He can get like this." He decided after all that he still would like to be invited to one of Jarvan's charity events.

"Just down the hallway, second door on your right," said Jarvan, stepping aside. "And oh, do be careful. The wooden stairs are old and we haven't got but one working light down there."

"Not so fast," said Gibson. "I said *show me*."

Jarvan acquiesced. As he led them he said, "I don't believe firearms are necessary; I am not as lithe and powerful as I once was."

"That's exactly why they're necessary," muttered Gibson. If he knew anything about the old millionaire, he knew the sinews of Jarvan's *mind* were still strong.

The two detectives, still wearing their chef's hats and aprons, descended the creaky steps behind Jarvan.

They were in the basement now and two of them were looking for clues. There seemed to be nothing spectacular about the basement; it was just a square room with all the typical basement stuff: tools and mementos, dust, cobwebs, secret switches to other rooms. *Secret switches to other rooms?* Gibson was running his free hand along the wall then a finger passed over a piece of stone protruding from it, accidentally lifting it up. In a time-span no lengthier than the duration of the average male orgasm, a secret room was revealed.

"What the hell is this?" Gibson asked Jarvan, whose face betrayed no emotion.

It looked to Cross like a torture chamber of some kind.

"Some of our guests– have different tastes," said the man of the house. "Nothing more."

"Sure," said Cross, mildly disgusted, but his eyes betrayed his wonder. The atmosphere in the room was unlike anything he'd ever witnessed. Sure he'd seen *Hellraiser* but he didn't believe those kinds of scenes actually existed in real life. Dozens of black, sooty chains hanged from the ceiling and from the four stone pillars that held it all up, and tiny black hooks curled up at the ends of those chains. Mounted on three of the four pillars were lit wooden torches, each casting its own show of ghastly shadows across the room's cold, stony walls. In the direct center of the room sat a single, tacky red seat.

"Swiscock was here," said Gibson, spying the chair. "I know the imprint of that man's buttocks like I know... my own... face." He reddened.

Jarvan and Cross shared a brief look.

The detectives proceeded to walk the room, each with one eye on Jarvan, and then they took turns sitting on the tacky red seat.

"Where is he?" said Cross's superior, running his fingers along one of the chains.

"What makes you think I would tell you where he was, even if I knew?" laughed Jarvan.

"Because we're corrupt policemen," blurted Cross from the tacky red chair.

"And we'll decorate this ugly wall with your even uglier brain matter if you don't start talking. He turned and pressed the barrel of the bright blue Desert Eagle against Jarvan's forehead. "You know what they used to call me back in the day?"

"What?" both Jarvan and Cross asked in unison.

"The Decorator."

Normally this is where a chapter in a story would end and you'd get to see what the other heroes of the tale are doing, but this isn't that kind of story. This isn't fiction. You can't make this stuff up.

Jarvan the Fourth moved fast for an old man; he moved fast like a young man. He slapped the Desert Eagle into the air and caught it, stepping backward easily through the doorway. A secret door slid closed and the two agents of Justice found themselves locked in a dank, sweaty room reserved for heinous sex acts.

"FUCK!" Gibson roared. "Cross, get out of that chair and help me with this!"

Both men pushed on the hard rock walls, grunting and moaning, like sex. They panted, gave up, and then restarted. The seconds felt like minutes. Were they trapped in here forever? Cross wondered.

Gibson searched for a switch. If there was a way in, there was a way out. He was sorting through a box of various sado-masochist devices when he noticed that behind one of the chains there was a short rope covered in old blood. Gibson pulled the rope and the wall let out a sickening groan and opened, and he snatched up Cross's .22, taking the lead up the stairs.

Stepping from out from the doorway, they saw Jarvan sitting, once again at the head of the dining room table, playing contemplatively with Gibson's gun.

"Ah-ah-ah, not so fast," the old man said, leveling Gibson's own weapon against him. "I'd like it if you both sit down for a nice helping of Cinna-Stix, before we all do something stupid." He made a grand gesture at the heaping, moist pile of delicious Cinna-Stix that sat before him on a ceramic serving plate.

Gibson pointed the .22 at Jarvan and made his way toward the old man, slowly, his heartbeat pounding in his ears. This was make it or break it, and he wasn't about to break anything. A lot of Jarvan's stuff looked expensive.

But Cross didn't exercise Gibson's caution. Lunging towards Jarvan, he tackled the elderly estate owner down over the back of his chair, and the Desert Eagle flew free.

"Where's Swiscock?" said Cross, nearly choking the old man by the collar of his silky satin robe.Jarvan chopped Cross in the neck with the side of his hand and the young detective fell off of him, sputtering. Jarvan rolled over on top of Cross, swiftly bringing a small dagger to the young detective's throat.

"Whoa there," said Gibson.

Jarvan felt the cold touch of the barrel of a gun to the base of his neck, a familiar feeling. He'd survived many assassins in his time.

"Je suis mon propre pére," he whispered into Cross's ear.

Cross felt the cool edge of the blade on his throat above his Adam's apple. He knew it was coming, the end of everything. Kendall Jarvan smiled. The old man's mouth was full of small, white teeth. He was pressing the blade now into Cross's flesh, almost puncturing it when, without warning, he leapt off. Rolling, he snatched the Desert Eagle up from where it lay, and fired it once, knocking Gibson's pistol from his hand. Cross didn't react; he merely ran his fingers along his throat where Death had tasted him.

"Now, I've got you both," Kendall said, on one knee, grinning. He pointed the gun and smiled at Gibson. "You two could have left well enough alone. But you thick-headed idiots came back and forced your way into my home, attacking my own help in the process, and then me. And you didn't even take off your shoes! I cannot tolerate such disrespect."

Gibson squinched his eyes shut. He was going to die like some stupid asshole here with this apron and chef's hat. But then enough time passed and nothing happened. He opened his eyes again and Jarvan was trembling.

"No. *NO!"* said the old man wearing a look of disbelief. It was as if some uncontrollable force was guiding him–

Gibson stepped in to disarm him, but it was too late.

"Swiscock," Jarvan had whispered in a defeated tone. He stuck the bright blue gun to the soft flesh beneath his jaw...

6 Villa 48

This time when Swiscock awakened, there were no windows for him to leap from. This time he knew where he was, despite the impossibility of its being. The room was somehow perfect, perfectly restored to his memory– the lights on the ceiling, the smoke stains on the walls from cigarettes, everything down to the small, fake succulents that lined the ledge beneath the two-way mirror. Would the bed on which he rested still recline with the push of a button and dump him into the raging sewer below? That idea had sprouted from Barnaby Weatherspoon's childhood obsession with a serialization of Sweeny Todd. Barnaby's ideas for the compound had always been the most cunning and the creepiest. *This place should not exist,* thought Pete, with a shudder. It had burned down, after all.

Yet places where the flames had ripped and torn appeared to have suffered no such fate. Walls that had crumbled and smothered the screams of those within now stood vacantly with the naiveté of virginity. Swiscock was in a room that had burned down when he, Barnaby Weatherspoon, and Patrick Gibson attempted to destroy the most dangerous menace to the modern world: former POTUS Jimmy Carter. They had failed. All Hell had come down on this place called Villa 48 and the few of those who had survived the initial destruction of the facility survived for much long after; Carter's most elite goons had hunted the Villa 48 staff and their families, slaughtering, torturing, and terrorizing in a broad, merciless sweep. And then, one morning, their pursuers ceased. Swiscock, Weatherspoon, and Gibson had managed to stay alive by staying together. It was over.

The three agreed, over some bitter arguing, that the price for their error against Carter had proven to outweigh the benefits of all their greatest efforts in the private world of espionage. Together they swore to lay low and shed any involvement in politics. In time Pete and Gibson took up localized law enforcement positions, Pete with his private firm, Gibson with C.L.U., and Barnaby— Barnaby had chosen to stay out of it entirely. (Or so Pete had thought.) After a while it seemed the heat had come off of them, they were looking over their shoulders less, but Pete knew the menace was always out there... like the great shadow in the space between Sun and Sea...

"Welcome back, Peter Swiscock," said a woman's voice through the intercom above him. He tried to sit up, but he was cuffed to the hospital bed.

Two days in a row, he thought in disbelief. "May?" he called out. "May, let me out of here." Swiscock struggled to get out of the bed but these handcuffs were military grade; he would need to pick them rather than break them.

"Relax Mr. Swiscock," said the voice again. "Your courier has completed her task and is no longer relevant to your situation."

"Who are you, then?" he said.

Silence.

A woman, her form a black silhouette against the well-lit interior of Swiscock's prison, studied the face that was reflected thinly back through the other side of the two-way mirror. The past nine months had put her under considerable stress. "First, I would like to assure you that you are safe here. You are back in Villa 48."

"Villa 48 wasn't safe the first time," said Swiscock.

"The first time Villa 48 was run by three foolish old men with dreams as big as their egos."

"We were in our twenties!"

"You got caught."

"We weren't old though."

"Well you're old now."

Pete blew out air. He was talking to a moron.

The intercom was quiet as the woman was conscious of her own ghostly features in the reflection. She'd struggled with vanity all of her life. Even now, in the midst of a crisis, she found herself judging herself. The woman cleared her throat.

"Villa 48 is now a data haven," she said. She brushed back her blonde hair. "We rebuilt it out of its own rotting corpse, restored it, modernized it, and all the while made it invisible from even the gods in the sky. And there's not a single paper trail leading out, not even to the potato chips in our vending machines. Do you know why?"

Pete shrugged, humoring her.

"We make our own potato chips underground. Villa 48 brand potato chips. Everybody loves them."

Most of Villa 48's employees agreed that the potato chips weren't good.

"I don't care about your potato chips," said Pete.

"That's because you haven't tried them. Where's Barnaby, Pete?"

"Barnaby? Barnaby got soft, got himself killed. Haven't you been watching the whole circus? He's got a pair of bullet holes in the back of his neck. He's as dead as his whole damn bird collection. Now my turn. Where's Autumn?"

"Barnaby's not dead."

"Oh what the hell is this?" Pete said, having already had enough. "Let me out of these shackles and I'll personally show you to his corpse."

"Listen, Pete," the voice said with unwelcome familiarity, "there were a lot of bodies at my– at Barnaby's home in Buena Vista. Most of them soldiers. But none of them Barnaby."

Pete said nothing. He mulled it over, thought of Autumn.

"You don't know what happened, do you?" said the voice, bearing, for the first time, the smallest hint of compassion. "You don't know then. You... are useless."

He thought he heard a sniffle on the other end. There were other voices talking, men. The overall tone was of concern. Abruptly, the lights went out in the room.

"Stay put, Pete," said the darkness. "Stay the hounds."

Swiscock shook his wrists against the handcuffs. He was losing time. Autumn was losing time.

"Let me out," he yelled. "May! Damn it! Let me out of here!"

But there was no one there to let him out.

7 A Warm Reception

There was a writhing movement beneath bed sheets in the master bedroom at the top of Jarvan Manor. May, moaning softly to herself, had been approaching something wonderful when the loud report of Gibson's Desert Eagle downstairs sent her catapulting into wave after wave of shuddering pleasure. She turned off the TV and closed her eyes, smiling at her mental image of Dick Clark and his famous family -friendly grin. She dozed for fifteen minutes or so in comfortable silence and then sat up, somehow aware that all was not right.

May Swallows threw on a plush pink robe and descended the spiraling dragon staircase quietly with her pistol drawn. At the bottom she saw the maids, unconscious, and then a pair of feet protruding from the dining room. "Jarvy?" she hollered. She crept down until she was met with the full horror of the situation: Kendall Jarvan was dead, the gray and red insides of his head were scattered across the floor.

"May," he moaned.

"Jarvy!" she said, quickly kneeling to his side.

"Am I going to make it?"

"Jarvy... who did this to you?"

"Swiscock."

"No," she said.

"Yes. Tell me I'm going to make it."

The back of Kendall Jarvan's head was completely missing. It looked like someone had spilled a plate of mashed potatoes on the back of the old man's head while he happened to be sleeping face down.

"Sure you are," she said, moved by Jarvan's resilience. "I'm going to get help." Help for the old man would be impossible, she knew, but her face set hard in determination for the next best thing. She went upstairs and quickly changed and packed an arsenal of weapons into a bag, and then she was out the front door and sliding into the driver side of her red Mustang. She took a long last look at the home she had surveilled and grown fond of, and then looked away, promising herself that she'd never look again. But there it was anyway, in the rear view mirror, and the drive down the hill away from the manor was pretty long, so she found herself glancing at it a few times just out of habit. She cut onto the main road and then Jarvan's mansion was out of sight.

The car was a spaceship disguised as a car but lacked the ability to fly or enter space. Scenery whizzed past. Her eyes flicked to the little *blip* sound emanating from the dashboard's LCD display. Swiscock's current location, courtesy of the nanite tracking device she had dropped into his tequila the previous night, appeared at the edge of the display as a small red dot. She thanked the heavens, quite literally, for her access to the state-of-the-art global positioning system. She wondered what Sturkey would think, but then quickly dismissed the thought.

She followed the roads until there were none. Dirt paths, barely visible, veered off here and there, until she found herself guessing which to take, as long as it seemed to head in the direction of Swiscock's red dot. The electronic map on the dashboard showed her nothing but a brown expanse of featureless mountains. Still Swiscock's signal appeared to be in range. She was going to get as close as she could in the vehicle before she would have to get out and huff the rest of the way on foot.

The woods were quiet when she finally came to a stop and cut the engine. Leaves crunched under foot. The hood of the Mustang ticked from the engine's heat. Wordlessly, May retrieved a suitcase from the back seat of the car and knelt. She assembled the sniper rifle and then placed the empty suitcase back inside the car. Next, she removed the global positioning system from the dashboard, noting that it would have several hours of battery power for use, now that it was unhooked from the car.

Equipped, she traversed the uneven terrain. She stepped over frogs and logs and even a family of sleeping hogs. The air grew chilly. Hours passed. She thought of Jarvan face down in the dining room, dead, and wondered what Sturkey would think, once he found out, or if it even mattered. He'd never approved of the situation, and they'd gotten somewhat distant for it.

blip-blip!
blip-blip!
blip-blip!

A quiet rage burned within her. Help for the old man would be impossible, she thought again, but she would get the next best thing, revenge. Swiscock on a stake.

She smelled burning. She was climbing a steep grade now, and the blipping of the GPS system increased in tempo. The tempo of her own heartbeat jumped with it; her excitement borderlined arousal. She came to the top of the grade and peeked over it. Nestled in the bottom of a valley that over looked a river, an enormous white building, wider than Hoover's Dam, was caught in roaring flames. The heat of an inferno pressed against her face. She grimaced, attempted to shield it with an outstretched hand. According to the dashboard display, Pete's blip was somewhere in the center of all that fire.

So he burns after all, she thought with a bitter smile. She'd wanted to be the one to light the torch. She shut one eye tightly and brought up the rifle scope to the other. The lens adjusted automatically to the brightness of the fire by dimming. She panned across the flames and then froze.

From behind the illusion, a woman in a small, paper white lab coat stood on the rooftop of the secret facility with her arms folded across her chest. Unconsciously she brushed back a stray curl of her blonde hair. Flanking her sides, a dozen sharpshooters had lined the perimeter of the rooftop and trained their lethal sights on May Swallows who was, unknowingly, looking back at them. *If she comes too close...*

It turned out to be no matter.

The tiny figure in the distance turned and fled back down the mountainside and the blonde exhaled in relief.

May, breathless, collapsed against a tree as soon as she was sure she had broken the line of sight. She didn't know how close she'd been to death, but she didn't want to find out. For the second time in her life she found herself amazed at technology she could not have conceived. One thing she knew was that Peter Swiscock was still alive and that she would have to play it smart if she wanted to pay him back for what he'd done to Jarvan. Shaken, but not stirred, she hurried back the way she came, though she did slow down to tiptoe past the family of sleeping hogs, and then she threw the gun in the back of her car. She punched her next destination into the GPS: 28 Washington Street, C.L.U. headquarters.

8 Within You, Without You

Pete hadn't fallen asleep in that cold room in Villa 48, not yet. He waited. Once the voice from the intercom had gone quiet for some time, he yelled out, thrashing against the chains to the point of exhaustion. He knew they were still watching him, monitoring his vitals through the darkness via night-vision and infrared cameras and subtle radar technology. Eventually, he'd collapsed and fell silent. It was time to give the observers nothing to observe.

He had called upon his training, whereupon he relaxed slowly into the recesses of his own subconscious, where language was without structure and meaning was as brittle as cobwebs. Thoughts and words and images and sounds came flicking past like lightning bursts, and Swiscock sailed along the electrical currents of his own mind, deep into the void. Alternating waves of reality and unreality dashed against port and starboard, nearly hurling Swiscock over, as a mountain of ecstasy rose from the depths and opened its yawning mouth to swallow him whole. He looked inside it and saw despair and desolation and dove headlong.

It was here that he had come for a reason. It was a quiet place, where the storm of advanced mental processes could not reach. From here he could review his own story in solitude and reflect as a mind within a mind.

It also happened that if those on the outside world were actively scanning Pete's brainwaves, it'd appear as if he was lost in REM sleep. Naturally, the observers behind the two-way mirror would dismiss all doubts that Swiscock was asleep, and they too would begin to nod off.

Swiscock raised a flashlight to his memories. Could Barnaby be alive?

He smiled grimly at the sight of his old friend who was hunched over, dead again, at the head of that table. In the realm of static memory, Barnaby looked to be at peace, a giant asleep at last. Quietly, Pete went over the shape of the blood that had dried on Barnaby's red tie; it resembled Death's bony scythe, but this might have been his memory embellishing the story. He flashed his light over the enormous crow and the sinister snarl it had been fixed with, to which he turned away.

He saw Autumn, mid-stride, frozen in time. She wore a look of disgust. A pang of guilt stabbed through him. He understood now what he hadn't before. How horrifying it must have been for her, on that January day, to enter that decrepit house in the middle of nowhere with its dead birds and awful stench, knowing not what Peter knew, to see the dead man, that lonely, bloody man.

His consciousness, and the pale beam of the flashlight, gravitated towards a detail he had not noticed nine months ago: before Barnaby lay a small, uneaten can of store-brand chicken noodle soup. The label, a cheap red and yellow, proclaimed that the brand used less than half the sodium of its competitors. Pete grinned cruelly. *Dear Barnaby,* he thought, *you could have had a heart attack. Yet you went the way of the dodo, anyway.*

It was then by the spark of some great insight that the memory flooded with color, as though a light much bigger and brighter than the one he had been carrying had been brought into it. Pete looked up. A small wisp of dust from the memory's ceiling fell down before him and crashed silently at his feet. The floorboards groaned and heaved beneath him, and he dashed around the hallway for the exit. The walls were falling in on him, as if a dozen bulldozers were pushing them in from the outside, and he slipped through the doorway to the lawn, tripping down the front steps. He looked over his shoulder just as the house behind him collapsed into a pile of debris.

He got up and reflected and smiled for what he had found. While the realization had nearly ended his dream, he was not quite ready to quit.

Pete sailed up, up, back up into the roaring currents of the storm, back into conscious space and then broke out into the pre-dimensional plane beyond it. Three thousand eternities later he paused at a place where the very real entanglement of consciousness and "outer" reality was illustrated in explicit, ancient patterns mutable only by those few who knew how to read them. Here in this vast, timeless space, he went to work. (To anyone in the outside world listening, they might have heard the faint feverish whispers that came from beneath Swiscock's lips, but as fate would have it, those who were supposed to be monitoring him had indeed fallen asleep.)

One by one, the handcuff's lock mechanisms moved and then clicked free. Swiscock was free.

Silence fell back upon him and now, when he slept, he slept a peaceful, uneventful sleep devoid of meaning or function and found simple solace in that tomorrow was a new day.

9 Swiscock

Pete blinked himself awake, all at once happy and alert. Today was a new day, indeed.

"Good morning, Pete," said the voice he recognized as from before. This time it took the form of a cute blonde with a ponytail sitting right beside him. She, as had May, seemed familiar. "I brought you coffee," she said.

Pete almost reached for it but remembered his cuffs were unlocked. He leaned toward the ceramic mug and she tilted it tenderly toward his mouth. The pleasant scent of a rich dark roast filled his nostrils.

"Villa 48 brand coffee," she said, triumphantly.

With his teeth he clamped down on the bottom of the mug and lifted it out of her hand, raising it vertically so all the scalding hot coffee could slide down his gullet. When he was done, he jerked his head sideways, releasing the mug from his jaws, whereupon it smashed to pieces on the floor. He flashed a smile, contented, with a fresh brown stain on his upper lip.

She turned and drew a picture out from a manila folder. "Recognize your girlfriend? This photo was taken yesterday." She held the photo in front of Pete's face, and sure enough it was May Swallows traversing the woods with a big rifle in her hands. "She walked all the way over here looking for you, and then turned around."

Pete's eyes betrayed nothing.

"I don't know how she knew you were here, but I know why she didn't come any closer."

"Are you here to gloat?"

"Yes, actually... and no. I want you to trust our technology, Pete. It's come leaps and bounds since you were last here. We have weapons and cloaking, and we're beginning to do things that I can't even tell you. But you have to trust me."

Pete made an obvious glance at the handcuffs. "You have a funny way of asking for trust, Honeycakes."

"The name's Felicia," she said sharply. "I'm sorry, but I can't remove them, not just yet. See, since you can't seem to remember anything about that day nine months ago, we're going to force our way in there, in to that old noggin of yours, and scrape it out. Once the procedure is over, you'll be free to leave, free to do whatever. It'll be simple and painless, as long as you remember your oath, that when you walk away from here you never come back."

A small part of Pete considered it: back to the life he'd led before nine months ago. The hospital, the hot cum, Jarvan's party and, now, this. It would all be just a dream, a glitch, a torn-out page in the notebook of life.

But none mattered, for Autumn was still out there, missing. To hell with anything else.

"If I consent to this procedure, I go free?"

She laughed. "Consent? It's out of the question. But yes, you will go free. Back to liberating cheap hookers and busting petty thieves to your heart's content."

Pete gave a look as if defeated. "Felicia, my dear." He held out his handcuffed hand plainly for her to take it.

"You have his eyes. Those bright blue sapphire eyes. Your mother couldn't resist those eyes."

"What?" she asked. Her voice wavered slightly.

"Let me look upon your eyes for the last time, as it will likely be the last time I look upon *his*. I loved your father," Pete said sincerely.

She placed her hand in his, and her grip was soft but strong. Barnaby had done well to place his daughter in charge of the new facility, Pete thought, though he regretted what he was about to do. "Do you know what he once said to me?"

"What did he say?" she whispered, looking, for once, very small and afraid.

"It doesn't matter what he said to me."

She gave a small yelp as Pete pulled her on top of him with the one hand and with the other slapped the button below the bedframe, causing the bed to tilt backward. The floor beneath them split apart and they fell into the maw. By the time the two technicians rushed into the room it was too late.

Pete and Felicia slid for several seconds in total winding darkness down a wet pipe that reminded Pete of a water slide except this one stunk like Satan's butthole. Without warning, the water slide released them into the open air, and Pete and Felicia fell several weightless meters into a churning river of sewage.

Pete was the first to emerge and he brought up Felicia with him, who was screaming, horrified, covered in filth. With his free hand he hooked one of the ladders that clumb to the raised platforms above the river.

"Come on!" he hollered above the rush of the water.

Felicia, sopping wet, ascended the ladder first and tried kicking down at him, but he grabbed her calf and squeezed. For a moment they locked eyes, and there was a mutual hatred. He climbed up after her and took her by the arm.

"Let me go!"

"Come on," he said, tightening his grip.

"You're hurting me."

"Shut up."

"Where do you think we're going? You're a dead man if you try to leave."

"Not if I take you with me. Walk."

They headed toward the light at the end of the tunnel. The light was a cloudless sky, the outside world dashing breezily into the muck. At the end of the tunnel the torrent of sewage was falling a hundred or so meters into the lake below. Despite the roar of the water, Pete could hear a team of footsteps growing behind them.

"Halt!" someone yelled.

They came to the edge, and not a moment too soon. Felicia shrieked at the height; it made her woozy just to look at it. Swiscock released his grip on her arm momentarily to shove her over the side—and then caught her by the front of her coat.With both hands she held tightly to his wrist and managed to keep her toes on the edge of the raised platform. Unable to resist, she peered over her shoulder at the fall below and nearly fainted; the white roaring water seemed to take forever to reach the bottom.

Pete dug his bare feet into the platform like an anchor, determined not to let the girl fall. He held out his other arm defensively, his open palm facing the clumping sound of the boots coming from the tunnel.

A group of deadly, masked soldiers appeared, first the one, then a second, then a third. In a triangular formation they approached Swiscock, weapons raised.

"That's close enough," he said.

The soldiers halted. Only the sound of the river could be heard. The winter air played icily with Felicia's filthy hair as she dangled over oblivion.

"Let her go," said the apparent leader, "you son-of-a-bitch."

Swiscock flashed a menacing smile. "Poor choice of words." He loosened his grip for a fraction of a second, letting Felicia experience the fall, and then grabbed hold again. The color had left her face.

The soldier-leader stepped forward. "Damn it!" he said. "Felicia, are you alright?" he called out.

"She's fine," said Pete. Her fingernails were digging into his wrist, drawing blood. He turned back to her and a twisted smile had crept onto her stricken face.

"What are you waiting for, Swiscock?" she said. "Do it! Drop me!"

"Don't you dare!" yelled one of the soldiers.

"Stand down!" She called out. "Drop me, Pete, and end everything for yourself."

Pete studied her for a cold hard minute. He threw her onto the platform in the space between himself and the three soldiers. She coughed and her body convulsed and the lead soldier immediately stooped to care for her.

"I don't understand," said one of the ones in the back.

"I'm not quite sure I do, either," admitted Pete. "But I admire her conviction. Definitely a child of Barnaby's. Tell your boys to get a helicopter ready, Felicia," he said, pushing past them, striding back into the darkness, unarmed. *"We're going to Africa."*

10 Goodlakes, ME

"Daddy, how long is the war gonna last?" said tiny Gibson. The future Director of C.L.U., then just a boy with shaggy brown hair, poked unhappily at his bowl of shredded wheat cereal. Vietnam was not an easy concept for anyone, let alone a young boy just trying to figure out this crazy little thing we call life. His father, a tall, stern man of great discipline and order, removed his spectacles and held them in front of himself, gesturing with them through a haze of cigarette smoke.

"Oh, Pat, Pat, Pat... Pat. Patty-Pat-Pat... I wish I had all the answers for you."

"Will you come back?"

Patrick Junior Gibson Jr. was clueless and worried. If something happened to Papa... Well who was going to show him how to fish? How to change a flat tire? How to correctly stimulate the female clitoris? Lately, at night, Gibson Jr. would sweat over such questions until they made him dizzy.

"What do you think about going for a ride in the boat tonight? Just you and me—"

"Don't forget Buddy!" cried little Gibson.

"And Buddy. We'll go out past Bluecliffe's lighthouse and I'll show you the ocean. The *real* rolling ocean."

"Gee, really, Pa?"

"Honest."

Gibson Jr.s face lit up like when you turn on a lamp in the middle of the night. "I'll go get Buddy."

A bright peal of lightning revealed the sky, followed by the thunder. Rain poured down that night, and the ocean churned dangerously. Patrick Junior Gibson Sr. was manning the helm with a glass of rainwater in his hand. The rain had long since displaced the whisky that had been in the glass, but he didn't notice; he took a swig anyway and threw the glass overboard. As a final gift to his son before leaving for war, he'd decided to get drunk and take him boating into a terribly dangerous storm.

"This is what makes a man!" he yelled, smacking his chest.

"Whee!" yelled little Gibson from atop the bow.

They crashed through the black tempest as waves ten feet high yawned and descended upon them. On both sides of his vessel Gibson Sr. had painted in blue the name PENELOPE, for the wife of the mythical man, Odysseus. Patrick Gibson's father had likened himself to the great warrior of Ithaca, a man endlessly lost in the pursuit of his home. This delusion led him to make reckless choices. Frankly, they should not have been out there on the sea that night. "Take the wheel, son!" he said.

Gibson Jr. climbed down from the bow excitedly and grabbed hold of the spokes. The wheel jerked violently to the side, throwing him onto the deck like a Raggedy Ann doll, and his father fell backward with a laugh and a burp. Another flash of lightning in the sky revealed to the boy a Monstrous Wave, and then the Monstrous Wave consumed them, turning the PENELOPE over beneath the surface of the sea. Cold, salty water stung his nostrils and the sea felt icy all across his body. He kicked his way to the surface, glancing at the lighthouse off in the distance.

"Papa!" he called out, but there was no answer. The black sea rolled around him, Poseidon without mercy.

"Papa! Papa!"

"—Gibson!"

Gibson snapped to, and realized he was back in the F-150. They were barreling down the highway from... he had no clue where they had been just now, he and Cross. He had been at C.L.U. looking over the Swiscock case and then there was a phone call... but now? How did he get here? He looked at Cross, who had one hand on the wheel, the other pressed up against his own temple; he was massaging it furiously. Gibson wondered what his partner was thinking.

"I thought your parents died in a freak water skiing accident," Cross said.

"What?"

"Isn't that why you hate the water?"

"I don't hate the water," said Gibson, startled.

"And where was Buddy that whole time? You said you'd bring him."

"My dog?"

Frowning, Cross shook his head.

"What?" Gibson asked.

Cross gave Gibson a look. "Your backstory always changes. And sometimes it's inconsistent. I just don't know what to believe anymore."

Silence invaded the space between them. Deep down within Gibson, a confession was bubbling to the surface. One that had been coming since the day the two had met.

"I, uh," he began.

"What?"

"Okay, I'll just say it. I'm self-conscious about my backstory. My real backstory isn't that interesting, or at least what I can remember isn't. I grew up on a farm. Mom used to sing this horrible song to me and my brothers when we were bad. I don't know, Garry. I've blocked so much of it out."

"Well, if that's the truth then that's a start," said Cross. "Not everyone gets to have some extravagant backstory where a single pivotal thing happens in their life that explains their thirst for Justice or Vengeance or Whatever. Some people just lead regular lives. Most people do, technically. I'll tell you right now *my* backstory isn't that impressive."

"What's yours?" asked Gibson.

"Fat kid."

Gibson laughed and then apologized.

"No, it's okay," said Cross. "You wouldn't think it looking at me now. But then here I am. And look at you now! Director of C.L.U., the premier crime-fighting organization of the East Coast!"

Gibson's cheeks reddened, and he leaned his head against the cold of the window.

"Are you really from Maine, though?" asked Cross.

Eventually: "Yeah, that much is true."

Cross chewed his lip. "Bet it's beautiful up there," he said.

It's beautiful here too, thought Gibson, as he relaxed a little more into his seat. "Hey Garry," he started, "you wouldn't happen to remember how we got here would you? I mean in this car?"

"Yeah, we got lunch at Sonic," he said, not taking his eyes off of the road.

The memory of eating came back to Gibson then, but he could swear there had been something else; the edges were still fuzzy. *All the way out here?* he wondered, quietly. They were still many miles from C.L.U., from D.C. Gibson yawned and dismissed the thoughts as they were beginning to make his head hurt.

Eventually the smokey capitol of the United States rose up to meet them, and they reentered civilization with all its honking traffic, curse-words, and stampeding children everywhere. People swarmed the streets and sidewalks and local Italian delis, each of them desiring a big log of salami. High rises belonging to Wells Fargo, Donald Trump, and Applebee's reached towards Heaven, each without quite getting there, but almost. On the ground, cars zipped around like tiny matchboxes.

Cross parked the truck back on the top story of the parking deck that was adjacent to C.L.U. headquarters, and they trekked the way down on foot.

"Welcome back, Mr. Cross," said the hot new receptionist, Mary, to Garrison, when he and Gibson entered the building. "Oh, and Mr. Gibson, there is an important client waiting for you in your office."

"I doubt it," mumbled Gibson and Cross gave him a sheepish grin. The two partners went separate ways, Cross to his cubicle down the hall, and Gibson to his office.

When he opened the door, Pat had to blink twice. A strong scent of perfume had smacked him in the nostrils and there was a woman sitting in his chair with her bare feet up on his desk like *yeah, I'm the boss now, little boy.* She wore a pair of dark, teal-rimmed sunglasses and her hair was cropped just below her jaw, and the skirt she was wearing was shorter than a midget's panties. On Gibson's desk rested a small .380, the silenced barrel of which casually pointed at him. As if in acknowledgement of the situation, the woman placed a finger over her lips in the universal signal for quiet.

"Gibson, is it?"

He stood frozen in the doorway, trying to contain his boner. He tried envisioning normal, everyday things in his head– toothbrushes, pancakes, coffee mugs– but each mundane image only made him harder than the last.

She floated out of the chair and advanced towards him.

She better not get too close otherwise she'll definitely know I'm at half-mast.

"Who are you?" he demanded. "Why are you here?"

She reached around him, pulled him to her so that her warm body was pressing against his. Like a mirror image, he caught her with his hand and his big strong fingers dug in to her deeply. The lavender scent of her perfume was intoxicating.

May Swallows said, "I'm here because I want what you want, Mr. Gibson." She was loosening his tie. "I want Peter Swiscock. And his head on a silver platter."

Gibson gulped thickly. *"Hors d'eouvers* are ready," he said and shut the door behind him.

11 Chapter Eleven

In the years before Villa 48 went down in flames, Barnaby Weatherspoon had been tracking a new evil from the deep verdant heart of Africa. A sudden child-turned-warlord known as The Grandmaster had earned a reputation for brutality and gained a cultlike reverence around himself, and was building a small empire. The warlord moved his forces by night, ensnaring village after village in an ever-widening grasp. Occasionally there were those who slipped away, however, and it was later rumored that The Grandmaster was in communion with the dead.

At the time it was thought that Barnaby had discounted such rumors. But now Pete was not so sure. He was not sure of much now, if even the dead man was really dead. He thought back to the memory of the crimson-streaked crime scene nine months ago, to the shape of Death's scythe on the fat man's tie, to what it meant. He had thought there were no clues but Barnaby had set one out for him in plain sight, and for that he was thankful.

To the benefit of his meditations, Swiscock had switched off his comms, and the loud motor of the black, stealthy deathcopter was drowning out all other sound. Amid the peaceful uproar he leaned over to survey the living, green undulations below and wondered what it was he was going to find down there. He looked back again at the girl, who remained expressionless behind a pair of dark aviators, and wondered at the relationship between her and her father. Barnaby had never mentioned a daughter, but then again, in the years after Villa 48, they had mostly avoided one another.

Suddenly the pilot reached back over his shoulder and tapped on Felicia's headphones. She flicked them to the on position and then Pete did the same.

"Alright, guys," said the pilot, "we're here. Now get the fuck out of my bird."

Felicia stepped into the bay of the helicopter and went over her gear one last time, by touch.

"See you down there, cowboy," she said, and left Pete alone.

She fell away into the green mass, gone from sight, until the clean white dot of a parachute unfurled. "Two days," said Pete, to the pilot, and then he jumped out after her.

He plummeted with exhilarating speed, darting through the cool air like a missile to the earth. He whizzed past Felicia, who was floating gently to the ground, and it was only at the last second, as the tree tops rose to meet him, that he panned his body back like a flying squirrel. He came crashing through down thirty meters of dense treeline, tumbling wildly and snapping branches left and right– the orange sunlight flicking in and out of his vision– until the final sudden stop, face down, at the bottom.

His ears rang out in silence while his vision came back to him, one eye at a time. He pushed himself to his feet and dusted himself off, calmly admiring the Swiscock-shaped impression he'd made in the mud between a pair of thick tree roots. Between the leaves on the trees, soft rays of morning sunlight caught here and there slices of steam rising from the ground. Pete sniffed it on his fingers, the earth. Wet with life, it crumbled easily. He listened to the sounds, as the dust fell away. His arrival had no doubt caused a great chatter among the forest's denizens. Gossip was being passed around in the language animals had spoken before man, in growl and birdsong. From around the bend, Pete heard an approaching crumple of leaves–

"I can't believe you're alive," said Felicia, with no real sense of urgency. She stepped down from a clearing. "Why didn't you deploy your parachute?"

"'Chutes only slow me down," he grumbled.

"Well come on," she said. "If your map is right, then we've got a lot of ground to cover before it gets dark."

They spent the better part of the day hacking their way across the forested hills in mutual silence. They stopped twice to eat, and several times to use the restroom, and then each time moving on at a brisk pace. It was a largely productive day. They had encountered no people to hide from, nor seen signs of civilization, and they had come across nary a woodland creature.

Still, Pete sensed the watchful eyes of the forest upon him. Once or twice he wondered if The Grandmaster was alert to them. Were heading too easily into the jaws of a trap? He knew they had no other choice, and that such worries were time wasted. Perhaps there was no Grandmaster at all and they would find nothing at all. This was somehow a worse possible outcome. Instead he thought of Autumn, and believed he was coming closer to her.

At nightfall, he heated beans over a fire. Felicia sat on the other side of it with her arms draped over her knees like a school girl. Her eyes were glued to the flames. Shadows danced on the trees and stones around them and high up below the stars came the menacing pitch of the sharp-beaked African Jungle Owl, the jungle's irrefutable apex predator. Pete pretended not to hear it and continued to stir the beans with his finger. Once he was satisfied with their temperature he sat down beside her and gave her a bowl full.

"It's been years since I've seen him," she said. "Since mom... He stopped showing up to work. He'd show up but it would be every once in a blue moon and he'd have these crazy theories. I could see that he wasn't sleeping. Everyone could. Eventually I told him just to stay home entirely. He obliged. But I know my dad. Even at home with his bird collection, his gears were spinning. And then, nine months ago, he contacted me on my personal line, the one we used to use when I was a kid. When you two were off fighting former POTUS Jimmy Carter. He told me things were going to get bad and that you were going to come to me."

She looked at Pete.

At long last, he smiled and said, "Barnaby, that poor, fat fuck, is the most brilliant person I know. A brilliant fighter and mathematician. One time, when he and I were imprisoned in Mexico, I saw him eat a Rubik's cube and shit it out five minutes later completely solved. Eventually word got around and the trick earned us our freedom."

"Huh."

"Yep," said Pete, reclining into a fallen log, "he sure had to eat a lot of Rubik's cubes to pull that one off. But the point is your daddy's a smart cracker— the smartest— and I trust him more than anyone."

"You think we're going to find him tomorrow?" she asked, rolling onto her side to face him. The yellow flames twinkled softly across the curvature of her bright eyes and Pete couldn't help but see Lola Weatherspoon, the love he too had lost, the love that he too had grieved, for which memory brought a bitter taste. But just as sudden it had come, the feeling was gone, and he remembered where he was. The night was calling him over and the beans were setting in. Swiscock permitted a low, rich fart to breeze out into his sleeping bag between his legs. He closed his eyes to the world and in a baritone he sang:

"I've been down to Mississippi. I've seen the stars above,
I know a lot about a little, and a little about love,
I wish that you were here to see the stars shine bright,
How I wish that you were here, here with me tonight..."

...Swiscock was also a musician

12 Evil Awakens After a Long Nap

By noon Pete and Felicia had placed several miles between themselves and the night's campsite, and they were coming up on the edge of a clearing. Tiny shadows darted past them on either side; trails of leaves fell gently in the wake of tiny scampering feet. Whisperings were heard; word was being sent out.

Felicia held her Beretta with two hands. Though her heart was pounding, she kept her composure.

Pete gripped his machete defensively; he was no longer using it to clear away the brush. Whatever waited for them, it would be here, in this clearing under the oppressive sun.

They had each stopped at the threshold, only for a moment's breath, though the sight was not what one would consider breathtaking. It was a village they had happened upon, one with little character save for its meek simplicity. A bright, dusty road split the village in half. Small brown huts made of clay and sticks flanked the road and Pete understood them to be for what they were: slaves' quarters. At the head of the road rose a large, grand structure like that of an old western saloon. The face of the wooden building was broad and dry. It very much was a face, for the two second-story windows glared like eyes and the wrap-around porch was fixed in a grimy wooden smile. A single rocking chair, like the lone survivor of a tobacco-stained set of chompers rocked idly as if it had been hastily abandoned.

They walked down the middle of the village, taking the road straight to the head. To the left and right, villagers had stopped mid motion in their menial, somewhat desperate villager-tasks to gape at the two intruders on their land.

"Alright you lazy scum," blasted the sound of a great voice, a voice deep and rich in the dry, empty air over this damned village, "back to work! That's enough damned gaping! And you two, state your business!"

They had made it halfway to the village square. They were now squinting up into the sky, looking at the ant that had shouted at them from the top of the structure at the head of the road.

Damn, thought Felicia. She had left her aviators at last night's campsite. She knew right where they were too, but by now it was too late to go back and get them. *Another pair, lost.* She shielded her eyes from the sun with her hand.

The figure was large and bulbous around the belly, and held items in each hand: in one, the long tendril of a lion-tamer's whip, and in the other, a double-barreled sawed-off shotgun.

"Well?"

"We've come from far away to see a friend."

This seemed to puzzle the man. Swiscock could tell that the brow of the silhouetted figure was furrowed. "There are no friends here," said the silhouette. "There is only work." Still, the figure said, "Wait there," and proceeded to scurry down the side of the roof and descend an iron ladder. At the bottom the man fell kind of awkwardly but managed to hang on to the whip and the shotgun. Then, he rose like a giant.

Pete walked briskly to meet him. The machete was sheathed, but he would have no problem lashing out with it, if need be. Turned out it needn't be.

"Pete... Swiscock?" said the man. "Pete-*Fucking*-Swiscock!"

The big, sweaty buffoon charged at Pete and hugged him up into the sky, nearly squeezing the life out of him. Feeling ambushed by this sudden affection, he pushed down against the shoulders of his old friend, Barnaby Weatherspoon, who, impossibly, was alive out here in Africa.

"Well slap me with a fish and fuck my dad!" cried Barnaby. "It's been years you old fucking dwarf! How are you? How's Autumn?!"

"She's gone, Barnaby—"

The bark of a gunshot butted into the moment, killing the dialogue before it could reveal anything important to the reader. The villagers ignored the spectacle.

"Now, now, my Barnaby, what's going on here?" said a silvery voice with a drawl. Barnaby set Swiscock down and all the youth and vigor went out of him in an instant. Between the hunched shoulders and sorry eyes this was a Barnaby that he'd never seen in his life.

The big man stepped aside so that Pete could meet his adversary.

The pistol, still raised into the air, was small in the grips of the long dark fingers of the man in white plush robes. He lowered the pistol into a pocket behind him and the hand came to join its sibling atop the smooth amber globe of an expensive hand-carved walking cane.

Livingston Bates was the spitting image of a wealthy black guy. His nose was long and his penis was even longer, as it hung out of the robe like a ferret.

Livingston realized all of them were staring. He looked down and tucked away his ferret hurriedly. He then resumed his impressive composure with a deep inhalation.

"Master Bates," said Barnaby, "My apologies for not introducing you. This is my old friend, Peter Swiscock, international super-spy."

"Ah, good, good. And finally Peter Swiscock, arrives," said Bates, with a perfect white smile. The next words oozed like toxic sludge: "I am grateful. I suppose if you had been killed in Buena Vista, I would not have gotten this chance to meet the legend in person. How you survived after so much bloodshed remains a great mystery to me—though I suppose every thorn has its rose."

Pete had caught Livingston's brief eye-flicker toward Barnaby with the word 'mystery,' and knew instantly that Barnaby had somehow been instrumental in saving his life.

"And who is this fine specimen?" he said, nodding at the only clean, white woman in a fifty mile radius. His eyes bared all the warmth of the inside of a working refrigerator, and an empty refrigerator at that.

"Felicia," she said, pronouncing each syllable through her teeth. "I'm Barnaby's daughter. And I am the head of a powerful organization which will bring you down."

Bates laughed. "I like your venom. But you will find mine is much more effective. My apologies. My name is Livingston Bates, though I have gone by other names."

"'The Grandmaster,'" said Pete.

"In an earlier manuscript that was my name, yes," said Bates as if stumbling upon an existential revelation. "Come. Barnaby, escort your daughter. Pete, come. I just opened a new bottle of Scotch and there are Cinna-Stix in the oven."

Bates turned and walked slowly toward the building at the head of the road. Pete, following cautiously, had noted that the man didn't need the walking-stick, and that it was likely a part of the man's grand, delusional persona. The narcissism was not surprising, but it would make him more dangerous. The mysticism, of course, was wrapped up in this persona as well. What this business about 'an earlier manuscript' was, Pete wondered. Though he did not know it at the time, he would learn by the end of the novel.

"Dad," said Felicia behind him. She was tugging at her father's arm. "No, let's go."

"I'm sorry, Honey. My time here isn't up."

"The hell it isn't," said Pete, glaring at his old friend. The odious sweet fragrance of lavender and Cinna-Stix blasted him at the threshold of the Bates estate. He somehow managed to keep the disgust from his face. Another first impression he had was that it seemed smaller inside here than its outside appearance had suggested, almost to the point of claustrophobia.

The hallway then opened into a wide living room that was furnished with an uncoordinated set of chairs and couches. The furniture was in a state of total disrepair. Pete guessed that nobody ever spent time in here anyway. On the wall leading past the living room into the kitchen were a few 14" x 18" posters of topless models. Faintly from another room could be heard Sinatra's "Fly Me too the Moon" and the casual tinkling of kitchenware.

In a moment of distraction, Livingston had slipped away. But before Pete could curse himself, the man reappeared with a pair of chilled glasses of scotch in one hand. The amber-headed cane was in the other. Against his better judgement, Pete took a glass.

"She's beautiful," said Livingston, motioning to the large poster hanging on the wall: a red swimsuit adorned Baywatch superstar Pamela Anderson, thrusting her sandy chest out on a clear skies day at the beach. "I've always wanted a woman like that."

"Autumn Summerfall?"

"No," said Livingston, nodding to the poster. They stood nearly shoulder-to-shoulder.

"She'd better be okay, Bates," said Pete, icily.

"Pamela Anderson?"

"No, Autumn Summerfall."

"Ah."

With all the sudden violence of a pulled ripcord, Bates lashed out with his cane. Pete drew his machete in the same instant and the blade embedded itself into the wood like a snakebite. They each put their raw strength into the stalemate, each determined to break the other's weapon. It was futile; all at the same time the pair of weapons and the scotches dropped to the floor, and the men squared off, unarmed.

Silence filled the space between Pete and Bates with such pressure that Pete couldn't tell if it was the blood in his ears that was throbbing or if it was the blood in his penis.

"This is the end of the first act," said Bates across his fighting stance in the white robe. His eyes shone with the certainty of a professional serial killer. "The end of you. And then the rest. You should never have come here."

"Well I can't exactly go back and change time, can I? So I guess you're going to have to deal with me!"

Pete sprung a fist out like the strike of a cobra, grazing Bates's lip, drawing blood.

"Your boys at C.L.U. are going to pay for that!" said Bates. He struck back at Pete with strength like a pair of twenty pound weights, dropping Pete to his knee. "The hit's already out, Pete!"

"No!"

They exchanged more blows and parries in a violent dance, as Livingston backed Pete up the stairs to the study. Bates shot out with an uppercut that caught Pete in the jaw, knocking him onto his ass at the top of the stairs.

"Punch punch Captain Crunch," said Pete, smiling. He got to his feet wiped the blood from his mouth. With the lengthy graceful strides like that of a praying mantis, Livingston ascended the remaining steps to the top, and again they faced one another. They locked eyes for what seemed like decades but, in fact, was only a half-second. Pete threw two quick left fists at Livingston's face– two hits. Blood leaked from Livingston's right eye.

"Is that all you got, old timer?" he taunted.

"I'm just getting started," Pete replied. He landed five consecutive punches on the man with the huge ferret cock. "How's that for a knuckle sandwich?" he said, but then, instead of waiting for a response, he pounced and continued to beat the living hell out of his poor adversary.

One punch.
Two punch.
Red punch.
Blue punch.

Livingston, with his back to the floor, was a battered man; his eyes had nearly swollen shut. His face was covered in blood the color of dark blood. He laughed, sputtering.

"What are you, some kind of Nancy boy?"

"Nancy *man,*" muttered Pete, placing the heel of his boot on the soft flesh of Bates's neck. "Tell me where she is, Bates, and I'll let you live!"

Bates cackled, spurting blood.

"Where is she?! Where's Autumn?!"

"You can't save her. She's in Hell!" With both hands he clasped Pete's ankle.

Pete frowned; the strength was still there; he couldn't lift his leg.

"Say it," said Barnaby, who had come halfway up the stairs.

"What the hell?" said Pete, tossing a sharp glance at his friend.

"Say it," said Barnaby.

"No."

"Say it, Pete! Say it!"

"I won't," said Pete, clenching his fists. But something primal and ancient stirred within him and it was too late to resist it. Pete calmed. A quietness that was louder than any military detonation enveloped the room, and the sunlight coming in through the upstairs windows darkened in anticipation of a great event.

The name was the fatal sound that slithered out from beneath Pete's cruel lips, and the name was *Swiscock.* The boot came down with the force equal to that of a train en route from Paris to Luxembourg in a satisfying crunch. Livingston's body went limp, but not before letting go a good buzzy fart that lasted a few seconds.

He removed his shoe from the lifeless body with a giant sense of euphoria. For an instant he swam in bliss. The euphoria came crashing down.

"I've lost her," said Pete, moaning. He turned away. "It's finished."

Barnaby stood alone at the top of the stairs now. "No, Pete. Like I said, it doesn't end here." Footsteps were coming up from behind him. Silently, the fingers of a dark-skinned hand crept over Barnaby's shoulder.

Said a voice that should have been dead: "I see you've met my hologram."

It was Livingston Bates. The real, human version.

ACT II: PEPPERMINT SHNISHCOCK

1 Uneven Tides

Long ago, Gibson had secretly installed in his office what is known as a Murphy bed. A Murphy bed is the kind of bed that folds up into the wall for space and concealment– and then back down again when you're in a hot pinch. This was Gibson's ace-in-the-hole, if you will. He took great pride in his Murphy bed. It was cool and sexy and he'd gotten a great deal on it, and, better yet, no one at the office knew about it, not even Cross. And in effect, Gibson's consistent long hours at the office, often from sun-up to sun-down, had garnered him an air of legend among some of the younger members of C.L.U., those who would vie one day to become the head honcho themselves.

But he knew he could not tell them about his Murphy bed, about the truth. That some nights he would lock the door to his office and change into his favorite tiger-print pajamas and then, quiet as a mouse, set down the Murphy bed. And he would climb underneath the cool blanket and watch the headlights from the cars as they passed beneath his window on Washington Street. He would count them, one by one, until his eyelids became heavy, until he could no longer remember, until memories became sounds became thoughts inside dreams– and then, with the morning light breaking in through the windows, a new day had begun at C.L.U. headquarters.

Happily, he would raise the Murphy bed back up into the wall, allowing it to click softly into place behind his oil painting of George Washington, and then turn around and start his day, first by changing back into his work clothes. By the time the morning crew was coming in, Gibson had already downed his first cup of Joe, and no one was wise to it.

Three days ago, it was in Gibson's Murphy bed that he and the spy, May Swallows, had become entangled in a fiery passion of such burning intensity that it was over in a matter of seconds. *The candle that burns twice as bright burns half as long,* Gibson had had to remind himself. Then, sadly: *I wish I had a longer wick.*

May remained a secret guest in Gibson's office and a constant reminder of Gibson's bedroom ineptitude. Though flattered, she'd refused Gibson's advances and his pleas to "give it another shot," which antagonized him to no end.

Co-workers noticed his grumpiness.

How he seemed to hide behind his office door now, more than usual.

How he was bringing more food back to the office than was usual.

Gibson, determined not to be put out by May's refusal to put out, slept at his desk chair with his feet on his desk. He could not kick May out; when he had tried, she had kind of playfully threatened him with the silenced .380. *Kind of sexy the way she points that thing at me,* he had thought, or something along those lines. It never occurred to Gibson that he was being held hostage.

For May this wasn't easy either; putting up with Gibson's constant come-ons was taxing, let alone her constant worry over the location of Swiscock, the enigmatic spy who had shot a man she had loved, Kendall Jarvan IV, in cold blood. She didn't know if she wanted revenge, or answers, or both, but she was now officially caught up in this tale and would ride it out to the end.

Night had fallen and Gibson opened the windows in order to usher in a breeze and to listen to the noises coming up from the streets. He sat by a window contemplatively. May was lying on her side, on the bed, smoking a fag, when the phone on Gibson's desk rang.

Now who would be ringing me at this hour? Gibson wondered as the late hour and line-chosen drew immediate suspicion. He looked at the blinking light without moving, and the phone rang out again.

"Aren't you going to answer it?" said May.

He frowned. He could only make the dame's silhouette against the billowing blue curtains behind her.

He picked up the phone, brought it up to his ear. "Hello?"

There was static, a roaring static, and yelling. It sounded urgent, violent, as if an action scene was being played out on the other end. *Not likely,* thought Gibson. But then he thought he heard gunshots, and the sound of glass breaking, and he realized the sound coming from the phone was actually pretty loud and that May, from where she was sitting, could definitely hear it too. Panicked, Gibson slammed the phone back down on the receiver as nonchalantly as one can slam down a phone, and was thankful that the room was dark, because he was certain May was watching him.

"Prank caller," said Gibson. "Heh. Just some goofball."

This man would make a terrible poker player, thought May.

"You need anything?" Gibson said, standing up to leave. "I'm going to get a bite to eat." He had to move, get the blood flowing. The call had given him chills. Strange things were happening ever since Swiscock escaped. "Maybe I'll grab something from the gas station. A taco."

He went to put his hand on the door handle, but then he felt May's presence right behind him, and he whipped around. She pushed him into the door. His back fell against it with a loud thud. She put her fingers on his lips and and ran her nails down the inside of his neck, and he knew the marks would definitely be there tomorrow. But Gibson was unable to think about such things. Three days of burning lust had reignited in him now and his head was already swarming.

"Tell you what, big boy," she whispered harshly, ripping into his pants. "Why don't you stay in, tonight. You can have my taco instead."

And yes, Gibson too might have cringed at that line if he hadn't been so fucking horny.

After another brief bout of lovemaking, May had fallen asleep and Gibson congratulated himself with one of her cigarettes. He wondered how he could be so lucky. He remembered that one time he scratched off a million dollar jackpot on one of those five dollar cards, but then the wind took it over the bridge and he seriously contemplated jumping after it. He looked over May's sleeping face and smiled, wondering what it was she was dreaming about.

In the dream, she was navigating the streets of London in her '84 Mustang, the one redder than all the red lipstick in the world. Heavy rain was pouring down, and the wipers were not wiping fast enough to compete with the rain. Her vision was blurring. Streetlights became streaks of painful light, and the needle of the speedometer was bouncing nervously a number spoken by no man but quickly understood as *VERY FAST.* She pressed her foot down on the brake, trying to stop herself from hurling into the traffic that was crossing the intersection ahead of her, but then she felt the brake pedal snap beneath the ball of her foot.

Brake-broke
I-need-a-smoke.

She lit a cigarette and cracked the window, but then flood of water came bursting in through the small opening like the way Mormons do if you're not stern with them. She was suddenly up to her neck in icy water. She fought to stay above the water's surface and held her cigarette high so that she could continue to puff it but then it was gone from her fingers, and then the water overtook her. She tried opening the door, but was met with such resistance as if a line of five hairy men stood on the other side of it, pressing it closed. She was going to die. By God, she was going to die in her dream. And, as we all know, if you die in your dreams, you die for real.

The car plunged onward into the rainy night, and through the liquid she was drowning in, she saw a man ahead of her. He was standing alone, in the middle of the street. He was holding a pistol and he fired it at her.

Gibson had noticed when May started squirming and he climbed on top of her, shaking her vigorously by the shoulders. He was shouting, not unlike he had done during the sex. "May!" he yelled. "May!"

"Swiscock!" she cried. She had balled up the bedsheet in white-knuckled fists of terror. She panted, scared and confused.

Gibson winced, but quickly went to one of his old young-Gibson tricks to calm her: a sensuous foot rub accompanied by an 8 oz. pour of Cabernet Sauvignon. When they were both at their respective resting heart rates, Gibson asked, "Do you always shout other mens' names post-coitus?"

Unwilling to dignify the question, May stumbled out of bed and put her clothes on. Her mind was racing. The dream had only encouraged her along her path. May grabbed Gibson's umbrella which was hanging from a rack next to the door.

Hey, that's mine, he thought.

It wasn't even raining, however; the dream was just fucking with her. She put the umbrella back and then paused for a moment to look back upon the old pile of man she had done unspeakable things with.

"Call me?" Gibson asked.

"No."

May was gone.

2 Evil is Love Backwards

Swiscock's escape from Bates's eerie residence had been nothing but cruel, dumb luck. Livingston Bates, the real human version, had set into action with a flurry of martial arts much flashier and quicker than his holographic predecessor, who remained dead on the floor. At Livingston's order, Barnaby, Pete's oldest friend and ally, joined Livingston in the attack against him, turning the evenly matched dinner for two into a dangerous party of three, the main highlight a surprise dish of betrayal, compliments of the Chef. For three sweaty minutes they fought, Swiscock mostly on the defense, keeping his third eye open for the chance to escape. He felt his time was wearing thin just when the big, fat oaf took a tragic misstep, sending Pete tumbling back down the stairs to the effect of freeing him from their grasp. At the base of the stairs, the back of his head struck the wall, and he saw Felicia lying down: her legs, sprawled over one end of the couch, her hands, folded over her stomach, and her mouth closed over the deep chasm of unnatural slumber. Likely drug-induced. "Felicia," he called. "Wake up! Fuck!" Two pairs of heavy naked feet stomped down the wooden stairs toward him. He got to his feet and sprang for the outside in an explosion of desperate strength.

Bates and Barnaby, both panting, stopped in the doorway to the bright sun outside, just in time to see Pete blast off in Bates's own black, 1972 Lincoln Continental, trailing a fat cloud of reddish dust in its wake. The car, partially obscured by the dust, grew tiny in the distance and then disappeared.

"Damn it, Barnaby," said Bates. "Will he come back for your daughter?"

"It's unlikely, Master. I'll send men to intercept him."

"Do it now. I can't have Swiscock escaping from me *a second time!*"

With his heart pounding in his chest like an African drum, Pete crashed through thicket and over the dry backroads of the sub-

Saharan countryside with what could be scarcely defined as a sense of control. But after his mind caught up to him, and after many stressed glances to the rear view he decided that he hadn't been followed, and that he likely had stolen the only vehicle in the village. Taking a chance behind some brush on a patchy hillside, he slowed the car to a halt in order to catch his breath, and to take a survey of its luxurious insides:

Both cheeks of his butt rested evenly on the white padded leather bench seating (which was quite firm on his back too); a wide berth of space beneath the dash offered his legs an expanse of comfortable breathing room; fixed to the dashboard, an array of robust silver dials for FM radio and amenities twisted sensuously at his touch; and in the center of the seat, an unusually heavy leather arm rest folded down to provide respite for the weary traveller. Pete reclined in the seat for a second, trying to get the feeling right, but the strange weight of the arm rest piqued him. He quickly discovered that the arm rest housed a cool ceramic telephone, one that would let him get a call out to Patrick Gibson at C.L.U. He held the device in his hand, looking at it as though he was unsure of what it was. Something of trepidation stopped him from dialing the number immediately. He *had* dodged his old friend at the hospital a few days ago, unwilling to bring Gibson into the whole mess. With Barnaby proven not only alive but traitor, to which the dual joy and pain seemed unreal, could he trust Gibson? He had to roll the dice.

The crack of a gunshot put a delay on everything; suddenly there was a massive Jeep, wearing a cheap green-and-gray camouflage paint job, barreling down upon him from behind. He threw the Lincoln into drive, and with a guttural cough it leapt into action.

He went nose-first down the steep hill, crushing small trees and other things loudly beneath the undercarriage. In fact the only sounds available to Pete's ears were that of the scratching of woodland brush, the furious engine of the '72 Lincoln, and the occasional missed gunshot from Bates's cronies. The Jeep was almost on top of him, eating his rear bumper. Swiscock could see that there were two masked men in the Jeep, a driver and a shooter. At the bottom of the hill he veered sharply, and the Jeep swept widely behind him, gaining him some distance.

From the Jeep a slew of machine gun fire erupted, cutting down almost all of the Lincoln's glass barriers. Pete ducked his head as bits of the glass rained down around the top of his head and his hands and fingers, but he managed to keep an eye on the side of the road. It occurred to Pete that if he lived and this little experience ever got put into a movie, he'd want *Achilles Last Stand* playing in the background, as he'd always thought it would make a good car chase scene song. This was his opinion and no one else's. It also occurred to Pete to check the glove box for a weapon, which– well, he was pleased when he did. In his hand he held an authentic Colt handgun, a well-balanced double action revolver with six already in the chamber. The length of the model's barrel was a solid six inches, which happened to be all the inches Pete needed to perform. Braving another round of gun fire, he turned in his seat and fired twice at the Jeep behind him.

The expertly placed shots dislodged the Jeep's windshield.

"Damn it," said the soldier driving, and the other kicked the spidery-cracked windshield forward. It bounced off of the side of the hood. "Keep at him!"

Pete ducked his head again at the third volley of badly aimed machine gun fire. He wasn't going to get so lucky for too much longer. Gun in hand, he dialed the number for C.L.U. Somehow, the dial tone sounded. Behind him: the enemy was changing his rifle's magazine. Inside: the receiver clicked.

"Pat!" he yelled. "Pat, can you hear me? Get away from C.L.U.! Get everyone away from–"

The top half of the phone exploded, just millimeters shy of his right ear, as machine gun fire marked up the dashboard. Now it was his ear that was ringing. He held the phone away from him and looked at it curiously. A pair of red and green wires stabbed pathetically into the open air. The momentary distraction would cost him a few seconds of his life, no doubt, for his heart stopped when he had suddenly gone over the edge of a small embankment and for a brief, small moment was nearly weightless. He almost bashed his face on the back of his own knuckles when the car splashed into the shallow creek at the bottom of the fall. The tires spun furiously and Pete spun the wheel frantically dodging a herd of alarmed cattle that had been drinking from the water. Once clear of the creek and the cows, Pete saw that he was at the edge of another village, one that was wetter than Livingston Bates's and shaded by the trees.

The Jeep was following along the embankment, which led to a wooden bridge. As Pete entered the village via the main road, faces curious, concerned, and disdainful appeared in the windows.

About a quarter mile ahead of him a big white van was waiting for him, facing him head-on. Pete slammed on the brakes and the Lincoln slid to a stop. Behind him the Jeep was already crossing the bridge. With his foes on both sides closing in, Pete shut his eyes and remembered back to what his *sensei* had taught him many years ago on the snow-covered plateau of a barren mountain. He had taught him not only to master his mind and emotions but even his involuntary bodily functions... the heartbeat, the breath, the knee-reflex when the doctor taps your knee with a mallet. He felt inside himself for the adrenal glands, felt them as if with his own hand, and then, very deliberately *squeezed* them. A fiery shock of adrenaline fanned out across his chest like a shot of Tennessee Jackson's famous hot whiskey (100 proof), and it spread until it was in his fingers and toes. He slammed his foot down on the gas pedal, turning the sedan from a thousand-pound driving machine into a thousand-pound killing machine.

Gunfire erupted from the big white van, putting little holes into the hood, but none of them in the target– Pete's face. He figured he had already flaked on too many invitations to Death's Great Big House Party to show up now. With his free hand he unbuckled his seat belt, and then at the last minute he dove out.

The black sedan smashed into the front of the van with a loud pop and the van's passengers, who hadn't been wearing seat belts, flew into the windshield which killed them instantly. The action was only half-over.

In mid-dive, Pete twisted around to fire two more professional-grade gunshots at the camouflaged Jeep that had been pursuing him the whole time. The driver fell aside not dead but asleep (a longtime sufferer of narcolepsy), and the jeep careened off of the road, missing Swiscock by a hair's breadth.

After lingering at ground level for only a second, Pete pushed himself up. He brushed the mud and clinging twigs off of his suit and jacket with all the coolness of a man destined to win a rigged poker game. From places in the shadows the villagers watched him. Some of them watched in awe, some in fury. He made his way casually to the Jeep, where it had gotten stuck, nose down in a ditch. As he approached it, the terrible monotonous whining of the Jeep's horn song grew louder, so Pete forced open the hood of the vehicle and used the remaining two shots of Bates's six-shooter on the horn.

He came back around the side of the vehicle, ready to reach in and strangle the survivors in a fit of vengeance, when he stopped short. The Jeep's shooter, who mindlessly struggled to escape his seat belt by tearing it with his teeth, was some freckle-faced kid. He couldn't have been older than thirteen. Pete frowned. *So this is who Livingston*

Bates sends to do his dirty work. A fucking kid? I should have expected no less from the bastard. The boy, sensing Swiscock, had frozen with fear mid-chew. Reaching in, Pete knocked the boy cold with a sudden punch to the jaw.

He awoke with pain in his eyes and a heavy, hurtful knee digging into the soft flesh to the side of his still-developing Adam's apple.

"What's your name, kid?" asked Pete. He eased the pressure of his knee only somewhat.

"Jerry," he choked out.

"Okay, Jerry, how's a young man like yourself get caught up in all of this?"

Pete waved his arms wide to emphasize. A crowd of villagers had gathered round and smoke was coming out from the small space between the white van and Bates's Lincoln. Overcast skies peeked down at Jerry from gaps in the treeline.

"I mean, don't you read, Jerry? Didn't you study me? You think you could have taken me out with a Hotwheels and a machine gun?"

Tears crawled from the boys eyes as he flailed and struck at Pete's leg. He was obviously in a state of discomfort. Swiscock relieved some more of the pressure and then said, "Look, I'm not bragging. I'm just saying that for future reference you have to study more. This applies anywhere. Now I'm going to let go of you and I want you to turn and run and live a new life. And start by finding yourself a new first name, one more interesting than 'Jerry.'"

"Thanks," Jerry managed.

Swiscock stood up and Jerry reached for his neck, rubbing it with his fingers. The blotches of red that had pulsed along the corners of his vision were already fading away; he felt himself returning to normalcy. His indoctrinated hatred for Swiscock was coming back too.

Just as soon as Pete had turned around to address the crowd of villagers on the evident importance of wearing seat-belts, a collective moan went out through them all.

"Hey, bitch," said Jerry, his voice weak from the strangulation.

Pete spun around.

"Je suis mon prope pére."

Pete's heart leapt.

Between the boy's grin, a flash of silver— a pin. Jerry held a primed Mark II hand grenade on his chest. A look in his eyes said he was going to throw it. Not one to waste time, Swiscock dove— onto the grenade— and the wind went back out of Jerry when he landed on top of him. Though most of the villagers had crouched and sprawled away, a handful of stoic and curious onlookers looked on. A loud but muffled bang went out from beneath Swiscock's belly and Jerry was dead.

Muttering profanities as he got his feet, Pete brushed at the blackened spot on his dress shirt where the grenade had gone off.

"Impossible," said one of the villagers, whose name was Clarke Armstrong. "But how?"

Pete tore away the cloth of his shirt and revealed underneath—

"*Mithril,*" observed Clarke Armstrong. The crowd gasped.

He and others exchanged astonished looks.

A short, stocky man with red hair stepped forward and said, "Well, it seems you are full of surprises, Mr. Baggins—"

And when no one laughed he said, "Did no one get that? I'm doing a Lord of the Rings bit."

Murmurs of recognition went around. The red haired man smiled, feeling validated.

"I need a favor," said the international super-spy. He unbuttoned his dress shirt.

Peter Swiscock, now adorned in the worn and tattered cloth that had just previously belonged to his newly naked acquaintance, Clarke Armstrong, waved goodbye to the village. Clarke Armstrong raised the new mithril coat above his head triumphantly and happy cheers went out across the village for their new weapon against Livingston Bates's oppression, and to their new friend.

The super spy zoomed off into the woods—

—and then out again.

Unto the wasteland.

Peter Swiscock, Midnight Desert Rider.

In the distance the high turrets of African International Airport shot up into the sky like a string of brilliant fireworks that never exploded, like Gibson when he couldn't maintain a sufficient erection. Lights danced everywhere: airplanes landing, airplanes taking off. A wave of industrial sound blared across the desert landscape, a reminder that progress came always at the compromise of peace.

Having arrived at the airport's front entrance, Pete parked the bike. He rubbed the seat gently and whispered, "You were one hell of a ride." He strutted past a confused valet and shoved his way inside.

"Good evening, sir," said the red-headed woman behind the counter with a smile as fake as her breasts. "Where to?"

"Washington D.C., I'm going to see an old friend."

"I don't care. Okay. Looks like we have a flight here leaving for Dulles in thirty. You should be featured in the next chapter of the book if you hustle."

"Just put me next to a window, damn it."

3 Backwards is Forwards Backwards

In a life not long ago, May Swallows had been an assassin. Quickly and efficiently and without question, she had done whatever her government had asked of her. Sometimes that meant taking a life. Other times it meant dropping a piece of mail into the mailbox or pouring a cup of coffee. In truth, she had only been an intern, but the experience had gone onto her resume, which was all that mattered.

Now, lying prone on the corner of a residential rooftop across the street from C.L.U. headquarters, she was ready to kill again.

With one eye shut, she peered through the scope of her rifle into the building across the street. Gibson, with his back to her and the open window behind him, was heavily invested in his Gameboy which he'd take out, from time to time, from a drawer in his desk. After spending several nights with him in his office she noticed that his routine hadn't changed much in her absence, leading her to wonder what his job at C.L.U. actually was.

At the present moment, his connection to Swiscock was all that mattered. Once the bastard showed his face it would be lights out. She licked her lips and caressed the trigger.

"I hope you don't mind, but I've already called dibs on the guy with the Gameboy," said a voice beside her.

May looked sharply, startled. It appeared that someone had joined her, a military man just a yard away, lying prone in the same position she was. He was adorned in standard all-black combat gear. A balaclava mask covered his face except for the eyes and mouth.

"Excuse me?" she said.

"Well since no one called it, I figured I'd lay claim to the guy on the Gameboy, for my first shot. After I take him out I suppose there will be an all-out war."

Did they think she was with them? And *who were they?*

She looked back at Gibson and was touched with a bit of sadness. Across the street and through the window he slammed his fist on the desk.

He'd accidentally pressed down on the directional pad when he meant to press left, and the Tetris block had shot down and stopped where it landed. Now there was no way for the 4 x 1 piece to make it where he needed it to go. In further testament to his failure, the display scrambled and he was received cheekily by the high-score screen. Gibson gave up. The new Gameboy was just too small for his thumbs.

May watched him hurriedly shove the handheld toy into the drawer and pretend to be working on something when Garrison Cross appeared knocking on the wall inside his office.

"Wait," said the soldier next to her, "I take it from your silence that you've already got your sights set on him and didn't want to raise a tiff by objecting to me. Well, worry not. As I see you were here first, it's only fair that you get first dibs. You see, I'm a respectful man, especially of women. I'm a man of culture. To be a man of culture necessitates some hanging back, some watching, not perversely, but observantly, if you will."

While the beta-cuck yapped on, May caught herself smiling at some of Gibson's mannerisms that she'd become familiar with over the past three days. Then she became aware of an approaching sound of boot steps. A second soldier, holding tight-gripped in one hand a weapons case, was approaching the two of them.

"Morning, Steve," he said. "Who's the chick?"

"Gibson!" said Cross, who was standing in the doorway to Gibson's office.

"What is it, Garry?" said Gibson.

"It's urgent. Everybody in the lobby is dead."

"Even Mary?!" Gibson demanded, rising to his feet. Mary had some *tectonic* knockers.

"I'm kidding," said Cross, with a chuckle. "But someone is here to see you."

"Who?"

Cross stepped aside and a tall disheveled man shifted into the room. His plain t-shirt was spotted with dirt and tattered and he wore a thick, bristly beard that went from ear to ear. The man's eyes, however, glowed like bright sapphires. Gibson shook the stranger's hand wordlessly in a way that wasn't awkward.

"You're in grave danger," the stranger grumbled. Gibson said nothing, keen to let his guest do the revealing. "I have knowledge that this very minute some of the world's greatest assassins are coming to kill you. They'll kill you and everybody in this building. In fact, I would move away from that window. They're– holy crap!" The stranger pointed out the window over Gibson's shoulder, and Gibson turned his body. It appeared that three figures were engaged in a dance on the rooftop across the street. It was two men and a woman, and the men were competing to dance with her. It looked like a very violent dance.

Wait a minute, thought Gibson, *I don't think they're dancing. I think they're fighting.* And then a gunshot went out, and one of the men the woman was dancing with appeared to collapse onto his face on the rooftop's ledge. A scream came from someone on the street below.

"Gibson!" shouted the stranger, standing up, yanking Gibson's attention back to him. "It's me, Peter Swiscock!"

Pete ripped off the beard and beamed heartedly.

Gibson grabbed Pete by the shoulders. "For Pete's sake, Pete– you're back! Why did you jump out of that window!?"

Pete had mirrored his friend's embrace. "No time to explain, Pat. Shit's about to get hot. So let's get out of here unless you want to get cooked!"

"You're a wanted man, Pete," said Gibson. "We can't go out the front door."

Swiscock attempted to reattach the fake beard to his face but it wouldn't stick. *"One time use only?"* Pete read from the back label. "Stupid Halloween Store piece of–"

"Enough," said Gibson. Halloween was his favorite holiday and he wasn't about to hear his favorite temporary retail spot badmouthed. "Let's use the fire escape." Gibson slid the glass window open and ushered the super-spy out. Outside, a choir of gunfire cackled and bounded off of the walls of the alleys. For some pedestrians, those who had been innocently going about their day on the streets, the quiet afternoon had quickly become a deadly nightmare.

Before leaving, Gibson grabbed hold of the microphone on his desk that was connected to the P.S.A. system, and shouted, "Listen up, this is the Director of C.L.U. speaking, Patrick Gibson. Effective immediately, I am rescinding my position as Director and will be taking an indefinite leave-of-absence as I have pressing matters to attend to. Thank you all for understanding, and good luck not getting killed as we are all under attack. Thank you."

Swiscock shrugged and then, ahead of Gibson, descended the rusty ladder to the alleyway below.

Though the soldiers, Steve and Bill, had been trained in karate, it was no match for May Swallow's judo. She dispatched Steve easily, using his own sidearm against him. He almost fell off of the rooftop, but landed stonily on its edge. Bill knocked the gun away, to the streets below and took on the role of the aggressor in the fight. But May was quick. Wherever he kicked, she parried. Whenever he swung, she leaned away from it. May was tiring him out under the hot afternoon sun.

Other members of that army, who were oblivious to the May Swallows / Bill / Steve situation, opened fire upon the C.L.U. building. *Damn it. Swiscock won't show up with this kind of commotion,* she thought. She twisted into a coil and then unleashed a spinning back kick that met the side of Bill's head with force. At that same moment she happened to turn and see, standing on the fire escape outside Gibson's window, plain as day— *well, son of a bitch! Peter Swiscock!* Fast as the devil, she drew her sidearm, a revolver with a mounted scope and squinted down the length of her arm and through the polarized lens—

But Bill kicked her hard in the ribs and she crumpled, dropping the gun. She looked again quickly and Swiscock and Patrick Gibson were scuttling down the fire escape that lead down and away from Gibson's office. Bill grabbed her from behind and put his arm around her neck, squeezing. Her fingers scraped blindly for the gun on the rooftop's gravelly surface, knocking it away farther. But then, just as her vision had started to go black, she found it. She fired it once over her own shoulder and the grip around her neck relaxed. She coughed, stars flashing in her vision, and then the door to the rooftop opened up. More soldiers were already pouring out.

Taking a chance, she dove over the rooftop's side, landing flat on her back on the metal bars of the fire escape. Consciousness whooshed out of her.

Swiscock and Gibson sprinted stealthily down the alleyway towards the parking garage which was located behind C.L.U. headquarters. They parkoured over a few ledges and did some cool tricks, and then Pete grabbed Gibson by the shoulder, stopping him mid-backflip.

"You guys didn't happen to impound my ride did you?" he asked with a hint of suspicion.

Gibson's expression read: "?"

"My Maverick. I take it your guys nabbed it from Barnaby's."

"Sure we got it, Pete... but we also have a hot Villa 48 issue Rolls that's just been begging for some action. Leather seats."

"Waste of a cow. We're taking my Maverick."

Next, there was smoke, screeching, and the smell of burnt rubber. They gassed out of the parking garage at a whopping eighty miles per hour, the elegant sedan careening over the emergency barrier. Pete's modified suspension caught them like a hand of God. He cut the wheel hard. Next thing you know, they were back on Washington St., leaving chaos in the rear view mirror.

They blew out of the city onto the dusty wasteland that was Northern Virginia. At first the huts and shacks stationed along the desert highway were plentiful but then they became fewer and farther in between. Years ago, former POTUS Jimmy Carter had nearly brought the whole world down, and this was the price the civilians paid. Unconsciously Gibson gripped the door handle.

When he was a child his mother, intoxicated on alcohol and painkillers, had spoken to him as an adult should only speak to another adult. She told him of the occult practices that often took place on the fringes of society and about a monstrous demon that lived by the strength of its name. Thankfully he could not remember the name. "The demon," she had said, however, "will return."

Bah! he cursed mentally. He struck his fist against the door, earning a disapproving glance from Pete. *Was this even true? Was any of his backstory true?* He couldn't tell what he was making up anymore. Gibson closed his eyes and leaned his head against the window. The glass was cold. He couldn't get comfortable. Something was poking him in the butt. *Oh yeah,* he thought, remembering the notebook in his back pocket.

When May had departed from his office several nights ago, she had left behind a notebook. Gibson found it hiding between the mattress and the bed frame. It was bound in tanned leather. Maybe the leather binding made it into a journal, thought Gibson, not a notebook. He couldn't be sure. He'd actually meant to get into it earlier, but then that same day the new Gameboy had arrived at his office at C.L.U. and he forgot all about it.

"What are you fidgeting for?" Swiscock demanded.

"May left behind a gift," said Gibson, cryptically.

May Swallows? Thought Swiscock.

For several minutes Gibson tried to get it out of his back pocket but it was wedged in there pretty tight, so eventually Pete had to pull the car over to the side of the road to help. With their pooled efforts, they were able to retrieve May's black notebook from Gibson's back pocket. They wheezed and laughed in exhaustion, and if you didn't know the context you might think something else was going on.

"This is her journal," said Gibson, handing it to Pete.

"It looks like a diary. Are you sure you want to go through a woman's diary?" Pete asked, fearing the worst. "What if she found out and got mad like women do?"

"Well..." said Gibson, shrugging.

4 The Past is the Opposite of The Future

The two old cohorts, Peter Swiscock and Patrick Gibson, hunched over the center console with May Swallows's diary spread between them. Swiscock read the words aloud. Pete loved to read aloud. Oftentimes he'd read to children at elementary schools. Reading to Gibson was a lot like that, he thought. As Pete spoke, Gibson's eyes lighted up. He displayed the raw enthusiasm of a small boy hearing his favorite tale told for the zillionth time and Pete couldn't help but find that endearing.

May's life, according to the diary, had been full of adventure and intrigue and many late night *liaisons* with eccentric billionaires and evil tycoons. Despite being heavy-handed on clichés and more than a few run-on sentences, it provided for some great reading material.

Swiscock peered ahead to see that he was almost at the final written page and became decidedly more animated:

"January 9th, 1988. Today was better than yesterday. I am starting to think I am an alcoholic."

Gibson frowned.

"January 26th," Swiscock said. "In two days I'm going to fly to Africa to spy on a Cinna-Stix dealer with possible ties to the occult. The briefing sounds farfetched but I suppose anything is possible."

"Bates?" asked Gibson.

Swiscock kept reading. "We all went out for drinks, Liam, Sturkey, and myself. The objective was to celebrate, by any means. By 08:00 hours we had accomplished our mission, however, I could not help but feel deeply troubled. In two days, I am the only one who will be setting foot in the southern hemisphere. The others do not share my intimacy with the task. Sturkey walked me home. We made out."

Gibson crossed his arms and looked out the window. A sign told him they were only twenty miles to Charleston. The stars had already begun to poke out from behind the red-grayish sky. Despite his emotional and sexual frustration, Gibson couldn't help but feel like a really cool dude, like one of the beatniks, a lone man cutting his soul open on the knife-edge of something Great and Expansive just to taste whatever poured out. He cranked the window down and allowed the dusky dry air of the wasteland to enter his lungs. He sparked a cigarette. "Finish the diary," he said.

Pete licked his thumb and turned the page.

"April 3rd, 1990. Hello diary, my old friend. I've come to write in you again. I will go mad if I don't. Bates has eyes everywhere. The villagers watch me at all times. They watch me when I sleep, when I eat, and when I bathe."

"Can't blame them," Gibson interjected.

"By Jove," said Swiscock, ignoring the comment. He had skipped ahead. "The Cinna-Stix trade is just a means to an end."

"Well what's it say?"

"May says, 'Bates has created something terrible. My hand shakes, my eyes water, and my bowels cramp as I write. I awoke last night to a small ruckus happening outside of my tent at the outskirts of the village. Peering from beneath the tent flap, I could see, by the light of the full moon, a small boy being forcefully carried away by two older men. It was obvious the boy was resisting. I listened at the edge of the tent as they went away, and then slipped out into the night to follow them.

'The moon was high in the sky and the night creatures were on the prowl, alerted to the sounds of the struggling boy and his captors. I tossed many Cinna-Stix to the ground to distract them, and could hear them greedily chewing the sugar-frosted side dish in the darkness behind me. I pursued the trio through the fields unnoticed. I came to the site of a big bonfire, which was apparently the destination. I watched from the bushes. There were men in robes chanting words I dared not remember. I realized immediately that the boy was to be offered as some kind of sacrifice. I was afraid for him. My stomach turned when the boy was forced onto a slab of concrete and a knife was raised— the ground rumbled beneath my feet. The knife went down. A sound came from the hills. It was so deafeningly loud that it blew my clothes right off me. I collapsed into a prickly bush, which probably saved my life, and I dreamt about what I saw. There was a light climbing into the sky.'"

Pete closed the journal and exhaled deeply. He looked at Gibson who was lightly rubbing his groin through his pocket. "Is that it? Read the part where the sound blows her clothes off again."

"No," said Swiscock.

"Pete," said Gibson in a half-whisper, like when you're playing laser tag and you want to tell your team what to do but the enemy team is nearby, "She wants you dead. For Jarvan. Quid pro quo."

"What?" said Pete, astounded. "Jarvan's dead? I just met him."

"The morning after the charity ball... She believes you killed Jarvan... Kenny, and the Jets."

"Autumn does?"

"No, May. I know you didn't do it, Pete, because I was there. I saw Jarvan take his own life." And then Gibson frowned at a sudden epiphany. He had to rethink his thoughts. *He had seen Jarvan take his own life. May wants you dead.* Something had happened back at Jarvan Manor to make both him and Cross forget, but now it had come back to him as clear as day. *What had been the reason for their amnesia?*

They were only a few miles from Charleston, West Virginia. They had been driving without destination. Swiscock struck a match and started a cigarette.

He, too, needed to think.

5 Cross Exits the Bathroom

He felt several pounds lighter, and satisfied, and winked at the man in the mirror. The automatic toilet flushed in the stall behind him. Cross flicked his wet hands over the sink and then opened the door to the hallway. He hummed a little tune all the way back to his cubicle and sat down at his desk. He didn't notice the silence or the general absence of personnel, but he wondered why the coffee pot hadn't been refilled.

"Mary!" he called out. No answer.

He poked his head over the top of the cubicle. "Mary? Gibson? Guys?"

Cross went directly to Gibson's office and had to do a double take upon entering. Sitting there plainly on the man's desk was his unfinished zip-lock bag of pretzels. But where was Gibson? *Gibson never goes anywhere without his pretzels,* Cross thought. *Whatever it was, it must have been urgent.* The window leading to the fire escape was open.

Cross went to the lobby and was shocked by the evidence of mayhem: shattered windows, the walls, riddled with bullet holes, the lobby snack machine, empty. A breeze was there that should not have been there. At the front door, the security guard, Teddy, lay dead in a pool of his own blood. "Mary!" he called out, hesitating to move over the broken glass. Even though he was wearing shoes he was no Bruce Willis and this was not *Die Hard.* He flicked off the safety on his Smith & Wesson. "Gibson!" he cried.

A tiny voice called out from behind the counter, "Garry!" Garry was the informal abbreviation of his first name, Garrison. The tiny voice belonged to Mary, who was hiding beneath the reception desk. "Is it safe?" she asked.

"I can't say." *I was... indisposed,* he thought cheekily to himself. "What happened?"

"They came for the boss."

"Gibson! Are you sure?"

"Yeah."

"Are you alright?" he asked, helping her up.

"I bonked my head when I first hid here, but that's about it. Oh, my god, Teddy!" she exclaimed.

Cross hugged her hard, willing his penis to remain flaccid with all his might. Both time and place seemed inappropriate, what with all the destruction and loss of life and stuff.

"Oh, Garry," she said like a true damsel in distress. "I can't stand to look."

"There's nothing we can do for Teddy the security guard," he said, wiping his tears with his thumbs. "But we can save ourselves. We need to get out of here."

The couple crept silently to the elevator, hand-in-hand, and Cross pressed the button for the basement-level parking. He didn't know if whoever was responsible for all of this was still in the building, and he couldn't help but force down a gulp of fear. The doors opened and the elevator swallowed them in.

Inside the elevator, there was no music, only dusty silence. The small, balding man whom C.L.U. had salaried to hide in the elevator's ceiling and play the ukulele had fled the building during the assault, never to return. The silence was broken by the small faint whisper of a fart. The back of Cross's throat instantly dried up and he coughed. Mary blushed. *Beauty, brains, and* damn*, this woman can fart,* Cross thought. The air in the small enclosure went rancid. He gagged.

The elevator came to a halt with a perfect C-note *ding!* and the two stepped out into the cleaner smelling underground parking deck.

"Mary," he whispered. "I don't trust my car. Let's use yours."

She nodded.

She was leading him to her van when, halfway there, an anonymous voice shouted from behind them: "Hey, it's them! Get them!" Gunfire barked in the concrete garage.

Cross had spun and fired the .22 instinctively, taking out the pursuers like a deft ninja. Mary grabbed him by the torso of his suit jacket and pulled him past a row of park cars towards her van.

"A *VAN?!"* Cross boomed.

"You're welcome to stay put," she said testily. A bullet whizzed past her ear. More bad guys were coming.

"I'm driving," said Cross. Cross slipped into the van and then turned the ignition key. A puff of black smoke exploded from the exhaust. Cross took them into reverse, peeling the van backwards and sharply to the left, and then threw it into drive. He pushed pedal to the floor and the tires screeched like a seagull on a mid-summer's day in coastal Massachusetts– one of those days where there's nothing to do the kids are all romping about just looking for a place to throw a baseball. The sun, friendly in the dry air, warms your face as you prop yourself up to take another swig of your Corona. Your best gal lies beside you and, even though this place means so much to you, you daydream about maybe one day getting out of this town. In the distance, a schooner drifts lazily on the water, the boat's captain waiting on one more catch before calling it a day.

Cross blinked as a pair of soldiers stepped out from behind a row of cars and opened fire. He drove past them without so much as a fuck to give. They went up a ramp that led them to the outside.

"Hold on to your titties, lady. I'm getting us out of here."

A pair of headlights in the rearview mirror caught Cross's attention. Behind them a black SUV was quickly closing the distance. His foot went down on the gas pedal so hard that he was practically standing on it.

"Hold on to your titties, lady," said Cross. "I'm getting us out of here–"

"You just said that!"

"FUCK!"

Mary's purple soccer-mom van whipped onto the street, nearly hitting an elderly couple, but actually hitting a younger couple. Dead on impact. Cross knew he was about to be in for the chase of his life.

He scowled determinedly, donning the expression of one unwilling to lose control of a situation. He was as stone cold as Stone Cold Steve Austin who wrestled professionally and had a few movie parts here and there.

They were rolling dice now, dodging traffic, taking one-way streets the wrong way, cutting through busy intersections, cinematic shit. Sparks flew to dramatic effect.

Up ahead, a railroad crossing issued warning. Yellow lights flashed as the long flat arm of the protective crossbuck lowered slowly.

"Do it," said Mary, bracing herself.

"You couldn't have picked a faster ride?" he demanded. To the right, a steam engine was fast approaching on its tracks. "Duck!" he yelled, and made a brief prayer for safe passage. They broke through the wooden crossbuck, snapping it at its base. The oncoming train bellowed hungrily. For one terrifying moment the behemoth loomed over them as they passed beneath its shadow.

The locomotive missed Cross and Mary by centimeters– nay, inches– but the pursuer was not so lucky. There was a crunching sound. In the rearview the SUV rolled to the side and then dropped out of sight behind the train.

The locomotive kept on pushing and it seemed to go on for miles. It created a barrier between them and whoever had been chasing them. Cross threw the overheated van into park and rolled the windows down to let the fresh air in. He needed it and he was sure Mary did too.

The two of them high fived.

"That train really came out of nowhere," said Mary, "plot-wise."

"You're telling me. That was a real *deus ex machina.*"

"Heh. It looks like our friends just bought themselves *two tickets to paradise.*"

Cross chuckled.

Twelve minutes later: "That was easily the most dangerous ride of my life," Mary said. She reached into her brown leather Louis Vuitton purse for her canister of Rouge Dior lipstick, and uncapped it discreetly.

Cross was leaning back, his eyes closed. "All that mess for Gibson, huh? I say we turn this van around in a couple minutes and go back. No doubt the government has gotten involved by now and scared those goons off." He looked at her. She applied the lipstick, slowly, *sexually,* to her lips.

"You know, you really know how to drive a car– err– van," she said.

Was she coming on to him? There was no way a woman of this breast size would ever, or could ever, find someone like Cross even remotely attractive.

"Well–"

Cross was cut off by the touch of Mary's pointer finger aka index finger on his upper lip.

"Shh," she said with a gaze that made his stomach turn to puddy. "I think the both of us deserve a reward." Mary ripped of her blouse and threw it on Cross's face, blinding him, which was perfect for what she was about to do to him. She reached over the center console and began working his khakis like a pornstar. She went down on him for hours.

And I mean *hours.*

Afterwards, they fucked straight hardcore in the backseat. We won't divulge all the details in *this* novel, however. Look for a steamy Swiscock erotica spinoff coming late fall.

And as the two slumbered together in the throes of a budding passion, a shadow passed over the window of the van. It was the shadow of a tall man with urgent business, the shadow of a man of cunning, of character, and of depth. In the shadow's hand: a pistol.

Tonight's forecast:

CLOUDY WITH A CHANCE OF STURKWISE

6 Cloudy With a Chance of Sturkwise

The gun tapped three times on the window. Cross blinked, surprised. A man was outside. Leaving Mary, he quietly clambered back into the front seat of the van and turned the key for just the power to come on. The man had followed him along the side of the vehicle. The window came down slowly.

"I guess this is it, huh," Cross said. "Just make it quick, for her."

The man with the gun pointed at Cross remained silent. He was very tall and he wore the austere look of a European well. Beneath the woolen fedora, a glint in the wintry green eye hinted at a joyful childhood in Essex, and the slender beige overcoat suggested countless hours hiked blindly along the River Thames, berating the locals for amusement. The fashionable black leather glove that gripped the gun pointed at his face told him the desperate tale of a bleak, year long voyage to sea– a suicide mission– but the man had returned. Scarred and dangerous, he had returned. This is what the glove told Cross.

"Well?" Cross said, suddenly agitated.

"You're Garrison Cross, aren't you?"

"Just 'Cross'."

"I've been following you for some time. I have questions for you. But we can't talk here."

The young detective pondered the implication. "And her?"

"I have a name," said Mary, from the back seat.

"She'll be safer if she comes too."

Against Mary's reasonable wishes, Cross and Mary abandoned the van there and squeezed into the back of the tall man's VW Beetle.

Once inside the vehicle, the stranger spoke. His voice was notably less serious than before. "I'm afraid we got off to a cold start. But it had to be that way." He reached over the seat to shake their hands. "The name's Sturkwise. Call me Sturkey."

"That's a beautiful name," said Mary, as Sturkey started the engine. The sound came on. The voice on the radio, deep and urgent, spoke from a place of fear. The speaker was detailing the death and destruction that had taken place on Washington Street five hours ago. After deciding that he had heard enough, Sturkey cut off the radio.

"I can't believe it," said Cross, full of sadness. He was referring to a tomato sauce stain he had just noticed on the belly of his dress shirt.

"Well man up," said Sturkey, his eyes peering ahead with grave conviction. "I have a feeling much worse is on the horizon– within the chapter, even."

Some time later the Beetle was drawing up to a parking garage. Cross stuck his head out of the window and looked up dizzily at the entire staggering height of the Trump Tower loomed over them. Quickly the sight was gone when the darkness of the building's bowels swallowed them in. The three took an elevator. Cross wasn't sure how close or far from Mary he was supposed to stand. The jingle in the elevator was nice but Cross missed the little ukulele man at C.L.U. and wondered how he had fared through all of the chaos.

The elevator stopped, and then Sturkey took the lead down a bleak and narrow hall. Like some kind of bad mushroom trip, the hall got narrower and narrower until they were shuffling sideways one after another. Then just when Cross thought he was going to get stuck there and die, the far wall began to drop.

"Oh my god, we're in another elevator!" Cross exclaimed, unable to contain himself.

"A secret elevator," Sturkey amended. "And listen."

He listened. He would have smirked at Sturkey if he could have, but the tight space prohibited any neck movement.

"Secret elevators always have better music. That's spying 101," said Sturkwise.

"They could have made this secret elevator more spacious," said Mary.

As excited as Cross was, he still wondered what this was all about and what he was doing in Washington D.C.'s Trump Tower.

As soon as the door opened at the top, these questions evaporated. They each squeezed through a tiny gap in the wall with considerable effort and suddenly found themselves in what was another world. Strange plants with big green leaves sat in ebony pots and wiry, red-flowered vines were crawling across the ceiling, some of them hanging down in groups. The air was cool and misty and had a slight mineral taste. Odd-looking moths with iridescent wings, each charming in their oddity, fluttered hither and thither.

"Don't touch the moths," advised the Sturkmeister, jerking sharply as one darted past his nose. "They're extremely poisonous."

"What is this place?" said Mary.

"Headquarters," he answered. "The penthouse suite."

Cross, Mary, and Sturkey came into a clean, empty room that was lighted by the great orange glow of the setting sun. The entire opposite wall comprised four large glass panels that afforded its occupants a view to die for. Mesmerized, Cross passed the flat-screen TV on the wall and the single table in the center of the room. He looked out. From the topmost floor of the Trump Tower, the D.C. cityscape was breathtaking. *This is it,* he thought, ready. *They're going to make me part of The Avengers.*

Soon the three were seated around the table drinking shitty black coffee, which dimmed the mood somewhat. That, and the topic of conversation:

"I don't know what you're talking about," said Cross, frustrated.

"I'm talking about a *psychic blast,"* said Sturkey, his frustration matching Cross's. "It's the only way to explain your amnesia, if that's what you're experiencing... You're telling me you still don't remember?"

"Remember what?"

"Your little trip to Jarvan Manor, when you and your big friend played detective and got the main man killed?"

"No... I don't remember," said Cross, swirling the thinly-flavored light roast in his Styrofoam cup. Images were coming back to him, but they didn't make any sense. There was a dragon... and a dungeon, and chains hanging from the ceiling. A tacky red seat. No, these were from last night's dream. He and Gibson had gone out for lunch at Sonic that day, nothing exceptional about it.

Sturkey recognized the change in the boy's demeanor. He said, "Well that confirms my suspicions, at least." He wrote something down.

"Excuse my tardiness," said May Swallows, popping in with a clipboard and some *loooong* legs. She had been through a lot today but she sure knew how to pull through in the looks department—which was important to society, especially in the era in which this story takes place. Frankly, Cross was wowed.

"Holy shit," said Mary. "You were at C.L.U. You went to Gibson's office. I never saw you leave."

"Well trust me, my extended stay wasn't exactly pleasure."

Cross shot Ms. Swallows a suspicious look.

"Everybody, meet my associate, May," said Sturkey.

Cross had stood up from his seat to shake her hand, but Mary did not. She was not interested in May. From behind the coffee cup she was watching Sturkey's mannerisms. His body language had spoken business, but his eyes were eating the young girl alive. She could tell that he was madly in love with her.

Earlier that day, Sturkey had come to May's rescue when she had flung herself over the rooftop after fighting the masked men. He had known where she would be because he knew her movements and had been keeping an eye on her. When she fell, he was there to catch her. Without a protest, he took her to a quiet place. There they had talked for the first time since she had left Jarvan Manor. Regrettably, some of the warmth between them was gone; their conversation had about all the character of a mere correspondence. Something had changed in her, he knew, and the best way forward would be through completing their work. Sturkey suggested that May, who had been unaware of the *psychic blast* that had occurred at the exact time of Jarvan's self-inflicted gunshot wound, was perhaps "jumping the gun" on Swiscock.

Having still been heated from the battle just minutes ago, she claimed she was getting blindsided. She didn't believe that such a phenomenon existed. He handed her the data in the form of a stack of fifteen or so papers stapled together. Furiously, she flipped through the pages until she stopped, abruptly. A pair of graphs, among dozens, stood out. They both indicated spikes in atmospheric electricity. One set of data bore the latitudinal and longitudinal coordinates for Kendall Jarvan IV's home at the time of the gunshot. The other, for Africa, in the same remote place she had stayed many years ago while she studied a man named Livingston Bates.

Presently, she clicked a small remote in her hand. The flat-screen television on the far wall of the conference room displayed a black-and-white image of three shirtless men on a boat, each arm-over-shoulder, each smiling at the camera.

"You no doubt recognize the man on the right," said May matter-of -factly.

"Gibson," said Cross, mildly intrigued. He had never seen this photograph before. In it, Gibson looked much younger, handsomer, and even spritely. The man still had hair on his head. He suddenly realized he really knew nothing of his longtime partner at C.L.U..

"...In the middle," resumed May, "is none other than the legendary super-spy, Peter Swiscock. We'll come back to him. And the one on the left—"

"Good lord, he's big," said Mary.

"That one goes by the name Barnaby Weatherspoon, although there are doubts that it's his birth name."

"That's where Gibson went, nine months ago, with a search team. To Weatherspoon's place. He forbade me to come, and then he didn't say much to me about it. And then it was very much under the rug. I had honestly forgotten all about it until Swiscock woke up. Does the name 'Autumn Summerfall' mean anything to you?" Cross asked. "Swiscock was looking for her when he escaped the hospital."

May wrote the name down. "No," she said. She shifted gears back to the topic at hand. "We need to know what Gibson saw at Weatherspoon's place. Your fellow agents must have taken pictures."

"I don't know."

"Damn it, Cross," May yelled, slamming her fist on the table.

"They're probably gone! C.L.U. was raided today. Don't you watch the news?"

May realized that he was right. Wordlessly, she sat into her chair. Any hope of knowing what had transpired was gone.

Sturkey leaned back and cracked his knuckles. "It's alright, May," he said. "There will be a way forward. We can go to Africa. See this ourselves, get closer than before."

"What is this about?" said Cross, invested.

"It's suicide," she said, ignoring Cross.

"They won't be expecting us," replied Sturkey.

"Excuse me!" said Cross, standing. "Tell us about this supposed *psychic blast.* How does Jarvan fit into the equation?"

"Might as well tell," mumbled Sturkey. "Nothing to lose."

"Except our reader's interest," said May, huffing.

"Come on," said Cross.

"Alright. It's a winding story but we'll get there." When no one said anything to this she continued. "As you know, Jarvan comes from money. But where does that money come from? Many years ago, Jarvan's family had invested in some socks that put the Jarv—"

"Stocks," Mary corrected.

"No, *socks,*" May resumed. "Jarvan the Fourth's father's father's father bought a thousand shares in a budding sock-company that has since become one of the largest in the world. With the development of nylon in 1938, both the industry and the Jarvan estate took off and never looked back."

"Everybody wears socks," interjected Sturkey. "It's a great thing to invest in." He spoke with the offhand certainty of a true pro. "I'm wearing socks now, see?" He pulled up a pant leg to reveal a long black sock that went halfway up the calf.

Thankfully, May retook control of the conversation: "With all that wealth comes fame, notoriety, and... eccentricity. If not for having nothing better to do, Jarvan IV dabbled in the occult. He would read bad literature and attended meet-ups with other wealthy types who fancied themselves 'spiritual.' He loved these societies so much that he created his own. It was called *Organization-Y.*"

Sturkey clicked the remote that changed the image on the TV screen. He clicked it a few more times and then stopped. Displayed was a picture of wreckage, flaming wreckage.

"I remember that photograph from the news," said Mary. "I was just a child at the time. But I remember it. That's Guantanamo Bay."

"From which all the inmates escaped," said Sturkey, filling in the blanks. "Organization-Y was behind that."

He clicked the remote again. Another famous photograph seemingly taken in Hell.

"The airstrikes of '78. You know the ones."

Sturkey's thumb pressed the button again. *Click.* More slides. More death and ruins.

"When money gets in the wrong hands, there's no telling how much destruction can be done."

"Tell that to our congressmen," quipped Cross. "But seriously, if you knew all of this was happening then why didn't you stop it? Why didn't you apprehend Jarvan when you had the chance?"

"May and I? We would have looked silly if we had tried," said Sturkey. "As far as the rest of the world was concerned, Jarvan's hands were clean."

"But evidently not clean enough. Hence the—"

"*Psychic blast.*"

The familiar sound of a television briefly flickering through a channel of static interrupted the conversation. One by one, they each turned to faced the TV which, apparently, had changed of its own accord. The footage was mostly black and grainy and the audio crackled like popping flesh. From the darkness of the image, a blubberous human-shaped monstrosity produced a smile that belonged somewhere in an insane asylum. At first, May, Mary, Cross, and Sturkey were each shouting guesses as to what they were looking at, and it dawned on Cross first: "Hey, that's former U.S. President, Jimmy Carter!"

"Yahtzee!" said the man on the screen as he shifted his considerable bulk. The suit and tie he wore suggested his power, authority, and freedom, though he appeared to be bound to a chair. His right hand rested casually over a joystick that stood up from the armrest. Pressing it forward, he, with the chair, came closer to the screen. "Pendleton," he bellowed. "And Maybel Beverly Swallows. May. What a pleasant surprise seeing you here." Behind him was a flag and an enormous picture of the Earth.

"Don't act like it's a surprise," said Sturkey. "You hijacked our system. You planned this."

"Truly," said Carter, "you are better than Swiscock."

Sturkey's face reddened a little.

"I am afraid to inform you that your time is up. I am pulling the trigger."

"What?" said Cross.

"See you in hell."

The television screen zipped into a white line across the horizontal axis and then faded away. One by one, Sturkey, May, Cross, and Mary each became aware of a faint chopping sound. It was not the kind of chopping sound an audience might hear throughout a Bruce Lee action flick, but rather the chopping sound of helicopter blades through the previously unperturbed air of the Trump Tower skyline! Someone burst into the room at that moment, a young redheaded boy in slacks and a white button-up that was way too big for him. An intern.

"Mr. Pendleton," he said frantically, his freckled forehead dotted with sweat, "we're under attack!"

"Get out of here you god damned intern!" grumbled Sturkey.

The intern hastily exited.

The overhead lights in the meeting room flickered and the floor rumbled, shaking the four of them about carelessly as if they were the crew members aboard the bridge of the *U.S.S. Enterprise* during a Starfleet / Klingon space battle. The rumbling subsided. Then, before they could stand, a shadow over them passed. Beyond the glass windows rose steadily the full fearsome form of a Black Hawk helicopter, eclipsing the amber sun behind it— and all hope with it.

"Oh my god," said Sturkey, soiling himself.

The helicopter turned ninety degrees so that the length of its body ran parallel to the room. The silhouette of a henchman stood in the bay window with something dangerous-looking balanced on his shoulder.

"RPG," shouted Sturkey, "hit the deck!"

This was one of those moments where time seemed to last forever. Cross dove onto Mary as the high velocity projectile penetrated the glass window and grazed the top of his shoulder. It embedded itself into the wall behind them with a loud crack. Milliseconds ticked like seconds.

Sturkey, with his hands over the back of his head, looked up slowly at the missile. The tail end of it fizzled out.

"A dud?" said May— and then it exploded into a ball of hot flame that gushed out, melting the glass as it shattered outward. The force destabilized the Black Hawk for a moment, and the shattered glass exposed a cold, blustery wind into the room. Other than sharing a significant loss of hearing, the four were okay.

"Nobody move!" yelled Sturkey. "But get to the door!"

May crawled to the exit on her hands and knees. Her clothes were torn to shreds revealing nipples and buttocks. Sturkwise had to look. He definitely wasn't as 'over' her as he had told himself.

Mary scurried out from underneath Cross and got to her feet. She was covered in blood. Her own? Cross's? Tears were streaming down her face and she was hyperventilating like a thirsty pug on a hot summer's day.

"Mary!" Cross shouted up from between her feet. "Mary, get back down!" He grabbed her ankle but the blood on his hand would cause him to lose her.

She wasn't listening nor hearing. She was in a state of panic. Bullets ripped into the wall beside her and she ran for the door. With each stride she came closer. The marksman in the helicopter was quicker; up and down she was peppered, until she was no more.

"NOOOOO!" Cross screamed like how characters in movies scream when someone they care for suffers a painful death.

Cross, May, and Sturkey kept their heads down while the machine gun continued to fire blindly into the room. Overhead sprinklers had activated, turning the thinly carpeted floor into a frigid pool of blood and debris.

Cross crawled to her as the dust and bits of hot metal ricocheted around him, and turned her over. She was gone. *No,* he wept.

At a necessary cessation of gunfire, Cross stood up. He was no longer himself, but rather an assembly of atoms that had lost consciousness of itself as being a distinct entity from everything that was not itself, and now felt not only connected with all other atoms in the universe, but *complete* as all things were one and he was all things. Cross charged desperately across the length of the room, ripping off his tie and buttoned-down shirt with each powerful stride. His chiseled pecks glistened by the light of the surrounding flames. Splashes of water by his feet caught the sun's final rays.

The henchman manning the mounted machine gun turret in the bay of the helicopter pivoted the weapon as the young detective passed into a plume of black smoke. When Cross appeared next, his .22 was held out across the length of his arm, and it was too late for the henchman to get an accurate shot. Both men opened fire upon the other. Cross sprang from the edge of the building as bullets whizzed by his ankles. Time dilated. In the ten feet of open air between the Trump Tower and the mercenary Black Hawk, Cross squeezed the cold trigger of his .22 five times. Each gunshot struck the henchman in the chest, staggering him backward to the other side of the open bay door.

Upon landing inside, Cross kicked the henchman squarely where he had shot him, knocking him clean out of the chopper. Without a word, he fell through the winter air many feet to meet a splattery death below.

Without stopping to look, Cross stomped quickly to the cockpit. "Clean-up on aisle five," he said, pressing the barrel of his pistol into the pilot's neck.

Click. Click.

"Fuck!"

Cross smacked the side of the pilot's helmet with the barrel, knocking him unconscious. He threw the soon-to-be-dead man into the bay behind him and climbed into the pilot's seat. "How do you fly these things?" he wondered aloud.

"Need a hand?" said a stern voice. It was Sturkey.

"I'm here too," said May. They were both topless as well. They had made the leap after seeing Cross do it. "I'm sorry about Mary," said May, placing a warm hand on Cross's right shoulder.

"This is no time for feeling sorry," said Sturkey. "Move over."

Cross sheepishly obeyed and let Sturkey and May assume the roles of pilot and co-pilot, respectively. "It's been a while since we last did this," said May, a little excitedly. Sturkey couldn't help but feel it too, the electricity in the air, as he familiarized himself with the controls.

Meanwhile Cross went back to the bay and pushed the unconscious pilot out of the helicopter. "Fuck," he said as he leaned over the edge, looking down. He contemplated the man's final moments of existence. Would he wake before he died? Was he dreaming? Would he die dreaming?

It was at that time that a second helicopter had come around from the east side of the building. With its confused occupants, it hovered idly some distance from theirs and the Trump Tower. "I think they're trying to make contact," he heard May say.

"Company!" hollered Sturkwise over his shoulder.

Cross reacted. He snatched the rocket-propelled grenade launcher that had been hanging on the back wall and placed it firmly on his shoulder. The soldiers in the other Black Hawk went from concern to panic, and began to scramble.

The young detective thought of Mary. He thought of their future together, the one that had been ripped away without warning or reason. He thought of their children, Ross and Jesse, their smiles Christmas morning as they rip open their presents. Ross's new bike (he'd always wanted one just like it) and Jesse's cute little sunflower dress. "Thanks, Mom and Dad!" Soon enough Ross is captain of the football team, and Cross is holding Jesse's hand at the abortion clinic.

"I'll never let go," he tells her. Ross becomes an electrical engineer and Jesse, after a few shaky years, gets it together and studies law at Princeton. Mary is so proud of them both and her love for Cross grows deeper with each passing year— as does his love for her. Time sees their children get married and eventually have children themselves.

Life is quiet. Come a calm, April evening the two are seated, side by side, on a bench that overlooks the freshly manicured lawn of the local park, when she goes. She would have been eighty-six, Monday. Cross holds her hand, knowing she has passed, and squeezes it. He is not sad, but full of peace. "I'll never let go," he tells her. The following morning they are noticed by a jogging jogger, and the beauty of their passing, and their story, enters town legend.

But that— all that— has been taken from him.

A single tear runs down his naked cheek, cool in the evening breeze. He closes his eyes and whispers, "for you, my love," and pulls the trigger.

The rocket fires out behind him at a downward angle and explodes at the base of the Trump Tower. The entire building leans into them a little bit.

"Shit," Cross mutters.

"Shit," Sturkey mutters. "Hang on!" he yells and he plunges the bird forward as hard and as fast as he can. All in all, they are lucky by mere moments; behind them the sacred structure falls forward, swallowing the enemy helicopter in one giant plume of ash and rubble.

May, Sturkey, and Cross fly away in silence, each taking a silent vow to never speak of what just happened ever again.

7 The Black Lotus

Pete and Gibson had spent their night drinking hard liquor and gambling successfully at the now world famous casino in Charleston, West Virginia, Moynihans. Not necessarily important to the overall story here but the two old compatriots had had a brush-up with the casino's security when they were accused of counting cards, which Gibson thought was funny, because he didn't know how to count.

The casino was lavish and wild and the drinks kept on coming. Pete could hold his liquor but Gibson found himself trying to play catch up the entire time, which led to him drinking to he could no longer remember anything at all. He presently woke to the cold quiet breeze of winter air in a cheap but expensive motel room. On the room's outdated CRT TV the news was flashing some kind of frantic alert, but the volume knob had been turned all the way down. Gibson looked at himself in the mirror to the left of the TV stand. Still fully clothed, he realized. He looked over at Pete, who was snoring snugly in the other bed with the company of two young beautiful women on either side of him. *Damn,* thought Gibson. *Where was I?*

Quietly he stepped out for a cigarette and pondered his life's meaning. He thought about the woman he had met, the one who called herself May. Memories and fantasies of her danced together through the long barren halls of his aching head. He wondered if he would see her again. Not that it mattered. Still holding a final lung of smoke, he tossed the dead cigarette butt onto the sidewalk.

When he returned to the room he couldn't help but turn the volume knob until the TV until it came at a full roar.

"Authorities have yet to confirm that this is related to the prior attack on C.L.U. headquarters, however the government is taking no chances and has issued a warning not to go outside for anyone living in the Maryland, D.C. and Northern Virginia area. The district is still under a State of Emergency."

The screen was shaky. A handheld video camera was filming. *Fucking amateurs,* thought Gibson. Still, he leaned in, his eyes close enough to the TV to fry.

He could make out the image of a black helicopter for a moment, and then the building came down like an avalanche. It went faster than he thought humanly possible. *That's cause an act like that– that's inhuman, monstrous. Was that Trump Tower?*

A reporter, a flabby-jowled guy with a tuft of blonde hair and dorky glasses, was live at the dust-covered scene:

"You're here with me now where last evening an act of senseless devastation took place. I'm sure you've seen the footage by now. It's incredible; two helicopters, multiple explosions, a whole lot to clean up, and a whole lot of questions. Unfortunately District Police Chief, Milton Wadsworth is unavailable for questions right now as he is on the ground assisting with the massive clean-up. All hands are on deck here, Lisa."

"Any word on casualties?" asked the attractive TV anchor.

"No word at the moment, Lisa, except that the building is known largely to be empty due to the fact that no one actually works in Trump Tower. The casualties are expected to be minimal."

"Right on, John. Well there you have it, folks. That's two D.C. attacks in one day. First C.L.U. headquarters and now Trump Tower. Needless to say the city is scratching its head metaphorically as to whether these events are related."

"Thanks, Lisa."

——

Gibson shut the TV off and violently ripped the covers off of Swiscock and his companions.

"We got to go, Pete," said Gibson.

"What?! What's happening?! Where's Autumn?"

"Time to go ladies."

Without words the girls dressed. They each slapped Pete a kiss on the cheek and left. *"Where's Autumn?"* Gibson said, sardonically, as he closed the door behind them. "Look, Pete we need to go back to D.C. right away."

"What's happened?"

"Another attack, while we were drinking."

"Seriously?" asked Pete, amused.

Gibson nodded.

"Then I'm gonna need another *goddamned drink.*"

8 Unadulterated Villainy

"Dad, let's go," said Felicia Weatherspoon as she tugged on her father's arm. They were alone at Barnaby's residence in the village. It was one of the larger wooden cabins with a fireplace, a kitchen, a dinner table, and a bed. Barnaby stood facing a full-length mirror.

"Let's go, let's go, *let's go!"*

"I can't," said Barnaby, withdrawn. The massive man, bare chested and powerful, appeared at once timid like a child, unable to face the girl's eyes.

"Damn it, Dad, we have to go now."

"I can't. He'll know."

"Dad!"

"I'm not your Dad!" he said, shaking her off of him with an effortless swoop. She staggered back and stared at her father.

"Well which is it?" she whispered venomously. "Is it cause you're not my Dad or because he'll know?" The 'he' they were referring to was of course, the sadistic mastermind Livingston Bates.

"I don't know," said Barnaby. "Both. Neither. I can't—"

"Look at me," she whispered, and the man turned abruptly to face her. He looked sullen and dejected. Had he forgotten his own reaction upon seeing Pete? His smile. How he had hoisted the man into the air. *Well slap me with a fish and fuck my Dad!* Felicia recollected. *It's been years you old fucking dwarf!* She shook her head and bit her lip. No, she realized. The man she was looking at was not her father.

"What happened to you?" she asked, suddenly unafraid. She had slipped into one of her comfort zones, which was gathering intel, working. Interviewing had always been one of her strong suits.

"I was fixed up by Roddy—"

"Who?"

"Bates's brother. He doesn't know what I am," mumbled Barnaby. "He doesn't know it worked. He doesn't know anything that poor son -of-a-bitch."

"Are you...?"

"Like Bates, yes. I am a copy. Roddy did this to me. Although at the time I would have phrased it as 'Roddy did this *for* me.'"

She reached forward and caressed the thick, touchable skin of Barnaby's face. "A hologram," she whispered.

"Yes." Barnaby placed his hand over hers, pressing it gently to his cheek.

"So the Barnaby Swiscock saw was..."

"Another copy."

Felicia took her hand back. "Where's my father?" she said.

"I don't know. I've done things, Felicia. With my own two hands. I've done things in the name of— *freedom?"* He spat. "You'd be ashamed if you knew what I've done."

"Dad!" she said, her voice was rising. "Talk to me!"

"You should go." Barnaby turned away from her, stood facing a corner. "We're going to be moving to the launch pad soon. You need to stay away from it. And stay away from that damned Villa. We should never have built it again."

"No, you're wrong. The work is too important."

"Villa 48 went down in the flames of wrath. 49 is destined for the same fate once Carter activates *Starshield Six*. God, I'm tired."

Felicia moved into the corner of her father's vision. "Dad what's *Starshield Six*?"

"Hell and high water, babe. You should save yourself."

And then the door to the cabin slammed open, shaking dust off of the walls. Felicia jumped, startled. Barnaby, on the other hand, wore a look of resignation and did not so much as put up his hands.

In strode grunting another Barnaby Weatherspoon wearing a dangerous grin and a sleepy, faraway look in his eyes. The black matte barrel of the gun he was holding was no larger than his pointer finger and was like a toy in his giant fist. He pointed the gun at the first Barnaby.

"Pull the trigger," said Bates in his white robe as he stepped into the cabin behind him.

The gun sounded off, and blood peppered the walls.

Bates quietly drew a pistol of his own and fired it into the back of the head of the second Barnaby. This one collapsed almost completely on top of the other.

Felicia Weatherspoon held her hand to her mouth, unable to scream or move. Her eyes went back and forth between Bates and the two dead bodies on the floor. *Dad?— was that?— was— who?— Daddy?*

"They're getting tough to keep track of," said Bates, mostly to himself, "like roaches." He pretended to blow the smoke from the barrel of the gun and then put it away beneath his robe. "You should have listened to your Daddy. You should have listened."

Felicia backed around the dinner table to the opposite side.

Bates grabbed the table's edges and shook it, making the legs dance off of the floor.

"Stop," she said pressing the table back down.

Bates laughed. His lean, lithe body moved quick like a spider, he had rounded the corner and was coming for her. She went the opposite way as fast as she could. Bates seemed to ignore the law of momentum and could alternate his direction on a dime, tricking her in the process. She wanted to sneak to the pile of dead Barnaby in order to retrieve the gun, but to her frustration it appeared Bates was able to sense this— his speed was quickest when she moved in that direction. She tried for the door. The result was no different. Bates simply outmatched her. She was panting from fear and exertion but Bates didn't have so much as a bead of sweat. *This isn't fair. This isn't fair. Ok, I'm going to get you, jackass.* She made a brief feint for the door, then made a sudden turn for the gun, putting everything into it. She stooped low and reached for it.

Bates swooped in and stuck his hand out, grabbing her up by the throat. He held her in the air and she kicked at him. It was just the two of them in that cabin. Both the gun and the door were very far away now. "Welcome to the Funhouse," he said. He held her face mere inches from his.

"They'll get you," she replied, a bloodied whisper.

"They'll try."

9 Paradise Lost, Then Found, in a Barren Parking Lot Where the Sun Don't Shine

Trump Tower, once a monument to wealth and power, lay in a pile of charred brick and ruination. Blue and red flashing lights of emergency vehicles gave color to the ashy fog that hovered about the Tower's carcass as all sorts of volunteers and government officials hurried to do something about the mess. Peter Swiscock and Patrick Gibson drove slowly into it, getting as close as they could.

"There," said Swiscock, like the old dude in Jurassic park. He pointed his finger across the dash. It was May Swallows's red Ford Mustang, parked on a side street two blocks down from the collapsed building. It appeared to be a mangled mess, a heap of steel garbage; a big chunk of cement had fallen on it, crushing the hood and whatever machinery that lay beneath. Pete shuddered– he loved cars. Even with the state it was in, and the crowd of bystanders in the way, nearly obscuring it, Pete was confident. "I know that car," he said. "That's May's car. I've been in that car," he added, unnecessarily. "What is it doing here?"

"We've got to get to it," said Gibson.

Two doors shut behind them, as they exited Pete's Ford Maverick. A large mass of concerned onlookers had gathered concentrically around the car, though this appeared to be mere bad luck. Nobody was paying attention to the Mustang. All eyes were upon the man with the megaphone, who was standing atop a small pile of rubble that resembled human skulls. Gibson rubbed his eyes and squinted. *Nope, just trash and debris.* He laughed to himself. Swiscock gave him a look.

Gibson shoved himself through the crowd, past the citizens and reporters and even past a troop of girl scouts selling cookies (and, while he believed the time and place of the cookie selling operation was horrendously inappropriate, he couldn't help but snag a box of Thin Mints.) Greedily he tore into the box. He couldn't wait. Three cookies later he was at the front of the crowd, with Swiscock at his side.

"Hey! Hey you!" Pete shouted at the man, who appeared to be a high-ranking official, all while waving his arms like when you're on a roller coaster and you go down that first exhilarating drop.

The official, unable to ignore Pete's dramatic display, grumbled silently and stepped down from the debris. "Yes, can't you see I'm extremely busy trying to get this crowd of idiots away from here?" he implored in a voice that was high pitched. Clearly puberty hadn't been good to him. "It's a danger zone, by Jove! Stuff's still falling out of the sky. We're lucky we aren't all dead right now! We're lucky–"

"Slow down, cowboy," said Swiscock.

"Thin Mint?" offered Gibson.

"Ah, that would be lovely," said the official as he reached for a sleeve. "Perhaps my sugar is low." After savoring a few bites he relaxed and introduced himself as Milton Wadsworth, Chief of Police.

"Gibson," said Gibson.

"Swiscock," said Swiscock.

"Say, that's an interesting name. Familiar too," said Wadsworth, airily. Swiscock was currently featured on the FBI's most wanted list.

"No it's not," said Swiscock.

"You're right."

"Look, Chief, we need to get into that car right there. Any chance your boys could lend us a hand?"

Wadsworth glanced over at the red Mustang beside him and then at his men, who were directing the crowd away from the scene. They were all so busy they wouldn't have the time for it.

"Well, what's in it for me?"

"Thin Mint?" offered Gibson.

Next thing you know, the boys in blue had helped pry open the doors and Swiscock and Gibson were in the front seats with Wadsworth hunched uncomfortably in the back. Swiscock traced his hand along the interior, and then the flash backs came, hitting him hard as if he was caught between two trains, with one train traveling from Tucson, Arizona, to Phoenix, Arizona at 55 mph while the other, from Phoenix to Tucson, was travelling at 60 mph, and both trains had left their stations at 4:58 p.m.: *Autumn is over and Winter is coming*– Barnaby dead, a blood spattered tie– Barnaby alive in the sun– Villa 48– the hospital bed– the hot cum–

"You okay?" said Gibson. "Let's hurry up and search this thing."

"Right."

The two of them turned over every inch of the front of the car while Wadsworth pondered the name: *Swiscock... Swiscock, Swiscock, Swiscock. Nope, nothing.*

"I wonder..." said Pete. "This car may be totaled but I wonder if we can still turn it on."

Gibson agreed, and reached beneath the dash. With some fancy jimmying, and a few choice words, the electronics in the car came to life. From across the atmosphere Kurtis Blow whispered promises of love into the quiet interior of May's car. Pete killed the volume so he could concentrate on more peculiar sound that was coming from the center console.

"It's a GPS," interjected Milton Wadsworth. "*GPS* stands for Global Positioning System. It's cutting edge. Satellites in space pinpoint your location on the planet. Provided you have some way to send a signal to them, of course."

Who the hell is this guy? Thought Gibson.

"So like a radar?" asked Pete.

"Kind of."

A yellow dot was blinking on the center of the screen that was otherwise blue. In the top right, two numbers appeared to be rapidly changing.

"Those'll be your latitude and longitude," said Wadsworth, pointing at the upper right corner. "Wow, and thinking back to my college courses, that puts the coordinates somewhere over the Atlantic. By Jove, that's pretty high tech stuff for a Ford."

Suddenly the silence was broken by the sonic signature of what could only be a pair of low flying F-16s. State-of-the-art military aircraft. Pete and Gibson shared a look, and in the next second they were out of the car and Pete was hauling the GPS box away from the scene, its wires drifting uselessly behind.

"Thanks for the Thin Mints!" called out Wadsworth.

Without wasting time, Swiscock tore out the cassette deck of his Ford Maverick, tossing it carelessly into the back, and wired the GPS system in its place.

"We'll never catch them in this piece of ****," said Gibson, pounding his fist against the window.

"Oh," began our main man, Peter Swiscock, as he turned the car eastward, "I wouldn't be too sure about that."

Pete pulled a lever just behind the steering wheel, one that Gibson hadn't noticed before, and the vehicle was suddenly tilting backward so that its nose was to the sky.

"Whoa," said Gibson, clenching his butt cheeks.

The rear doors of the green sedan flung open and then rotated so that they were outstretched parallel to the vehicle's body like a pair of wings.

"Wait a minute," said Gibson. His heart was pounding a million miles an hour. "This thing can FLY?"

"It's the nineties, Pat," answered Pete, smiling. "If you didn't think Man would have invented a flying car by now then you'd be a total fucking idiot, an utter shit-for-brains. I won't say more. Now sit tight and hold on to your titties."

And they zoomed.

10 S & S

"Where did you learn how to fly?" Garrison Cross asked Sturkwise Pendleton over the roar of the helicopter. He was amazed at how smoothly they were tearing through the air.

"Are you stupid?" was the indignant reply. "It's on autopilot you nitwit. I just figured someone ought to look the part. You know, keeping up appearances."

"Oh."

"Just kidding. I'm a pilot, born and raised by the counter-intelligence community. We both were," May was asleep in the copilot's seat, snoring soundly. She was still topless. They all were.

"You two– uh?"

"We have a history," said Sturkey.

Cross clapped him on the shoulder and walked back to the bay, to which the doors were now closed. He looked out the window. "Where are we going?" he called out. By the scenery, or lack thereof, he knew they were travelling over the Atlantic Ocean (Cross had studied large bodies of water in college.)

"Africa, my boy. To settle the score."

Cross gulped. Whatever was going to happen, he realized, was going to happen to them and them alone. He thought of Patrick Gibson. He pictured his dorky smile and his beer gut poking out from beneath his favorite sea green L.L. Bean crew neck shirt. Cross hadn't gotten so much as a chance to say goodbye. With heavy thoughts he slumped into a seat and buckled himself in. "Just going to close my eyes," he announced, and that was it. Cross was out.

Nine hours later and the chopping sound of the helicopter blades had winded down to a small clapping sound like that at a sporting event with few fans present, maybe a preseason WNBA game or local tennis match. Groggily, Cross unbuckled himself and stood up.

Outside, tall, spidery vegetation lining a field of golden grass waved at him happily in the afternoon sun. Cross, May and Sturkey, had landed.

"Put these on," said Sturkey, tossing a bundle of thick clothes at him. "It'll be hot out there right now but there are bugs you don't want to mess with, and when the sun goes down this place turns into a tundra without the snow. It'll be cold, in other words."

Sturkey was a natural born leader. It was in his bones. Hey, guess what else was in his bones. It's milk. Strong bones he had, and he owed it all to milk. *Thanks, milk,* Sturkey had thought on more than five occasions throughout his life.

Cross saw that Sturkey and May had dawned matching uniforms and it made him feel pretty special that he was about to join the team. Almost giddily he stuck his leg through the right pants hole and began to dress. "Wait," he said. "These are what Carter's men were wearing."

"All the better for us," answered May. *"Incognito."* She tapped her skull, knowingly.

She took the lead when they abandoned the helicopter, following a map she had drawn from memory. It was really just a picture of a curvy line and some trees on a cliff, and a couple squiggles that indicated some water they would have to cross. She had lost her old map along with her diary. After all, she was unable to remember where she had last placed it.

A soft breeze played through the grass, and the afternoon was pleasant and without purpose. They walked silently, each lost in his own thoughts. Then, they heard the explosion.

Cross whirred his head. In the distance, it appeared that the helicopter they had rode in on had gone up in a ball of flame. "No, why?! What happened?!" he pleaded to the vast, indifferent clouds above.

"I sabotaged it," said Sturkey.

"Why?"

Well, Sturkey hadn't thought of that. He pretended that his answer lay somewhere in his cool silence.

Unhappily, they continued. To Cross's further dismay, the ground took on a twenty-degree gradient as they found themselves ascending the foot of a mountain's spine.

The day drifted into night. The jungle closed in around them. The canopy was thick, blotted out the stars in the sky and the air grew cold, just as Sturkey had said. And then came the first of the weird *hee-hoos* of the notorious African Jungle Owl. The sound, coming from all sides and distances, reminded Cross of the undertaking of a vile pagan witch-orgy in which he had accidentally partaken during a field trip for his Large Bodies of Water class in college. Cross smiled back upon the fond memory, and opened his mouth to share—

"Shhh," warned May. "The African Jungle Owl is extremely aggressive. If we're not careful—"

"We might as well be birdseed," whispered Sturkey.

Cross decided to keep the NSFW flashback to himself, and the three pressed on despite the birds' haunting chants. Eventually, to their great relief, the sounds went away. They finished the rest of the night camped at the base of a great Kapok tree. They kept warm by the flames of a small fire.

Not all scenes need be action-packed, Sturkey reflected. To take it further, some literature was quite boring and even got away with it, like *Ulysses.* Jesus, what a headache. Two thousand pages all for some schmuck just to climb back in bed with his wife. Perhaps he didn't get the nuance of it.

They awoke at once to the harsh sun and to the sound of a loud *THUMP,* and a vibration that shook the leaves of the Kapok above them. The three were stunned motionless.

"Let's move," said May, and they gathered their things quickly.

She led at a brisk pace, with Sturkey right behind her and Cross struggling to keep up.

"What was that?" asked Cross. "Sturkey?"

"Just keep moving, Cross," said the Sturkmeister between grim strides. They went some time hastily through the jungle.

The young detective had only begun to forget about the sound and the earthquake it had made when it came again. This time it was closer.

"Get down," ordered May. She knelt. "It's tracking us," she confided in Sturkey. She glanced around, alert. The woods were awfully quiet. No birds, nothing. Only the passing wind through the trees made a lifeless rustle. A few leaves fell to the floor with a soft patter.

Cross crawled up to the two of them.

"I heard what you said just now," he whispered. "What's tracking us?"

"The Modong... the fucking Modong," was her vague reply.

The way she said it scared Cross. He'd never seen a look like that on anyone's face before. Never heard that kind of fear in a person's voice. "What's a Modong?" he asked.

Another *THUMP* rumbled the ground. Dust and crumbs of dead bark fell from the tree shafts. A shadow, hideous and deformed crept over them. The air was as cold as night.

"In the States, you have a different name for him," said Sturkey. He had unconsciously grabbed Cross by the shoulder. His grip was hard and nervous.

"What do we call him?"

Behind them a rolling tree fell down with a tremendous drawn-out crash, and Cross fell back in horror, unable to think, feel, or even sneeze.

"You may know him," said May, looking upon the monstrosity, "as Bigfoot."

11 Air Assault 2.5

A rough, 50/50 mixture of glee and terror coursed through Patrick Gibson's veins. His back was glued to the passenger seat of Swiscock's Ford Maverick, because, as like 99.9% of human beings to walk the Earth thus far, he had never before sat shotgun in a car that could fly. The grip he had on the sides of his chair would have qualified him for the Olympics, if a competition that tested such an exertion were to exist.

Swiscock pressed the gas hard in order to catch up with the fighter jets that were ahead of them in the sky. They were turning the tables on Bates, taking the fight to him. There was nothing to hold over him now. No threat to his friends that would hold him in check. *Autumn, I'm coming for you.*

Two F-16s appeared before them.

"Gotcha, motherf****ers," said Pete. His demeanor was cold but his overall body temperature was on the warm side because Gibson had complained about his lips being chapped and insisted on cranking the heat.

Pete flipped the glove box open, revealing a set of three metal switches. Above each switch a small light box glowed a dull green.

"When I say so, flip the first switch," he said over the roar of the wind around them. "We've only got one shot at this, Pat. This is no time for hesitance."

They gained fast. The sleek, aerodynamic forms of the fighter jets came into sharp focus. Gibson could almost read some of the markings below the wings.

He cracked the window to spit out the gum he'd been chewing. It flew right back in and smacked him in the face.

"Happy now?" said Swiscock.

"I'm nervous, Pete. Jesus, I'm not thinking straight. What the hell are you doing?"

The flying '71 Ford Maverick had reached the same altitude and speed as the fighter jets, and crept into formation between the two. Gibson watched the pilots of the fighter jets exchange looks.

"Now!" Pete shouted, and Gibson jumped. He flicked the switch to the *on* position.

Without warning, the car shot into *hyper speed* and leapt ahead of the two jets.

"Jesus, Pete, we're in their sights!"

"Stay cool. This'll be just like Villa 48."

The reference to their old times together brought Gibson a bit of comfort, but only a bit. He was still incredibly unsure about this.

Swiscock dug his hand into the center console and groped through a mess of cassette tapes that he'd meant to organize but never got around to. His hand stopped around the cool, familiar handle of his single shot, bolt action Winchester pistol. Despite what he had just said to Gibson, he hesitated. He realized that a gun would not solve his problems. *No, too much blood has been shed this way.* As his eyes found the horizon before them, he resolved never to use a gun again or at least until the next time he used a gun.

"Listen, Pat. When I say, you need to hit that second switch okay? And then the third. I'll let you know. It's easy. A mistake here, however, will cost us both our lives and, most importantly, this dope ass car."

"You got it, Pete," said Gibson. "Give me the word." He trusted Peter Swiscock. In times like these, it's all one could do.

"Hit it!" Pete shouted, twisting his body in his seat. Gibson flicked the second switch.

With a loud crumple, the Maverick's roof shot off of the top and then disappeared behind them. Pale wind swept into the car, a full gale. Gibson, with all of his might, reached forward in order to crank the A.C. to the highest temperature possible.

"Gibson!" shouted Swiscock, above the deafening air. "Stop fucking with the air conditioning. Hit that third switch for me, would ya?"

Grimacing, Gibson flicked the final switch. "Now what, Pete?" he said, turning to his friend. But Swiscock was gone.

Up above, having ejected from the craft, Pete was a small, singular mass in an infinite ocean of sky. The atmosphere passing around his body and through his hair soothed him and caressed him like an overly affectionate babysitter. He closed his eyes to drink in the moment, to drink in the long, overdue dose of serenity. There was a solidity to the whole experience as his feet planted squarely on the nose of an F-16.

Inside the cockpit, the pilot, a young man by the name of Scotty Dorman, was dumbstruck. *"Uh, did he just do that?"* he called over the comms. There was a genuine note of panic in his voice. And for good reason.

Swiscock was fully zen. The muscles on his neck, arms, and chest swelled, bursting violently through the fabric of his tailored Armani suit and dress shirt.

"Oh, God!" cried Dorman, as this impossible, clearly wild person standing on his aircraft plunged his fist in through the reinforced glass window of the cockpit and into his own living chest.

Across the sky, Dorman's wingman, who shall for legal reasons remain nameless, watched in silent horror. The wingman had heard over the comms the breaking of the glass and the sickening crunch of Dorman's chest cavity. He had heard the hollow, hollow gasps of a dead man, for Scotty couldn't shriek, couldn't cry out. The abrupt change in pressure had collapsed Dorman's lungs.

Swiscock drew his hand out of the man's chest, bringing with it the still-beating heart. *Warm,* he thought. He took a chunky bite from it and let the blood slide down his gullet.

"What the fuck," said Gibson, peering uneasily into the flying car's rearview.

With thunderous speed Swiscock hurled the half-bitten heart across the sky to the other F-16, where it got sucked into the jet's air intake. The belly of the flying machine caught fire and exploded, sending it into a nosedive straight into the middle of the Atlantic ocean. Swiscock admired the hole he had punched. The pilot, Scotty Dorman, was gone now. Twenty-seven youthful years, and this poor corpse in the sky was the sumtotal. Dorman, once an adventurous boy with dreams of becoming a famous airshow pilot, was instead an ill-fated extra in a larger tale that might one day sell, like, six copies. The pilot, frozen in his fear and in his death, held still the control stick. The flying jet kept even.

Pete signaled to Gibson up ahead. The car pulled up alongside the jet.

"Need a lift?" said the old friend.

Pete strode calmly across the length of the F-16's wing, and slid back into the driver side door which Gibson had held open for him. Just thirty seconds prior, the back seat of the Ford Maverick had mechanically slid forward, in a cunning technological display, to replace the driver seat that had ejected into the sky along with Swiscock.

"You look like a bloody mess," said Gibson as he watched Pete get situated.

"Was that a fucking pun?" said Swiscock.

"Does a Modong shit in the jungle?"

"What?"

"Nothing."

Somehow, Gibson knew.

"No, no!" said Cross, as the gigantic monster peered at them through dark yellow eyes from behind a bush. The three had pressed themselves up side-by-side against a big tree. Behind the tree the ground simply ended, giving way to a stark hundred-foot drop to the valley below. He continued: "Bigfoot lives in the backwoods hills of West Virginia, not out here in the lush jungles of Sub-Saharan Africa!"

"Tell it to that guy," said May. "Your fried-chicken smeared photographs of a big, hairy man dancing about Hickville, USA are nothing to the real thing. Sturkey, I'm going to need you to cause a distraction."

Thinking quickly, Sturkey procured from his backpack a small capsule filled with brown, finely ground Sickleberry, a fast-acting and highly effective hallucinogenic. He ingested the capsule dry and gulped dizzily.

"What's that?" asked Cross, nervously. "May, where are you?"

May had started climbing up the tree, leaving Cross below with Sturkey, who was already beginning to have mild hallucinations. "Let's throw rocks at it!" shouted the Sturk, excitedly. Sickleberry also produced blind euphoria. "Wait!" he cried. He sprinted away, disappearing into the thick.

"He'll be back," said May.

"I'm back," said Sturkey, nearly out of breath. He released from his arms a pile of rocks and watched as they rolled and clacked together so innocently at his feet. To Sturkey, the whole fascinating event felt like hours.

The monster huffed. Behind an immense rustling sound it came forward into a wide ray of stray light. The beast with yellow eyes had a face uglier than finding a pair of mole rats fucking unexpectedly on your birthday cake. At a fully-realized stance of twelve feet, it was twice the height of a six-foot man.

"Fuck," muttered Sturkey and he snatched up a rock.

Cross followed suit. *This is stupid,* he thought, holding feebly such a primitive weapon. *That monster's huge. Why don't we have guns?*

Sturkey, who suddenly appeared to have the same reservations, did the only sane thing to do and, without a word, turned and ran over the side of the cliff behind them.

Great job, Sturkey, thought May.

Fuck you, dude, thought Cross.

Clearly incensed, the beast took to all fours and bounded towards the helpless young detective, grunting hungrily with each motion.

Cross, already sensing the touch of Death's cold skeletal grip, cowered feebly behind the palms of his own hands. The ground shook more and more as the Modong closed in.

This was the moment May had been searching for. Calmly, she let go of the tree. Now, May wasn't a heavy woman– not at all– but science proves that any sized woman can fall from a height of 30 feet and inflict some serious damage by landing onto even the biggest of creatures. She crashed directly onto the giant's back, sending it face forward into the dirt just before it could reach Garrison Cross.

This pissed the Modong off.

"Punch it in the balls, Cross," said May.

When Cross realized that he wasn't dead, he opened his eyes to the stunning action before him. The beast was roaring and stomping in place. It was blindly reaching back to grab May, who had it tangled in a rear naked choke, but for some reason it was struggling.

"Do it," she cried. She was hanging on, desperately trying to cut the beast's circulation.

The monster's poor innocent grapefruit-sized cojones were completely exposed as it thrashed about. Cross, knowing what he had to do, cracked his knuckles and went to town on Bigfoot's testicle sack with a flurry of powerful jabs that would make even Mike Tyson think twice about entering the ring.

It took a second for the pain to register but then the monster howled with a fury that inspired fear and quiet in the jungle for miles.

Armed with nothing but hope that the monster would pass out, Cross kept pounding away the thing's potential future children.

And just as the monster appeared to be slowing down, its fingers found May and it slammed her back to the ground with a vicious arc of motion. She did not get up right away.

"May!" yelled Cross, defeated.

This caught the Modong's attention and in one foul swoop it grabbed Cross by the top of the head and lifted him off of the ground. It roared angrily in his face, revealing in clear relief two rows of long sharp teeth, and then it simply hurled him over the edge to the fall below and, possibly, to Sturkey.

May could barely open her eyes. The light that came in was painful. Where was she? She remembered holding on fiercely to a coarse shag carpet in the sky. No, that didn't make sense. It had thrown her down. The Modong. Her heart leapt in her chest. She felt the hot breath of the Modong press against her neck, felt the insidious heat of it climbing into her skin. And the smell— wasn't too bad.

A large hand slipped behind her waist, wrapped itself around her. But it did not squeeze when she expected it to squeeze. The monster moved her into a sitting position against the tree and then released her. She let out a small fart, relieved. She opened her eyes.

The beast's pink, human-like face was close to her own. It seemed sad. She watched with fascination as the great yellow pupils of the beast swelled and narrowed, taking her in.

"Mo-dong," it grunted sleepily.

"May," she responded.

She reached forward and grazed the giant's face with her fingertips. Tenderly it placed its hand over hers.

"May," it said, and there was, undoubtedly, a smile.

A breeze passed over the place on the cliff's edge, and then a shadow. May tried to turn her head, but it was stiff. A crashing sound like that of thunder interrupted the silence and then the blurred figure of a man crashed into the Modong, knocking it onto its back. The figure was on top of the beast, poised to strike.

"No, Peter!" cried May, instinctively leveling her pistol at Swiscock's chest. *Oh yeah, I guess I did have a gun this whole time.* Her hand trembled. Her heart was pounding against her ribcage. The savage monster implored her with a vulnerable look, as it knew it was beat.

Peter Swiscock glared at her through the corner of his eye, challenging her to shoot him, as he raised his hand to impart the fatal blow. The very air around them began to stir as Swiscock, without hesitation, whispered

Swisssc–

–BLAM!!

The stark silence that followed the single close-range gunshot was as deafening as any that had ever preceded it. Before the international super-spy could complete his lethal sentencing, May had shot him square in the chest.

12 Easy Cum, Easy Go

Pete held his own blood in his hand, stunned.

"I'm not sorry, Pete," said May. "I owed you that for Jarvan."

"For whom?"

She shot him again.

"Fuck." He fell from atop the Modong.

Gibson came charging from the clearing where he had parked the flying car after Swiscock had leapt from it. He stopped as quickly as he had been running– his attention went from May holding the gun, to the enormous ugly beast on the ground, and then to Swiscock lying down next to it, with two growing red circles on his chest of his perfectly tailored Armani dress shirt.

"May," said Gibson. He desperately ignored the barrage of sexually -charged flashbacks to their time together at the beginning of Act 2 of this book. "What did you do?"

"She acted in my defense," said the giant beast in a voice that was rich and sonorous like that of a morning radio talk-show host. The beast rolled gracefully away from Swiscock and got to its feet.

"No," she said. "I shot him for what he did to Jarvan."

"You're wrong to do so," said Gibson. "I was there for what happened. What happened didn't make sense, but I was there and saw it with my own eyes. Jarvan shot himself... all on his own. Although it wasn't on his own. Something coerced him. Something forced his own hand to do it."

Tears came to her eyes. Sturkey's stupid little *psychic blast* theory was coming back to haunt her, she just knew it.

"But it wasn't Pete," concluded Gibson.

"Pete," spoke the Modong. "Wait here."

"Eyy, look at that. It's Bigfoot," said Gibson as the lumbering beast disappeared into the woods on all fours.

The Modong returned, rumbling the ground with its mighty motions. It came to Swiscock's side and produced an item silver and impossibly tiny in its hands: a pair of tweezers.

No way, thought May, regaining her composure. *Legend tells of the steady hand of the Modong.* She held her breath, unable to believe she was about to witness the famed surgical prowess of the Modong in action.

In compliance with unspoken orders, Swiscock unbuttoned his shirt, exposing the pair of wounds for everyone to see.

Quietly the Modong drew close and studied him with its big yellow eyes. It smiled.

"It's not bad," said the beast. "One of the bullets completely destroyed your right lung, but that's why God gave you two."

"And the other bullet?" asked Pete.

"Nothing vital."

Pete squinched his eyes shut as the monster went to work. Its mission was to extract the bullets with the tweezers.

May couldn't watch and Gibson went to her in an effort to console her, but she brushed him away.

Dejected, he paced. He thought of Cross and wondered where Cross was in all of this and had he made it out of the C.L.U. building alive. He couldn't wait to tell his old friend about the flying car. Perhaps the next time they got together, he would finally tell Cross about Villa 48. The boy deserved to know. And then Gibson remembered for the thousandth time why he couldn't, for he had signed an NDA. *Damn. Well, whatever.* Gibson glanced about his surroundings and saw Pete thrashing beneath the Modong's crouched body. A chill ran through him. *Wherever Cross is it's got to be a better place than here,* he thought with a touch of dramatic irony.

Swiscock groaned as the Modong pulled the first bullet from his chest and placed it into its own palm. Then it went for the bullet that had struck Pete's lung, and pulled that one out too. It was over.

May clapped her hands together quietly, suddenly aware she'd been rooting for Pete's recovery.

The Modong held the two bent pieces of metal before him like they were a goddamned Christmas miracle. Pete, visibly relieved, picked one up and examined it. "Well, slap me with a dead fish and fuck my dad," he said. "Look at that."

"No," interjected Gibson, seriously. "Look at *that."* He pointed to the sky over the valley. As the other three turned their heads, a steady thundering grew until it was impossible to hear anything else. Down below, between the mountains, some kind of cylindrical object was ascending toward the heavens. *Like a space shuttle*, thought Gibson. Except there was no flame, no trail of smoke behind it. *What was powering it?* Then, at somewhat a farther distance, a second appeared. The trees below swayed violently side-to-side beneath the objects immense force. A third came after it, joining the other two in their climb.

"It appears Bates has accelerated his operations," said Pete, clutching his chest. The pain was present but by many degrees it had lessened.

"Then he must know we're here," said May.

"Come," said the Modong. "Follow me."

Sturkey, thought May. *Follow the noise.*

13 Separation Anxiety

"Gibson!" Cross shouted, inexplicably terrified.

He was sopping wet. His whole body was shivering. He shot up into a sitting position and forced his eyes about his surroundings until they focused. It appeared that he had plummeted from the sky into a small shaded cove beneath the face of the cliff, and that the water had carried him to the shore. There was no sound here, save for the lapping of the pool, and a small breeze that rustled the leaves of the trees lining the jungle beyond. There was no one else. Certainly no Gibson. Cross missed his old C.L.U. buddy badly. Realizing a desperate, innate need for the warmth of the sunlight, he bumbled his way to his feet and stripped off his jacket that he had worn over top of the black turtleneck, both courtesy of Carter's helicopter goons. He threw it into the water. Cross climbed wearily out of the cove to a high place, to the top of a mountain of boulders that stood prominently above the tree line. He gazed out far across the vast verdant forest before him and promptly collapsed under the sun and fell back asleep.

A great rumbling nearly shook him off of the side of the boulder. He came to as his body was scrambling. On all fours, he peered across the same treeline. In the distance, a fire, a bright white fire, was going up into the blue sky. *Are we in the space race?* he wondered, bizarrely. The rumbling died down.

"Cross!" called a voice from below. It was Sturkey. "It's me, Sturkey!"

"Sturkey!" he cried and then hurried down the pile of smooth boulders. The two embraced in a strong, emotional hug. Then Cross stood back, holding the other at arms' length. Sturkey looked bad. Parts of his face were bruised and swollen, and bore red slashes across right cheek. He, too, had removed his jacket and his black turtleneck was riddled with long tears in the fabric. He had fallen a long way as well, but had not such a gentle landing. Cross sucker punched him hard on the nose.

"Fuck!" said Sturkey, stepping backward as he cupped his newest injury with his hand.

"What were you thinking?" Cross demanded.

"I don't know," he said, his voice muffled. "I took too much of that damned Sickleberry. My damn head still hurts."

Cross didn't know what the hell he was talking about.

Sturkey waved his free arm resignedly. "That pill. It's a hallucinogen. Among other things. I swear I've used it in combat before. But that damned thing– I thought King Kong was gonna eat me."

"Yeah, well lucky you it didn't," said Cross sardonically. He huffed. He was dizzy from anger and from having fallen off of a high cliff.

"Don't worry. This is a good thing," said the Sturkmeister, calm and wise.

"How is this a good thing?"

"In this instance I think we were meant to get separated, us two and them... so that maybe we can come in and save the day when it's least expected."

"So like a plot-device in a story?" asked Cross, a little deflated.

"Exactly," said Sturkey. "You and I both saw that rocket climbing into space– therefore we both know where to go. After our little exchange here is over, the story will switch to them, or someone else– god forbid they introduce any *new* characters at this point (Sturkey had no idea)– and then when shit's hitting the fan for them, we'll pop in, shitting on a shiny goddamn fan of our own! Everything will be covered in our shit!"

Cross folded his arms across his chest and appeared to contemplate. He had to admit the Sturkmeister's logic was sound. But he was still upset. "Alright," he said. "Let's try it. But don't think this redeems you for running off the cliff like that. You're going to have to do a little something more, like sacrifice yourself or something."

"I know, mate," said Sturkey. With a grim smile he patted Cross on the shoulder. "Don't I know."

"Alright then. You lead the way."

14 Delusions of Grandeur

A knock resounded on the steel door and it hissed aside. Roddy Spayceman didn't look up from his computer. He was elsewhere. The genius, Roddy Spayceman, adventurer extraordinaire, adored by the ladies and admired by the men, a true legend, was on the final flight to STARSHIELD SIX, former POTUS Jimmy Carter's fully operational lunar research compound. He would touch the heavens... and maybe more. There were thousands cheering him on as the vehicle left the ground, roaring–

A cold hand with a strong grip had found his shoulder. He saw the arm on his shoulder reflected, and then himself. He appraised the blurred colorless face that gazed back from between the green phosphor symbols rolling across the monitor. He found it wanting. When was the last time he had eaten? Who was he kidding? Roddy Spayceman? He was only the poor nerd who somehow got suckered into building a space station. There was no fame for the spine. The skin always got the glory.

"Brother," said Livingston Bates. "I wish you the best of luck down here. We are so close to victory I can practically taste it." Beyond the CRT display was a long glass window over looking the inter-terrestrial shuttle that would take Bates away. Many men at work, tiny as little ants, were preparing the vast machine for launch.

"I want to go with you, brother," said Roddy. "You will need me up there. I mean it. The engineers you hired are idiots."

"Careful, Rod."

"Trust me–"

"No. That's final. I need you down here."

Frustration nearly brought tears to his eyes. He was glad that his back was turned to his adopted brother. When Roddy was only a year old, the Spaycemans had tried for a second child. They tried and tried for years and then, fruitless, went in for advice. They were told they would simply be unable to produce. So they chose to adopt.

The boy, young Livingston, who was older than Roddy, proved to be a nuisance and a menace. He fought at school and neglected his homework. But the Spaycemans were very loving. They signed him up to be a boxer and he quickly developed a liking for it. While Roddy pretended to fly airplanes and tinkered with budding computer technology, Livingston learned how to fight and became obsessed with the topic of war. Despite their differences Roddy and Livingston were amicable to one another. When Livingston dropped out of school to join the military, the Spaycemans embraced his choice. As he rose through the ranks, they were proud. He was making something of himself. And when he deserted the military of the republic to raise his own militia of murderers and psychopaths, they were alarmed, but they forgave him. The pivotal moment, however, the only straw that mattered to Roddy's parents, was when Livingston altered his last name to Bates. The child had forsaken them. They could not forgive him that, and neither party had spoken to the other since. The whole feud made Roddy sick. Perhaps he would not want to go up with Bates, after all.

Now that he was feeling fairly resolute, he placed a hand on top of Livingston's. Livingston then placed his other hand on top of Roddy's. In a swift counter, Roddy placed his other hand above Livingston's topmost hand. Livingston slipped his bottom hand out and regained the highest position with it, and this went on for several turns. Despite the awkward angle, Roddy persisted until Livingston got fed up with it and threw in the towel.

"Shuttle #151 will be ready in twenty minutes," Roddy said, eyes focused on the monitor. "I suppose it's time you suited up." He swiveled in his chair to face Livingston, and was embarrassed at his slight reaction to Livingston's unusual appearance. His adopted brother seemed to have aged in the past couple days. He was thinner than usual, and he was unshaven. Flecks of white stubble had appeared beneath his dark neck. He looked like a vagabond.

In truth, he did not look fit for a launch into outer space.

"Are you sure you're ready?" asked Roddy.

At that moment, the two brothers' final rendezvous was interrupted, as the room went suddenly dim, illuminated only by the faint red glow of the emergency lights poking out of the walls. A siren began sounding loudly, its wails echoing off the vast cylindrical walls of the launch chamber. The launch site had gone into red alert.

Bates had a far off look in his eye. "Swiscock," he grumbled. He cracked his fists.

"Swiscock?"

Bates said nothing more to Roddy before he turned and left the room. The metal door slid shut. Roddy Spayceman was left alone in the dark, both literally and metaphorically.

"May, have you set the charges?" asked Pete, pistols drawn, his back to one of the towering ancient trees that were enclosing Bates's compound. The trees, dark and mysterious, had formed a thick forest for hundreds of feet around the octagonal stone structure, providing it with an effective layer of camouflage in addition to its position within a deep prehistoric crater. The only fault in its concealment were the launches themselves. But now, as Bates's men were rushing to initiate the final takeoff, it was eerily quiet; only faintly could be heard the steady rising and falling sound of the base's red alert signal from over its towering walls.

May nodded quietly, from behind another tree some distance away. Gibson, who stood shoulder-to-shoulder with May, squinted up at the hundred-foot wall. A look of mild apprehension passed over his face. He squeezed the grip on his bright blue Desert Eagle. It had been a long time since he'd done something like this.

"This could get ugly, guys," said the titular hero. "But if we stick to the plan we can come out of this with the skin still on our dicks and a story for our grand-kids. When we get to Bates, remember, I want him... alive."

Halfway between the inner and outer walls of the white stone fortress, Bates's #2 man, General Gunther "Spoons" McTavish, was preparing his dutiful men for the coming standoff. Spoons wore a full suit of battle armor, much like the juggernaut-class from the highly popular first person shooter video game, Call of Duty: Modern Warfare 2, available for the Xbox 360 and Playstation 3 gaming platforms. With two hands the warrior cradled the M-16 assault rifle, and over his back was slung a heavy M249 that clacked against his munitions belt as he walked long, heavy strides. A half-smoked cigar hung loosely from his lower lip, and threatened to fall out when he spoke.

"Alright boys, just like in training. You've all watched the videos; you've read the play-by-plays; you know Swiscock's sole advantage is his utter unpredictability on the battlefield. And his versatility, his ability to adapt to any situation. Also, he is an unparalleled marksman."

McTavish's men exchanged worried glances.

"Oh yeah," said their fearless leader. "I forgot. His disadvantage will be his compassion for his allies which, according to the radar, numbers to two." He was reading feed on the optical display that hovered just over his right eye. "They are approaching the outer south -east wall now. Ten seconds. What are we gonna do when they get here?"

"Rip off their heads and shit down their necks!" answered the small army of flunkies in unison.

"I can't hear you!"

"We're going to beat them so hard, their clothes'll be out of style!"

"That's my boys," roared Spoons– he ducked his head. An explosion had rumbled into the peace. The green grassy plain between the two stone walls became thick with clouds of smoke and the smell of burning rubber. "Form up!"

Hastily and efficiently his men retreated to the inner wall and ascended the stone staircase that ran along its side with their guns drawn and leveled at the breach. McTavish waited until the last of his guys reached the top before following them up and then posting crouched behind the four-foot barrier that crowned the top of the wall. He held his breath. *Come on you son-of-a-bitch,* he thought, reworking his grip on the trained M-16. As if in response, a pair of yellow– *headlights?*– headlights appeared through the smoke. Spoons's nostrils widened.

Within the dark and quiet control room behind the inner wall, Roddy Spayceman watched these events transpire soundlessly on the closed circuit monitors. The frame-rate was choppy but he was able to make out the bright lights and then the truck bursting through the opening.

"Fire!" ordered McTavish. "Wait! Don't fire!" He held up his hand, which was the signal not to fire. "What the hell is that?" asked the mercenary. Obviously, it was a truck. But *why?*

The man in the big brown truck leaned his balding head out of the driver side opening and shouted, "UPS!"

Spoons's men on the inner wall shifted uneasily in their positions and exchanged confused looks.

The general pondered. "Did anyone order anything?" he barked.

One of the men, or rather a youth, who was standing at the far end of the formation raised his hand shyly. "It might be my paperback, sir," spoke the boy. He looked a little frail compared with the other men who were big and brutish, and his posture, head ducked down between his shoulders, was submissive. *You have to start somewhere,* thought McTavish, gravely. "Go on," he ordered. The young henchman hurried down the stone steps that ran along the inner wall and then jogged lightly across the grass.

"Sign here," said the postman, "and here. Okay, thanks."

The boy gave the man in brown a nod and then hurried back up the steps with his package in hand. He returned to his firing position and then held his rifle. Still, it seemed that all eyes were on him.

"Aren't you gonna open it?" yelled McTavish all the way from the other side of the formation.

Damn it, thought the boy, setting the gun down. He fumbled through his pocket for the knife until he grabbed onto the familiar contours of the wooden handle. It was the knife his grandfather had given him the night he passed away. He studied it for the thousandth time. Everything he had ever sliced, stabbed, or cut into with it came back to him at once. For him it held memories. And mystique. The knife had been handed down along the paternal bloodline, beginning with his great-great-grandfather, who had purchased it from a hooded merchant on one of his many travels across the Mojave Desert. The best part about the knife was that it was still sharp as ever. The boy pulled the blade open and then used it on the tape that bound the cardboard box. His nervousness gave way to excitement. He opened the package then discarded it to the wind for what had been inside. He held in his hand a smaller white box. Definitely not the book he had ordered.

He frowned.

McTavish: "Well?"

Hesitantly, he peeled back one of the flaps—

"Wait!" McTavish was saying, but it was too late.

The bomb exploded, killing the boy and one other henchman who had been peeking over his shoulder.

Inside the truck a familiar voice quietly said, *"Burger time."*

Swiscock emerged from the rear of the UPS vehicle first, practically bursting through the double doors, and rounded the side as he fired into McTavish's men with both of his two .22 caliber Berettas in tandem. Normally you'd see this kind of thing in the movies and think, *whoa that's badass,* and you'd be right on the money. Pete swung the semi-automatic weapons in beautiful arcs, depressing the triggers in rhythmic staccatos. The henchmen fired back. It was song to him, the gunfire, and he danced all the way to it.

The grassy ground between the walls of the compound was littered with outcroppings of rocks and small boulders. Swiscock darted from one to the next, using their cover to his advantage.

Next out of the truck was Gibson in his brown UPS uniform, but he was a lousy shot and might as well not have even come. He did nick a guy in the shoulder though.

May split out from the truck and she, like Swiscock, expressed a profound aptitude for warfare. With one eye she aimed coldly down the elongated sight of a lightweight French FAMAS assault rifle, firing it up at the men who stood garrisoned along the top of the inner wall. She walked forward, adjusting herself almost robotically, taking lives with each methodical step.

One by one, McTavish's men fell victim to the onslaught, tumbling over the wall to the grounds below, or rolling to a lifeless stop along the white stone stairs. Some simply hanged over the lip, their limp arms draped over it, hands clutching at nothing.

"Damn it!" Spoons cursed. He was watching his men die down around him. His little army of trained soldiers was quickly becoming a litter of useless corpses. He unhitched the walkie from his belt. "We need back-up, Bates!"

Meanwhile, within the walls: Livingston Bates, who had been eyeing the scene closely from the shuttle grounds as his men put the final preparations on the launch, bent low to the desk-mounted microphone. "PETER SWISCOCK," boomed Bates's voice, amplified a hundred times. "I should have killed you when I had the chance. This is what I get for fooling around. Listen Pete, I'll give you this one opportunity for you and your company to turn back. Turn back, run away, and live the rest of your days as best as you can, right now. This is your one free chance. Take it, or I'll kill you, Pete. I'll kill your friends too. I'll kill them just the same as I killed old Barnaby and his daughter. I enjoyed the girl. There's something special someone you can kill only once. I made sure it lasted." With trembling hands and averted eyes, the two technicians nearest to him continued lifting equipment and entering data into their scanners. "Final warning," concluded Livingston Bates as he withdrew from the microphone rather rapturously.

Damn it, thought Spoons, who was crouched behind the inner wall. He was hoping for real backup, not some weak fucking plea.

The gunfire had ceased. Silence pervaded the compound. A gentle wind passed swept into the grounds between the walls. It was summer here, in the Southern hemisphere. McTavish listened. It sounded like Swiscock and his cohorts had halted their assault in order to listen to Bates's speech. As had he and his men. He thought furiously. Where he was once a knight– or at least a rook– had he become simply another pawn in Swiscock's real life version of the popular board game, chess? *No*, Spoons decided. He would move like a bishop; that is, he would advance diagonally. He was down to fifteen men, and he would need them *all* to draw Swiscock's attention even if it cost them their lives. Spoons was prepared to make the sacrifice. He switched the channel on his walkie to address his platoon.

"Boys," he said, speaking firmly but quietly. "I'm going to need you to relocate to the south, south-eastern vertex. Be quick and don't be seen."

He frowned sentimentally at his men from across the distance and shook his fist in silent cheer. Two of his men returned the signal and then turned, following behind the other thirteen. Spoons peeked over the wall as carefully has he could. He couldn't see Swiscock or the other two, though he could hear them debating something behind an enormous white boulder.

"We're in position, sir," said one of his lackeys over the walkie-talkie.

"Can you see them?"

"I think so."

"Good."

Spoons crawled to the edge of the staircase with the powerful M249 machine gun balanced on his knee. In theory, when his men opened fire on Swiscock and them, forcing them out of their hiding place, he would appear with quite the volley of his own. He pulled the cocking mechanism backward until it went *click!* "FIRE," he ordered, and his men popped up like a line of deadly wack-a-moles, raining bullets.

Swiscock made to escape the sudden barrage from the left but had to quickly reverse his steps as second attack opened up from McTavish's M249 on the right. He pulled his back to the boulder as tight as it could go.

"We're trapped," yelled Gibson, who was squished in the middle between Pete and May behind their only source of cover. The report of McTavish's machine gun at such a close proximity was nearly deafening. "Why did we have to stop to listen to that asshole? We were doing *great!*"

"Stow your whining, bitch," said May from over her shoulder. "You're forgetting the plan."

"You're right," said Gibson, cutting the conversation short before she could call him any more mean names.

Behind them, the UPS truck rocked on its suspension. Even to Gibson, who knew what was about to happen, the sight of the vehicle bouncing around, seemingly of its own accord, was jarring. Again, the gunfire ceased. The package-delivery truck fell onto its side with a dull, heavy crunch.

Roddy Spayceman shot backward in his chair at the appearance of the Modong, and then pulled himself even closer than he was before. He watched as the ferocious beast closed the distance to the wall and scaled it. Without mercy it ripped the fragile limbs from McTavish's men, tossing them into the sky behind it like discarded toys.

"No, no, no," he said and he turned to flee the room. He collided with the steel door and ended up in a backwards somersault.

He rubbed his forehead, confused. The door should have before he'd reached it.

"Door, open," he said.

There was no response.

"Door, open," he repeated.

"Vocal pattern not recognized," said the door.

Roddy's eyes spaced in disbelief. Was he trapped here?

"Fuck!" Livingston swore, his eyes on the same footage. He motioned to the two technicians with a sharp snap of his fingers. "You two, double time. Or one of you, quadruple time. GET ME THE HELL OFF THIS PLANET!"

The inner walls of the compound extended towards its center, into which had been hollowed the enormous cylindrical area that housed Bates's final rocket. Within the walls snaked the labyrinthine corridors that connected the many crews' quarters, operation rooms, and lavatories. Pete and the gang, having followed the Modong up the wall, descended behind it through an exposed hatch that lead down into the dimly lit bowels of the base. Once inside, our heroes reloaded their weapons and checked for any gunshot wounds, bug bites, or poison ivy, and then they each took a bathroom break.

"*Pussy time*," said Swiscock, after washing his hands and drying them beneath an overly loud air dryer.

"They're heading right for me," said Roddy to himself, horrified. The closed circuit display showed the monster leading Swiscock and his two companions down the hall way toward the control room. *Where was security? Who is permitting them to pillage us?* The monster kicked down door after door, wall after wall, with no resistance.

Roddy ducked and covered his head with his hands. There was a loud *BANG* and the steel door that hadn't allowed him to leave suddenly flew into the room and over him, over the station controls and through the glass window that separated the control room from the launch pad. Tiny shards of glass slid past his fingers like a hundred cat's claws, drawing thin lines of blood in an instant.

Swiscock marched heavily into the room and pressed the mouth of his Beretta into the top of the man's head.

"Stop the launch," Pete demanded. He smacked the young scientist with the pistol.

"I can't stop it! The machine– it has full control! Full control of everything!"

Pete ejected his entire clip into the computer switch-board. The furious barrage of gunshots rang out like the horrible screams of the children you could have saved if you donated back that nickel they sent you in the mail instead of spending it on the children themselves.

"Stop it!" yelled May, covering herself.

"Yeah, cut it out!" said Gibson.

"Mo-dong," said the Modong.

"It's all over, Swiscock," said a voice over the loudspeaker.

The pounding of a dozen or so boot-steps announced the arrival of another of Bates's militias, as they lined the observation balconies that ran along the inside of the hollowed-out launch structure. Secure in their higher ground, the soldiers crouched and took aim down at Pete, May, Gibson, and the Modong. In the hallway that led to the control room: more boot-steps and quiet orders issued over a radio.

Gibson's heart sank. They were surrounded.

Midway up the starch-white, convex face of Shuttle #151, one of the shuttle's rectangular panels faded away. Standing in the foreground of the ship's interior was Livingston Bates. He wore some kind of silver, retro space suit regalia that probably wouldn't pass as realistic nowadays.

"Brother," said Roddy into the fat end of the spiral-corded walkie. "Whatever you've gotten us into, you need to stop it!"

Bates's eyes widened. "Whatever *I've* gotten us into? Don't feign innocence, *Spayceman."* He practically spat on the name into his own corded microphone. The sound elicited a horrible feedback screech that echoed off of the walls. "Poor, innocent Spayceman. You know I can't stop when I have all the cards."

Swiscock reached over Roddy's shoulder and snatched the Walkie. "You don't have this one," said Pete. He pressing the Beretta into the side of Roddy's face. He pulled back the hammer with his thumb.

May was in disbelief. Were they taking the boy as a hostage?

"Tell me where she is Bates. Or your brother bites the bullet."

Gibson whispered to May, "He's not using that idiom right."

Behind the stretched cold glare of the florescent lights on the glass, Livingston folded his arms, appearing to chew things over in his mind.

"What's there to consider?" Roddy's heart was pounding in his chest.

"Just tell me where she is," said Pete. For once it was a terrible struggle to keep his desperation hidden beneath the usual, gruff bravado. "Where's Autumn?"

"Oh, don't pretend you came all this way for *her*," said Bates, smiling broadly. "Please. This whole thing, this adventure, it's been a big barrel of fun for you. *You don't want it to end.*" Bates paused for a response, but then he was unable to withstand the silence. "Face it, Swiscock. You're a killing machine. You're murder, romanticized. Idolized. A crippled child's dream. The way you executed my mercenaries, bullet-by-bullet– I watched it all from here. It was quite fun for you wasn't it?"

"No."

"Don't lie to me. The way you move, it was pure joy. I admire your skill, a skill borne of a love for the craft. A skill unattainable in the absence of such a love."

Swiscock's gun hand was shaking ever so slightly. He had come all this way. *Was it fun? No. But it was, wasn't it? What was Bates doing to him? Coming on to him? No.* He was making him see the truth. Swiscock blinked slowly. "Yes, it was fun," he admitted. He thought about when he bit a chunk out of that dude's heart. *Maybe I have a problem.*

"You've got a problem, Pete," said Bates, "an addiction. I know because I have it too. It's a shame we're not on the same team."

"You don't have a team, Bates."

Livingston Bates gritted his teeth. "Right now, I'm going to make you a deal," he said. "Kill your companions, all of them– starting with Roddy Dearest– and I promise you'll be reunited with your precious Summerfall by the turn of the next page."

Pete glanced at May. Her FAMAS, which she held casually at her waist, was pointed directly at him. He then looked at Gibson, who stood expressionless with his infamous blue Desert Eagle at his side. The Modong cracked its big, hairy knuckles.

Meanwhile the young scientist whom he held at gunpoint stood with his hands up in quiet surrender. There were no options for a person in his position.

"Time is running short, Swiscock," said Bates. "I know you can make the right choice."

Swiscock stole a peek at the next page, just to see if he'd taken Bates up on his offer. Turns out he didn't.

"Well, I've considered your offer, Mr. Bates," he said. "And, as enticing as it is, I have to... disrespectfully decline!"

He pivoted and fired up clumsily at Bates.

In response, a deadly barrage of bullets hailed down into the control room. The four heroes and Roddy slid into the leg space beneath the rather large computer station. The Modong, usually a fearless beast, curled into the fetal position beneath the bits of bouncing glass and broken metal. Pete, May, and Gibson held their weapons at arm's length, for a separate component of Bates's mercenaries would surely be pouring through the open doorway behind them to flank them. It was a deadly and time-worn strategy that would make this their final stand. The mercenaries on the balconies ceased their attack in anticipation of the maneuver.

Swiscock, May, Roddy, Gibson, and The Modong waited, panting, staring at that open doorway.

Flashes of light and mini eruptions of gunfire sounded in the hallway.

An atmosphere of confusion had penetrated the climate of dread.

"What? What's going on?" hissed Bates over the loudspeaker.

A mad whooping and hollering from above resounded throughout the launch pad. Bates's men craned their necks up at the sky and pointed at the strange silhouette that was descending upon them.

"It's a bird," one of them shouted, like some kind of dumbass.

"It's a plane!" offered another.

A barrage of machine gun rounds hailed down, cutting through those of Bates's men who had stood bewildered just a moment too long.

"Neither a bird, nor a plane!" cried the voice of Garrison Cross, falling quickly with the aid of a large red parachute. "It is I, Garrison Cross!"

"And I, Sturkwise Pendleton," said Sturkey, as he stepped swiftly into the control room and fired a FAMAS out at the rest of Bates's ill-fated flunkies out on the balconies. Just in the nick of time, he had single-handedly taken down the team of soldiers that were poised to flank Swiscock and the others in the control room.

Continued Cross: "Get your cameras ready, folks because you just witnessed a miracle! How'd we do it? I'm not quite sure! I'm not capable of telling you where I found this parachute, let alone a point high enough that would allow me to parachute in, but here I am anyway!"

With the end of the hearty monologue, Cross crashed into the room, releasing the chute behind him, and took his forward momentum into a perfect somersault. He and Sturkey high fived.

The button on Gibson's Levi jeans came popping off as the abrupt force of his erection almost completely removed his pants.

"Look, May, I told you it was a one time thing," he said proudly, but she had already ran to Sturkey and was embracing him with kisses on the neck. "You're not even looking. Give me one more chance, please!"

From the interior of the spaceship Livingston had watched his men get cut down. Spoons was nowhere to be seen. *Coward.* In a vast understatement of his anger, he slammed his fist against the glass panel before him. The sudden burst of emotion told the vessel that it was time to go. Its engines kicked off, roaring loudly. His foes shrank below and disappeared beneath the view of the window.

After the crushing sound of Shuttle #151's departure, Pete collapsed. He resigned to let himself weep into his own arms. It was over. Yet it was worse than death. He would have preferred to die just now, for Barnaby was gone. Felicia too. And Autumn was... Guilt bent him at the back of his neck. *Autumn.* She was out there, helpless or worse. He tried to remember her, to even think of her face, but he was having trouble. Was his subconscious preparing him for the inevitable truth?

"I'm sorry, Pete," said the Modong in its deep, unnatural voice. The rest of them had gathered 'round: Gibson, May, Sturkey, and Cross. They knelt beside Swiscock and put their arms around one another. I guess you could say friendship, or at least companionship, was the silver lining to the somber scene, but who cares?

The stranger, the scientist betrayed, had fled to the far wall, but remained a part of the company, as he was coming to terms with a grief of his own— and a course of action. Roddy raised his chin as one who had seen beyond his own past. "I can get you up there," he said weakly.

Only May appeared to notice.

Roddy cleared his throat. "I said I can get you to space."

Swiscock was startled. "Come again?" he said.

"There's still an old hunk-a-junk lying around here, in a silo just three miles east. It's an older ship, and will probably explode and kill us before we can leave the atmosphere. But if it works..."

"My boy!" Swiscock exclaimed, beaming life from his blue eyes. The vibes in the desecrated room lifted instantaneously.

"It'll be a long shot," said Roddy, unable to maintain his cynicism in the face of Pete's infectious smile.

"My boy—"

"Roddy."

Pete walked over to Roddy and lifted him to his feet.

"Roddy, my boy, I could kiss you right now."

He did.

The seven of them sped across the jungle in a hurry, led by Roddy Spayceman, brother to the adopted Livingston Bates, formerly Livingston Spayceman. *I'm going to space,* thought Roddy, with a major grin, as he hacked his way through the foliage.

They reached another stone fortress that lay hidden just on the other side of the crater. This one had been abandoned some years back and had already been overtaken by plants and wildlife and hookers. Once at the outer wall, Roddy dusted off a panel and punched in his old PIN. It worked (not gonna tell you what it is though). They wandered into the base, each trembling with a nervousness of his or her own. On the launch pad rested a shuttle much taller and fatter than the one Livingston had left in. Roddy was first up the large steel ladder that led into the ship's anus. *It might not be fast and it might be rough, but it'll be worth a try,* thought Roddy, using his PIN again on the shuttle itself.

"Follow me," he said, pulling the air tight hatch aside.

They filed in after Roddy.

"Do I need to close this?" said Gibson as he was last to get inside.

"Don't worry about it. The ship will pull the ladder into itself and then close the hatch securely once I power it on. Which..." he trailed off.

"What is it?" asked Pete, concerned.

"I'll have to explain something once we're all strapped in and ready to go. Okay. Now that we're all strapped in and ready to go I'll explain something." Roddy, at the head of the space shuttle, turned away from the blue sky beyond the viewport. The chair he was in rotated a full 90 degrees but would go no farther. "You see, this ship is not powered off of any previously utilized energy source like hydrogen or even coal, but purely off of bad vibes."

"Bad vibes?" said May.

"Anger, maliciousness, judgement, those sorts of things. Negativity, fear. My brother is so positively *teeming* with horrible emotions that he was able to power Shuttle #151 almost completely on his own, all the way to Starshield Six."

"I see," said Swiscock, though he didn't.

They sat in silence. This seemed kind of stupid.

"Is despair a bad vibe?" asked Pete. He was feeling pretty low just sitting in this cold, dead piece of metal now that it wasn't going to work the way he'd first envisioned it.

"It'll do. Try to feel more of it."

"Does hopelessness count?" said Cross, who was sitting several rows behind Pete. *The moon is pretty far away, and cold. And space is cold, far colder than any body of water.*

"Kind of the same thing, but yup."

"What about frustration?" asked Gibson.

"What *about* frustration?" said May. Without waiting for a response, she went into a tirade. "Patrick, those three nights I spent stuck in your office were the most horrible, depressing nights of my life. Between all your lousy advances and the cheap Chinese "dinners" you kept bringing me, I hit a career low. You know there are other items offered on the menu. Not just kung pow, right?"

"But I like kung pow," said Gibson, timidly.

Sturkey spoke up: "Well Dear, I doubt it was good for Mr. Gibson here either. Putting up with you is hard work. Christ, it's no wonder Jarvan ended up offing himself."

"Whoa," said Pete.

"What was it about a *psychic blast*?" countered May.

Sturkey folded his arms.

Cross snorted. "Hey May, I just realized your name is May B. Swallows. Remember when Carter said May Beverly Swallows? Get it? May B? Get it?"

"Shut up, you idiot," snapped May. "How does it feel to know your closest friend is an impotent moron and your girlfriend is—"

Cross became tense. "Don't," he said.

"You know, lying down with the rubble where Trump Tower used to stand."

"Jesus Christ," said Sturkey.

"THAT'S ENOUGH," yelled Swiscock.

Cross fumbled furiously with his seatbelt, ready to attack a bitch, but the Modong pressed him back into the seat with one heavy hand, unwilling to see things escalate physically between his new friends.

"Let go of me you hairy turd!" Cross shouted.

A roar went out beneath them. The lights came on. The ship was fully juiced. Automatically the ladder had begun to retract itself into the ship's anus.

"Hold on!" cried Roddy, pivoting back in his seat to face the front. He reached up and pressed a few square shaped buttons overhead, and suddenly they were moving. The sound inside the flight deck was deafening.

The shuttle climbed into the blue sky, alone in its voyage, but strong in purpose. Our heroes grimaced beneath the weight of the intense g-forces. Blue steadily faded to black, and they did not explode. The atmosphere cleared out around them. The pull of Earth's gravity gradually lessened. They had separated from their homeworld.

And as the sound of the engine finally died, the Modong observed with a smile the gentle dance and sway of the hairs on its arm. Thought the Modong: *It's better this way.*

ACT III: SPACE RACE

1 Black Friday

"Sensors online. Drilling equipment online. All systems nominal, Captain Spayceman," said the computer to Roddy. "All eight passengers are in good health. Time to destination: one hour and forty-seven minutes. You are currently taking the fastest route."

"Stay uncomfortable you lousy pieces of shit," barked the young captain over his shoulder. "You fucking ugly wastes of time." His eyes flicked over the Vibes Gauge nervously; the orange needle was now vibrating in the negative space between the yellow DISCONTENTED and orange AGGRIEVED. He was worried. *Would this bird fly on worry?* He was grateful that Sturkey, who was seated to his right at the foremost of the flight deck, appeared to be lost in heavy thoughts of his own.

Behind them Swiscock and May shared the same row that was separated by a narrow aisle. Then directly behind those two sat Cross and the Modong. Gibson occupied very back in a row all by himself. "Does anybody want to sit next to me?" he called up.

"Wait a minute," said Roddy, shaking his head.

Cross pulled himself away from the view of inky black space, feeling inexplicably tense and alert. Something didn't smell right, and it wasn't the Modong.

At the very front, Roddy turned in his seat and counted with his fingers. "Me, you, you, you, you, you, and you. Shit, Computer, did you get the correct headcount? I count seven."

"My systems detect seven passengers on the flight deck and one passenger en route from the main cargo bay."

"Oh shit," muttered Gibson, as he was the one furthest from the group and closest to the cargo bay. He struggled with his seatbelt. "Shit."

Pete, eyes fixed in determination, said coarsely: "Gibson, with me. We're going to the cargo bay."

"No need," answered someone else.

That someone else was Gunther "Spoons" McTavish, floating at the entrance to the flight deck with his machine gun poised to fire at the crew. His combat fatigues were ripped and torn and a string of red blood drifted away from his face from a gash in his forehead. "I've come to you," he said.

"You," said Pete.

"Me," Spoons replied.

"Him," Gibson said.

"I," Spoons answered.

"Spoons," the Modong grunted.

"Gunther," McTavish shot back. He spat into the zero-g. He was salivating. He squeezed the machine gun's trigger, but alas he had used up all his ammunition in that big battle scene just a couple pages ago in the book. *Cripes!*

While Gibson worked on his seatbelt, Swiscock glided towards Spoons like a phantom, like a balloon that you get at a carnival when the wind is blowing violently and you're too young to understand why it's being lifted out of your hands. He collided with the battle-dressed soldier, immediately pressing his thumbs into Spoons's eyes, ("*Why?!*" Spoons cried) carrying the mercenary forward into the bowels of the ship whence he appeared.

The two fought in the zero-g corridor, exchanging karate chops for roundhouse kicks and swan kicks for sleeper holds, all as Swiscock attempted to steer McTavish back toward the ship's anus.

At the flight deck, Roddy and the others crowded together nervously. They watched the camera feed on the monitor. Much to their dismay it appeared that Spoons, thought to be outmatched, was as tough as or tougher than they came. Twice he slashed out at Swiscock with a hidden blade. It appeared and disappeared at the masterful mercenary's will.

"He's fighting dirty," said Cross, making to leave.

"Stop," said the Modong, again shoving his long, hairy arm in the way. "You will only compromise the fight for Pete."

Reluctantly, Cross agreed to stay put.

The concealed dagger came up again in a steely flash, but this time Swiscock was prepared. He caught Spoons by the wrist and twisted it backwards. With a grunt of pain, Spoons released the knife and it floated away, clanging cleanly off of a wall. Swiscock, with his other hand, shoved Spoons into the airlock and then pulled down the heavy door.

Spoons banged his fist in rebellion against the glass window that separated him from the rest of the ship but the sound of it was inaudible. The entire ship lurched forward from the surge of negative energy. Swiscock grabbed one of the interior handles to brace himself. When the ship steadied, he stared coldly at the figure on the other side of the airlock.

"Should we keep him in there?" asked Roddy over the intercom. "We could use his anger to power the ship." He would admit to himself that the idea, as quick as it had come, was ugly— but it was novel.

May was equally as unhesitant in her response. "No," she said. "Slimeball that he is, it would be sadistic."

"You know him?" asked Cross, arching his neck.

"He's a McTavish," filled in Sturkey, as knowledge from his early intelligence gathering days was coming back. "The name is almost synonymous with murder. Assassinations, torture, petty larceny. At war crimes, McTavishes don't even blink. Worse yet, there are hundreds of them, all spread across the globe. A whole network of wetwork. A wetwork network."

"They aren't all as evil as you'd like to believe," said Gibson. "But the family is a dangerous family to be in. And yes," he said, eyeing Sturkey carefully, "murder tends to run through it."

"Sounds like you guys are setting up for a sequel," said Cross, enthusiastically. "So what do we do?"

But it was too late. Swiscock had already sacrificed Gunther "Spoons" McTavish to the blood-boiling abyss of outer space.

"That was resolved quickly," observed Gibson. The ex-director of C.L.U. went on. "Imagine if, like, McTavish went undetected longer, until we got to the moon, and then surprised us right at our moment of victory."

"That would have sucked," chuckled Cross.

For the next few minutes our heroes excitedly debated possible alternate plot scenarios. The Modong's rapt silence eventually stole their attention, however, as one by one they followed the yellow-eyed gaze. The bright, pockmarked face of Earth's most luminous satellite was rising up towards them. The sheer size of it, now that they were so close, was astonishing. For the first time for Swiscock, at least, Earth's moon appeared to him as a *place* rather than an ornament in the sky.

From within a deep black recess in the moon's southern hemisphere a small light blinked on and off. If you weren't looking, it would have been almost impossible to catch. The light belonged to one of Starshield Six's many space traffic control towers. It blinked again solemnly.

"That's no space station," said Gibson, breaking the sound of a collective awe. "That's a moon."

"That's *our* moon," Cross exclaimed.

"Autumn is there," said Swiscock, rubbing his chin.

"How do you know?" asked May. She realized with embarrassment that she had never met Autumn Summerfall and had forgotten that finding her was the title protagonist's chief motivation.

"I don't know, but I can feel it." Pete turned to Roddy. "Okay, Roddy. We're at the end of this now, no turning back. I don't suppose you got us into space without a plan."

"Yes, we're going to board that bad bitch of a space station and blow it the hell up."

"So you've got the grit for it, eh?" said Gibson, trying to sound badass.

"You betcha."

"But *how,* Roddy?" asked Pete emphatically. "And, I mean, fuck, what does that space station even do?"

"Well it's a research station."

"Go on."

"For the dark arts."

Gibson gasped.

"Wait here," said Roddy, and he glided past the group towards the rear of the flight deck where Spoons had appeared so recently. He reached up into an overhead bin and, after some fumbling around, procured a blue plastic binder thick with leafy documents. "Gotcha," he said, and shut the overhead bin.

He glided back and sat down again.

"This has everything we need to know. Blueprints for the entire space station. It's got everything from structural to electrical to amenities." He opened the binder and flipped through the pages. They all gathered around him to peer over his shoulder. "I've already got an idea of how we can do it. I just want to be sure—"

"Stop," said Pete. "Is that the space station?" He was pointing at the open page.

May said, "Looks like a—"

"Pentagram," finished the Modong.

"It *is* a pentagram," said Roddy. "Makes sense, right? It's the only way the station's power distribution ever worked without having overloaded. This is the first and only working model."

"I sense there's more to it than that," said Sturkey wisely.

"You're right on. Each midpoint of the star's triangular limbs houses a massive Power Cell that works in tandem with the other four. Energy runs along corridors that connect each point. It's complicated math, but it works, and it's all to power *this.*" Roddy stuck his finger down in the pentagon at the center of the sketch of the station. The space was blank, however. There were no notes to indicate what it was.

"It's all to power what?" asked Pete, annoyed.

"A telescope," said Roddy. "I think." It was thus with a screeching stop that his moment of spellbinding charisma ended. "It's not mentioned in this blueprint."

"A telescope?!" demanded May. A small burst of negative energy shuddered through the space shuttle.

"Well obviously it's not a *good* telescope."

"Like it doesn't see far?" asked Cross, concerned.

"No, I mean good as in *morally.*"

"Wait," said Sturkey. "How can a telescope be moral?"

"I mean... in the wrong hands..."

"You don't even know it's a telescope," said the Modong, getting in on this.

"Look, guys," said Roddy, and he threw up his hands. "It doesn't matter what it is as long as we can blow it up, right?"

The gang pondered this.

Roddy placed his hands behind his head and leaned back. "Computer, ETA to port sector Lambda?"

The voice of the computer replied, "You should reach your destination in five minutes, Captain Spayceman. However, my self-diagnostics reveal a critical issue that may challenge the landing."

Roddy exchanged an impatient look with Pete.

"Well? What's the issue?"

"A power issue, Captain Spayceman. Since breaking free from the Earth's atmosphere, my sensors have detected a serious positive inflection in the vibes. Furthermore, the loss of critical negative energy due to the elimination of the eighth passenger may prove to be damning."

"Spoons!" said Pete and he smashed his fist against the wall.

"Not good enough, Passenger Swiscock," advised the computer. "I need more feeling."

"What happens if we run out of power before we get there?" asked Gibson.

"Then we won't be able to make the thousands of tiny course corrections necessary to properly dock," said Roddy.

"That is correct," said the computer.

"Wait, so we're going to *miss* the moon?" Gibson was astounded. He sat down as best he could in the zero gravity cockpit. "You were right, Roddy, we should have kept him as a prisoner. If only the good girl here hadn't opened her mouth."

"It would have been wrong," she asserted.

"Shut up," said Gibson in a rare display of attitude.

"It's my fault," began Swiscock. "I let the man out of the airlock. It was a rash decision." He turned to look out at space in a way that rather justified his actions.

"Computer," said Cross. "Are you sure the vibes aren't bad enough? I think we're all feeling pretty lousy."

"I'm not," said the computer, "but then again, I'm just a machine. To answer your question, Passenger Cross, no the vibes aren't bad enough among the seven present."

"Maybe I got a little excited at the prospect of blowing up a structure on the moon. That couldn't have helped."

May and the Modong each murmured shyly in agreement.

Meanwhile Gibson brooded in silence. Flashes of something sinister flickered across his mind. Memories– *future* memories?– like prophecies filled his vision. Fire and flashes of gray steel, and a beast from beyond Hell. He heard his mother's voice, telling him, "a sacrifice, Patrick. A sacrifice." He bolted awake, suddenly aware that he was sweating and that the others were watching him. *A sacrifice, this dark magic ship of Livingston's requires a sacrifice.* He knew it without knowing how. He was trying to form the words. He sputtered. *If we can get the ship close enough to the port, I can pull us in with*

"A tether," said Sturkey.

"What?" said Gibson.

"If we can get this ship close enough to the port, I can go out there and pull us in with a tether."

"How?" May said. "No– don't be stupid. You'll die out there, Sturk. Are you crazy?"

"I'm going to pull us into the station. The shuttle should automatically dock itself with its remaining power."

"You don't know that," said the Modong. "You don't even know."

"Yes, I do. I'm right, aren't I, Roddy?"

Roddy jerked suddenly as if he'd been falling asleep. "Yeah, he's right. Right, computer?"

"He's right," said the computer. "If I reduce myself to a minimum power state now, I should be able to launch Passenger Pendleton towards Starshield Six's surface at the precise moment needed to pull the shuttle towards the dock. Once we are close enough I will cut the tether and dock us."

"See, love?" said Sturkey.

"Sturkey."

"Don't, worry... I'm just a supporting character in this story, when it's all said and done. It's not like it's my name on the cover, after all."

"There's got to be another way," she whispered.

"There should be space suits on board here somewhere," said Roddy kind of quietly.

"No." The Sturkmeister shook his head. "This dark magic ship of Livingston's requires a sacrifice. A price for everything!"

Gibson couldn't take it anymore. "Damn it, let me sacrifice myself! I was thinking the exact same stuff that you just said except that you said it faster." Gibson crossed his arms.

"Yes," said May, looking brightly into the depths of Sturkey's eyes. "Let Patrick do it."

"I'm sorry, love. I'm afraid it has to be me."

"Attention Captain Spayceman," said the computer. "Vibes are sufficiently bad. Maintain vibage to reach port sector Lambda in two minutes."

She pulled him to her and placed her head against his heaving chest. She was crying silent sobs. The rest of the crew couldn't bear to look.

"Look," said Roddy. "Once Sturkey gets us in there we're going to move quickly. Factoring in the condition that my brother will believe that he was on the last vehicle bound for the moon, and that this will be a silent docking procedure automated by the shuttle's and the base's respective nervous systems... he shouldn't know we're coming. So we'll have the element of surprise. Once we get in we'll need to destroy three of the five Power Cells in order to shut down the station. I suggest we break into groups..."

As Roddy gave the briefing, no doubt to save himself from becoming emotional, some thoughts occurred to Gibson: how composers can spend their whole lives searching for the kinds of moments from which they can draw beautiful music. This was without a doubt such a moment. Beethoven would have killed to be alive during this. For lack of the master's presence, Gibson thought he'd try. He attempted a melody in his head. *Bah–* it was something he'd heard before when he was young. His mother sang it to him, her mouth wide, bellowing great big noises. It gave him chills now to picture her doing it. It went *bah-ah-laal– bah-ahlaaaal–* It was not a beautiful sound. No, he was hearing it wrong. He clenched his fists, miffed at his own incompetence. It should be *he* going out there to die, *he* into the end as a permanent sacrifice. *He* to never see soil again. *Wait, what am I thinking?* Everything seemed so cold. The reality of it suddenly struck him anew.

The tall Englishman had passed several broad loops of government standard Flexi-cord around his waist and then yanked the whole line taut. The Modong saw the pain in his face, and could almost feel it around his hairy stomach, himself. He was pulling the rope too tight. The girl sat before Sturkey as he performed this ritual. She remained silent, but her eyes were noticeably moist. The one named Swiscock merely placed a hand on Sturkey's shoulder and then glided away to the airlock.

Cross gave Sturkey a knowing nod (please refer to the prior chapter, "Separation Anxiety").

"Thirty seconds," said the computer.

"No," whispered May.

Sturkey pulled her to himself and kissed her hard and with unnecessary eroticism– wishing only for more time, if not at least a cameo in a prequel novel– and pushed her away. He joined Swiscock at the airlock's threshold. Side-by-side they gazed out as the pale lunar landscape passed beneath them. Soon the Lambda vertex of the Starshield Six pentagram would appear. By then Sturkey would be gone, descending hundreds of feet towards the evil-built superstructure.

As far as music goes, maybe this moment would be best left alone, for it was completely quiet aboard Shuttle #22 when the hatch finally opened and Sturkey shot out of it with thousands of feet of Flexi-cord squeezing his torso. The computer had calculated the launch to a millisecond. Perhaps human error would render it all for naught. What remained was for Sturkey to plant his feet near the docking bay and yank the cord as hard as he friggin' could.

The computer slowed slow the rate at which the shuttle was moving parallel to the moon's surface. Swiscock and crew felt the jolt of Sturkey's landing– and then his immediate tugging at the tether.

Impossible, thought the Modong, in a mix of relief and sadness.

Sturkey's forceful landing had raised only the faintest cough of dust from the surface of Starshield Six's outermost point. Below him, just inches from his toes, another thousand feet of the structure ran down to the surface of the moon. He took the briefest opportunity to appreciate the audacity of the enormous space station–its mere presence was an affront to all he thought he'd known about humanity's progress in space– and wondered about the pale dome shape rising from the center of it, off to the lunar East. *It could be a telescope, after all, like the kind they keep in the observatories.* In the sky, the tiny Earth stood curiously still, as if expecting him to move. *Right.* With the tether in hand, he strode towards the nub-cylindrical protrusion that was the port Lambda airlock and went to work.

Sturkey pulled the entire ship towards Starshield Six. His skin was turning blue. Ice had already formed on his muscular forearms. The whites of his eyes had begun to crystallize. The effort became more difficult as he alternated with each arm. There was no air to breathe, no more resources from which to pull. Never again would there be. Yet he could not let such thoughts affect him; if he failed, then those depending on him would fail too. he pulled. He grimaced. *Closer*, he urged the shuttle from across the absolute desolation of space. As the last of his vision faded, he saw the ass-end of Roddy's old mining vessel growing before him. Sturkey heaved, summoning strength that he never knew he had. Once the vehicle had made it to him, the computer would do the rest. It would cut the tether and mate the locks. The shuttle would stand erect over the southwestern point of Starshield Six, and the rest would be left up to its crew.

"It's working," said Roddy.

"Duh it's working," said the computer.

"Of course it's working," said May.

Sturkey reached out and touched the ceramic surface of the mining vessel with the tips of his fingers. *May,* he thought, *why is this so absurd?* He recalled the glimpse of her pale thigh beneath her skirt on that first summer date. That day had turned colder than either of them expected. *I'm sorry.*

He ceased to move then, as he had become more icicle than man. All that was left of him was silence, and then echoes of silence.

3 Mama-Se Mama-Sa Mama-Ku-Sa

For several eerie seconds, the banging and crumpling sounds were heard throughout the ship. When it was over, Gibson opened his eyes and blew out all the air he'd been holding in his chest. He felt sickeningly guilty. Cross, who was now sitting aside his old partner from C.L.U. said to him, "We've come a long way."

"Alright," began Roddy. He was climbing down the ladder that separated the rows of seats on the flight deck, handing each of the crew a pair of heavy, iron-footed shoes. "Sorry," he said to the Modong, when he realized there would not be a pair of shoes big enough to fit the giant's feet. He spoke as he moved down. "This is it, everybody. Get your climbing muscles loose because this is going to be a long descent through darkness. We're lucky the low gravity will make it easier."

"How long is it?" asked May, matter-of-factly.

"It's about thirty stories."

He led her gaze down between his feet and jammed a button to his right. For the third time since leaving Earth, the shuttle's rear airlock door swung open. Below them, where the ship had connected to the surface of Starshield Six, a quiet maw of total black awaited. Only the first few rungs of the ladder and the concrete wall around it were visible within the shortest reaches of the shuttle's interior lights. "Yep, down there is about thirty stories of offline maintenance shaft that leads to the Lambda complex."

Cross's heart had been beating quickly. He rubbed his palms together and then on his shirt in an attempt to dry away the sweat that had formed. He licked his lips. He was hanging on to Roddy's every word as Roddy described how the station had been built in six major steps, with the Lambda triangle being the first, and therefore the oldest. Apparently it had been mostly abandoned, except for its use as a detention center for Starshield Six's unruly personnel. Still it housed one of the five Power Cells.

"At the bottom we'll be at the back of the security station, which will be out of commission. Should be. Worst case scenario, I'll hack through the door. Once we're on the other side, we'll have our options for how we want to do this. The station's crew traverse the pentagram via the five railways which we can use—"

"Let's get on with it," said Gibson, anxious.

One-by-one, the crew of Shuttle #22 took to the ladder that led directly from the shuttle's flight deck down into the farthest reaches of Starshield Six's Lambda vertex. Roddy passed into the utter darkness of the shaft that led into the station's bowels. Just meters away, on the other side of complex machinery and insulation, the cold corpse of Sturkey stood motionless in the soundless void of space, the undrifting clipped length of Flexi-cord still in his left hand. Swiscock was next to follow Roddy through the threshold into darkness, stepping down one cautious step at a time. The trembling intuition that he was finally going to see Autumn again was tainted by the gnawing sense that he was walking— or climbing down, rather— into a trap and that things would get worse before they could get better. He said nothing. Some strange force compelled him to stay quiet. May, climbing down after Swiscock, watched above her as the ring of light that was the illuminated ship's interior became distorted by the mass of silhouettes produced by Gibson, then Cross, and finally the Modong. It was very likely the last of light she would see for a long time. The thought made her tense, and she hung onto the idea of the light extinguishing. *Entropy will make everything dark,* she mused, envisioning the starless sky of a time-distant civilization. Yet the light was still there, still reaching the top of her arms and shoulders. The light would stop Bates, master of darkness. The lower half of Gibson was fully submerged in blackness. He felt for each rung with his foot, then his hand, and noted the sensation of the slick steel in his grip, how the temperature almost made it feel wet. He had climbed down many rungs of many ladders before on his secret reconnaissance missions with Villa 48, but never one that was *what did the scientist boy say? Thirty stories?* Meanwhile, Cross thought about the time he was crossing a street and he saw a penny that was face up, and when he stooped down to get it, he staggered and accidentally kicked it beneath a truck. He never saw that penny again and often wondered if the luck associated with discovering a penny face up was contingent upon actually acquiring that penny. As the image of the penny faded, he realized he had been staring at the top of Gibson's balding head. He smiled and wondered what he could have been so scared for. Then, dang it, just as he started to regain his confidence there was a loud, resounding *–BANG!–* and the darkness was full and absolute. The Modong jerked to a halt. Even with its excellent night-vision, it could see nothing. The airlock above them had swung shut, effectively closing out the little light that had shone down from Shuttle #22's anus.

This, Roddy had expected.

The wild rumbling that ensued, he had not.

Desperately he clung to the violently shaking steel, forgoing all descent, and was thankful that the others had appeared to do the same. Up above him he could hear Cross and Gibson shouting. The sound was like that of a dozen fires– no, make that *two* dozen fires– blazing in his eardrums. And then abruptly, the sound and the vibrations ceased. Six frightened breaths heaved in the darkness.

"What the hell was that?" said Gibson. Though he could neither see nor be seen, the accusing glare that he aimed at Roddy and Swiscock, below him was definitely tangible. "Well?"

"I believe it. Shuttle #22," Roddy panted, "has left. Departed."

"How?" said May. "I thought it didn't have the energy. What the hell was Sturkey's sacrifice for?"

"It appears we've been betrayed," said Swiscock. *Damn, I called it*, he thought. "Shuttle #22 is no doubt alerting the base to our presence. Maybe it already did."

"Damn it," said May.

"Then let us get down this damn ladder with haste," urged the Modong from high up. "And do what we came here to do."

They climbed down now, a little faster than they had been when they started. At first the only sound was of their hands and feet landing on and leaving the rungs, but as they neared their destination, the inner machinations of Starshield Six became audible. Big groaning sounds like that of metal bending, grew from within the walls. They passed between the sounds of turning gears. Electrical currents whizzed by. There were organic sounds. Sounds like the pleading of souls trapped just on the other side of the chasm. The temperature oscillated between the extremes. For meters at the time the steel rungs would be unbearably hot. And then they would be cold. After a while the changes became intolerable. Gibson felt as though he were passing through a time-loop. The thought of simply letting go and falling freely to the bottom had appeared several times to him as a peaceful alternative to this slow, physically demanding descent.

When Roddy's foot struck the bottom he was hardly prepared for it and he fell onto his butt. "Pete! Slow down, we've made it!" he shouted, and then he leaned back. God, he was tired. Pete, however, appeared not to have heard, and stepped onto Roddy's leg, and then fell on top of him.

"Oof!" he said.

Roddy giggled.

The two of them scurried backwards mischievously and listened in the darkness as the rest of the crew all crashed together into a pile at the bottom, culminating in the sudden heavy descent of the Modong.

"Ouch!" said May.

"Sorry," said the big guy.

Roddy and Swiscock were too busy laughing at the others' grunts and confusion to notice the third laugh join them– that is, at first. They froze. The others froze. But the third laugh continued. Its *hee hawing* cackles bounced and leapt around them ghoulishly. May suddenly recalled the terrible *hee hoo* cries of the African Jungle Owl, but this was something much worse. The lights came on, blinding and white.

Pete shielded his eyes. He then lowered his hand as the blurred figure came into focus. Livingston Bates, donning the same bleach white robe he had worn when they'd first met in that oppressed African village, stood with one hand atop his walking cane, and removed the night vision goggles from his face, revealing a gleeful smile. There were soldiers behind him now, faces hidden beneath yellow storm trooper masks, pointing their guns at the party.

"Welcome, my friends," said Bates, "to a space station on the moon."

4 Our Gang is in a Heap of Trouble!

Moon Prison, the toughest slammer of them all, thought Gibson, channeling his best Clint Eastwood. Desperate, he grabbed onto the bars and tried to squeeze his face through them. "Guys?" he called.

"What?" said Roddy.

"Just checking if you're still there."

"We're still here," answered Cross, who was sitting beside Roddy on an uncomfortable metal bench. He looked at the Modong, who simply shook his head. It had been over three hours of Earth-time, though they had no way of knowing.

Three barred cells divided by thick steel walls comprised their prison. Roddy, Cross, and the Modong, had been put into one of the end cells, while Gibson had been thrown, by his lonesome, into the middle. This, apparently, had been a calculated move.

He will drive us insane, realized the Modong.

"Let me out!" Gibson called. "Hey! Damn. They took my gun. Hey guys, they took my gun!"

"We need to get out of here," said Roddy. "I can't take this anymore."

"Modong," said Cross, getting to his feet. "See if you can bend those bars."

The Modong lumbered over to the cell door and pulled the thick vertical bars away from one another with all of its strength. It heaved and strained and rearranged itself several times, even using its naked, hairy feet to push off of the ceiling, but ultimately it was not successful.

"I'm sorry," said the Modong.

"It's okay."

They all sat back down.

Why did the madman spare us? Cross wondered. *Where were May and Swiscock?*

"Did you guys get out yet?" asked Gibson from the other cell. He could not see them, only hear them next door. "Hello? Let me out of here!"

The Modong pounded its fist against the outer wall. A hollow thump shook white flecks to the bench. Curious, it inspected the curl of its fist, and then brushed more pieces off.

"Fucking plaster," said Roddy. "I don't believe it."

Cross grinned.

"Sounds like you can punch a hole in the wall," observed Gibson, his hands clenched around the bars of his cell.

The others confided quietly.

"What are you whispering about?"

"Shut up!" cried Roddy.

Cross said something inaudible to the Modong. The Modong nodded to Roddy. The Modong placed its big hairy hand on the place it had knocked, straightened its arm out and then leaned forward on it. Roddy and Cross then pushed into the Modong's hairy back from behind. Thin spidery cracks in the wall emerged in all directions leading away from the beast's hand, as the palm of the hand sank a little into the wall. And then the entire monster fell through.

The sound had been like tearing an entire phonebook's worth of paper at once, a party trick Cross had used, with mixed results, to impress chicks. He and Roddy laughed together quietly, both joyous at such a stupid, fortunate turn of events.

Then, Cross, with his shoulders hunched, stepped up to the jail bars. "Listen, Pat, old buddy," he said, knowing full well what he had to do. "Just hang tight while we do a little reconnaissance. We're gonna come right back for you." Behind him, Roddy Spayceman was already stepping through the black Modong-shaped tear in the wall. Cross moved an inch closer to the bars. He knew that Gibson was just on the other side of the wall, listening intently. He said, with more conviction this time, "I'm going to come back for you. Right away."

He was answered with silence from the other cell.

As the door to the Lambda-Tau tramcar slid open, a rough hand shoved Swiscock from behind. It was an unnecessary, impatient, and cruel gesture. If it happened again, he would twist around and break the fingers on that hand. Even as his own were cuffed.

May stepped out beside him, her hands cuffed together too, and he saw the same flash of emotion pass over her face. They merely nodded at one another. The tram station was empty except for the soft moans of air coming from the tunnels.

Livingston Bates stepped around them to lead the way. While Bates's bare feet padded softly, the other four pairs of footsteps clicked brightly on the smooth moonstone floor. Behind them, the tram car screeched and hissed and left, disappearing into the shadows. They passed diagonally between rows of structural support pillars that had been plastered with heaps of redundant pro-Starshield Six propaganda, and then Bates showed the small crew up a wide set of steps obviously meant for large quantities of foot traffic.

Do people actually live here? May wondered.

"This station is at the exact midpoint of the Lambda-Tau rail line," began Bates, ascending the steps. "It is the fastest way to reach The Core."

"The Core?" asked Pete.

One of the bodyguards hit him from behind. "No questions."

"No it's alright," said Bates, waving his hand absently as he lead the way. "The Core is where the magic happens. It's what all this has been leading up to." They were about halfway up the stairs when Pete realized he was sweating from exertion. *Aren't we far above the moon's surface? The gravity should be weaker here, not stronger.* Bates, a psychopath but not telepath, continued: "I admit I was sorry I couldn't have killed you on Earth. Twice. But then in the time since our most recent encounter I thought of something better. I'm always thinking of something better. Carter wanted you dead too, and tried to shame me for my failure when his men alerted him that you were coming aboard that infernal Shuttle #22. That's why I had him put into Moon Prison, *the toughest slammer of them all.*"

"That's where you sent Gibson and the others," said Swiscock. It was not a question, more a statement of fact in order to help orient the reader.

"Yes, sir. It was on the way, so it was no hair off of my back."

"I doubt you ever had any hair on your back," said May, trying to sound cool. Even though she maintained a calm outward appearance, her heart was beating like a drunken raccoon that had woken up in a bird cage with no way out.

"You're right, Ms. Swallows. It's true. Except for my eyebrows I'm as hairless as a babe. Always been that way. Old Roddy and his friends used to call me Smooth-Boy back when we were young. I hated that nickname, Smooth-Boy... you see, oh— we got ourselves off-topic." Bates cleared his throat.

They had reached the top of the stairs which opened up to a wide corridor leading away from them on either side. On the far wall, directly behind Bates, was writ in a large bold letters BIG DOME OBSERVATION ROOM, a long black arrow leading to the right. Below it read BIG DOME LVL 2 (COINTEGRATION CHAMBER) / CONCESSIONS with a red arrow leading to the left. The hallway seemed to go on for quite a distance in both directions, as each side of the pentagram's interior pentagon was three miles long. Bates spun around and bowed slightly before speaking. "We used to call it 'The Big Dome.' Old paint. That was while Carter still mattered. We call it 'The Core' now."

Pete rolled his eyes. *How many names can you have for the same thing?*

"Anyways, I hate to say it but this is our final meeting. I'll be headed to the Observation Room now to see you off. My loyal guards will escort you to the Cointegration Chamber."

Pete smiled. "Escort nothing. You know that the moment you are gone from sight these lackeys are dead men. And then you will bring me Autumn Summerfall." He heard an amused grunt come from behind him.

"Perhaps," said Bates, "She will come to you." With that, the tall black man in perfectly white lounging robes turned on a heel and walked away.

Pete, glaring, started after him but May placated him with a cuffed hand on his arm. "Let's see this through," she whispered.

Pete had one eye on Bates, who was getting away quickly. "We're playing into his hands, May," he said through gritted teeth.

Before she could respond, they were being ushered again into the opposite direction. Pete shrugged. He felt strangely out of control of the situation, as he had been once he fell from that ninth story window at Scooberdoo Hospital a lifetime ago. May was with him then. God, how everything came back in an instant: Autumn, the red hot end of a cigarette, Kurtis Blow, the hot cum. Seated across from him in the passenger seat of his Ford Maverick she had asked him, "Doesn't it ever get boring to you?"

When Cross stepped through the Modong-shaped tear in the wall he was taken by surprise at the violence on the other side. Roddy's back was to him. Hunched forward, the skinny scientist had his hands around the big monster's waist as best as he could, looking as if he was trying to pull the monster off of someone else. There was a pair of booted feet kicking and screeching against the floor.

"Modong, stop it," said Cross. Their big, hairy companion suddenly relented and stood away from the youth it was strangling. The would-be casualty, a boy with innocent looks— freckle spotted cheeks, a smooth, wide brow, and a wave of fair, auburn hair that fell thickly to one side of it— hacked and convulsed. The pain on his red, crying face was evident, and yet his size (for he was tiny in the black-and-white camouflage patterned combat fatigues he was wearing) produced a comic effect that undermined any authority he might have. Roddy was simply thankful that the boy was alive.

The Modong apologized in its deep, otherworldly voice. "I just fell through that cheap plaster wall and my hands landed on him and—"

"It's okay. Your primal instincts kicked in. You alright?" Cross asked the boy. He offered a hand, but the poor kid was still coughing.

"Give him a minute," said the Modong. It shrugged.

"I'm alright," said the boy. "Sc—scared me, th—that's all," he said, glancing up at them. "Say, who are you guys? Ye—you're the prisoners, are—aren't you?"

"I don't know. Do we look like prisoners?" answered Cross, again offering his hand. This time the boy took it and got to his feet. "The name's Cross."

"Roddy," pitched in Roddy. "But you can call me 'Rod, or El Dorado." *God why was he trying to impress some kid. The little shit couldn't be older than thirteen.* Roddy then realized then that he had probably spent too many nights cooped up in the forests of Africa doing his brother's secret bidding. First thing he would do once he got back down to Mother Earth would be to go to America, hit up some bars and hit on some babes.

"Modong," said the Modong.

"Jerry," said the freckle-cheeked kid. His eyes widened in evidence that he'd suddenly remembered something. "Shit, I've got to go. I've got to get to the CC ASAP. Shit, I'm a dead man." he said, glancing at his wristwatch.

"The 'CC?'" asked Roddy, an eyebrow cocked.

"The Cointegration Chamber. The Big Dome. The Core. Look, I've no time to explain—"

Cointegration. Roddy had mouthed the word almost immediately upon hearing it. He said to Cross, "This is starting to make sense now. The Big Dome, it's not a telescope. Of course it's not a telescope." He'd said the last sentence almost inaudibly. Something darker than a lack of sleep shadowed his eyes. He lunged out to grab Jerry by the shoulders. "Boy, listen to me. You don't want to be in that chamber when the thing starts. You don't know what you're getting yourself into." He glanced sidelong at the Modong, pausing to think for only a millisecond. He spoke quickly. "You and Garry, take the tramcar on the Lambda-Delta line all the way to Delta Labs. Don't worry it's automated. There will be weapons stored in the labs, the highest tech available. Use them to destroy the Power Cell like I talked about." He returned his gaze to the boy, appraising him for his trustworthiness.

"How will we find it, the Power Cell?" asked Cross. "And what of Gibson?" He nodded toward the tear in the wall behind him.

"Remember it lies at the triangle's midpoint," said Roddy. "You'll know it when you stumble upon the security there. And Gibson... Damn him. Listen, Jerry, I need you to stay away from 'The Big Dome' or whatever you call it. In the meantime help get my friend out of the middle cell back there. Do you know where you can find the keys?"

Jerry shook his head no.

"I need you to find them. Your life depends on it. Do you understand?"

Jerry shook his head no.

"Free the man in the middle cell and prepare two escape pods. Once I'm done with my business we're going to blow the Power Cell here and leave. Time is on our side."

Garrison Cross, ignoring the boy's watery eyes, asked, "And what is your business?"

Roddy said without turning, "I'm going to kill my brother."

5 Villa 49

The pale disc of the winter sun lent a spectral beauty to the sky above the shrouded hills of Virginia. And indeed it did now– however another spectre had intruded upon the scene on Villa 49's roof. The spectre of Death. The unmarked, black matte deathcopter, the same that had carried Felicia Weatherspoon and Peter Swiscock to Africa many chapters ago, was now returning from another, more terrible mission. Its deep, steady chops pushed away dust and dead leaves that had fallen to the helipad and surrounding areas and drowned out any possibility of conversation between the three men waiting upon the deathcopter's arrival. Not that they had much to say that hadn't already been said.

As the winding of the 'copter blades slowed, a soldier, tall and masked, jumped down from the bay door. The soldier's arms cradled a woman's lifeless body. The three men, all top officials at Villa 49, moved aside to let Frederich McTavish pass through.

"I am sorry, brother," one of them had said, though it didn't matter who. Frederich thought of Swiscock and only Swiscock, murderer of his kin and now murderer of his love. He played back the memory: Peter Swiscock holding Felicia over edge of the rushing sewer dam that continued to rush below them many stories even now. He recalled her bravery as she threatened suicide: *Drop me, Pete, and end everything for yourself.* And later that day he'd been sick with jealousy as Swiscock helped her onto the deathcopter. From a distance he'd stood at attention, aching to accompany her for this mission. But she said no. She sensed his feelings for her and his disdain for Swiscock. So he was made to stay.

As he carried her down the ramp to the enclosed stairwell that zigged and zagged to the earth, he replayed that last image of her as best as he could remember. It was her profile with the drab, olive colored fatigues, her tiny hands sticking out of the sleeves. It was a flash of her perfectly white teeth. From beneath the black padded cup of the flight comm headset, a cascade of blonde curls and wisps fluttered past her cheeks in that afternoon breeze. She had looked his way then, maybe at him, smiling fully as she said something absently to Swiscock. She'd stepped up into the black shadows of the Villa 49 deathcopter, leaving no trace behind her. Frederich's astonishment at the way she had disappeared had caused him to physically reach out in pain. Ashamed, he'd glanced around, but it seemed no one had noticed, or no one had dared to make comment. That had been the last time he ever saw her alive. Up until her death the foolish girl had referred to this facility as Villa *48.* She hadn't fully accepted that Villa 48 had been destroyed as a consequence of her father's actions. That her own actions here would have consequences, too.

In truth, he didn't know where he was taking her. It didn't matter; there were no protocols for this event. Barnaby had long been absent and she had no next-of-kin. He walked with her all the way down to the grounds, and carried her across the lawns and into the woods that formed a natural perimeter around the secret installation, Villa 49. At a respectful distance the three men from the rooftop tailed him. Two of them were his brothers, Immanuel and Hans, and the third was the occultist, Liam Portobello.

He set her down gently and turned her so that she was facing out into the forest, her cold body still as stone for rigor mortis. He reached into his pack behind him for the iron spade, remembered using it to smash the tiny, predatory skull of an African Jungle Owl mid flight as it darted for him. He remembered opening that cabin door and seeing her lying on the ground, alone, impossibly quiet...

"Talk," said Frederich, fully aware of the silence of the woods, and of the men standing behind him.

His brother, Hans spoke. "As of yesterday at about this time, our sky scanners have been detecting unusual lunar energies emanating from somewhere within the Mare Fecunditatis. We're talking heat readings that rival the sun."

Frederich would have laughed at such a dramatic comment if he hadn't been busy digging a shallow grave. He listened on.

It was Liam Portobello's cue. Portobello, once an infamous whistleblower on government conspiracies and supposed expert on all things occult, had been shamed into hiding by one of his rivals for stretching a truth. Later on, it had been the fine eye of Felicia Weatherspoon that had plucked the recluse from his favorite shadows and offered him a job as a consultant at Villa 49. The others had long thought the skinny, malnourished man useless until now. His voice was small but firm. "On a hunch, I took the sky scanners' recordings and transposed the wavelengths into audio. Most of it is unintelligible, but some of it... some of it is clearly *language.*"

Now this was strange enough to jar Frederich McTavish out of his trance. He turned to face Portobello, and rested his hand on the shovel. He merely stared, waiting for the little occultist to continue.

"*Je suis mon propre pére,*" said tiny Portobello. "Does that mean anything to you?"

"No."

Hans whispered something to Portobello. He made a move to push up his glasses but then realized he wasn't wearing them. He stepped forward, confused, and asked, "How about the name, *Ba'alal?*"

"Belial?"

"No, not Belial. Ba'alal. With an apostrophe in the name."

Frederich frowned, unsure.

"The Betrayer," said Hans.

"Yes," said Portobello. "Ba'alal, the Betrayer."

Frederich turned back to the dirt. He dug the shovel in with his foot, loosened up a clump of heavy mud.

"Mother used to sing us a song," said Hans to his brother's back. Hans wore a mustache that would make Tom Selleck blush and, understandably, it guaranteed him a certain level of authority. "She would sing it to us when we acted unruly. Do you remember it, Frederich?"

"Yes," was all he was willing to say. For years he had fought off any such recollections of his disturbed childhood. He preferred not to think of his current self and the boy with those memories as the same person. To have his mother's evil song resurface now while he prepared a grave for the woman he loved... to hear again in his mind's ear her painful, prophetic wailing... he scowled.

Said Portobello, "You must remember it."

Frederich McTavish whirled violently. "One more word from you and I'll bash your head in with this spade, you brazen, overpaid nut-job."

"Please, brother," said Hans. The youngest of the three present McTavish brothers entreated with moist eyes. "Listen to the recording. We all have."

"Fine. Fine, I'll listen to your stupid recording." He tossed the shovel to Immanuel McTavish, the mute. "Bury her properly. I'll be back to inspect." With that, the silent McTavish went to work.

6 Nightmare Machine

While a lone tramcar carried Garrison Cross and the Modong towards the high tech laboratories in the Delta triangle of Starshield Six, Swiscock and May were being escorted by their two captors to a pair of imposing black double doors. Across the two doors, bold, angular letters, in red ink, read: COINTEGRATION CHAMBER. They moved in slow motion. Bates's henchmen were a little too close for comfort.

Pivoting on a dime, Swiscock brought the side of his cuffed hand up in a slicing motion. It clapped against bodyguard #1's jugular. The bozo, wearing a face of surprise, put his arms up in defense only after the fact. Swiscock then kicked the inside of the guard's leg, right below the knee, which dropped him down six inches. Then Swiscock brought both of his fists down upon the back of his neck. At the same time May had swung low for bodyguard #2's crotch and missed— as the guard stepped back, but followed through with an upward arc, turning and catching the underside of the guard's jaw. The heavy man, chosen by Livingston Bates for his cruelty rather than his intellect, drew the pistol from his hip holster with an evil grin. Spinning from out of nowhere, Swiscock kicked the gun from his hand, and then May kicked the brains from his head. Bodyguard #2 fell alongside his colleague into a silent heap.

Nine seconds later: Swiscock rubbed his wrists where the handcuffs had been and said to May, "I'm telling you, this is a bad idea." He picked up the bodyguard's pistol from the floor and stuffed it into his pants.

"I don't think we have any other choice," said May, looking up. The two were dwarfs standing next to the massive doors. Rather than waste time with any argument, Swiscock grasped one of the door handles and forced it open.

May went through first. She hadn't known what to expect but the view made her dizzy. The interior of the Big Dome was much larger, much vaster than any American football stadium or any Olympic stadium she had ever set foot in. The interior wall of the dome went away and then out as far as the eye could see and then turned in on itself and came back to them in the broad sweeping arc of a perfect circumference. Grey panels and big, steaming tubes stuck out from the curved wall in shadowed relief. Up above, the Earth, an impossible blue jewel, lingered in solitude amid the deep black sea of space and the patches of small, white stars twinkling behind it. There was no roof above them separating them from the frigid death-grip of the abyss. *How was this possible?* she wondered. Space, hanging above them like that, was too terrifying to bear. She stepped forward.

Before her stretched a six-foot wide path of carbon-steel alloy that ran forward over four-and-a-half miles, the entire length of the dome. Two miles and something to the thing at the center. There were no railings on either side of the path. It merely ended. She went over to the edge and gasped. Swiscock caught her as she fell back. Below them, tens of thousands of Livingston Bates's soldiers stood idly like so many chess pieces. None of them uttered a word, none of them so much as shifted in their boots or scratched an itch. Even though the distance was too great to truly tell, she was sure they had all been looking at her.

"Come on," whispered Pete, into her ear. "Let's stay close to the center of the path and press on. I have a feeling that army down there won't do anything. Not yet, at least. Our host is here for a show."

"Thank you, Pete," she said, glad for his presence. "I know I haven't said this but... with what's ahead... just in case... I'm sorry I tried to kill you back in Africa."

"Happens all the time," was his stoic response.

"You asked me what motivates me, back when we first met, back in Jarvan's shed."

"I did?"

"Something like that."

"Ah yes, right before you drugged me. And?"

"And my answer hasn't changed."

Pete laughed, taking her hand. "Money, huh? Maybe I was wrong about you Ms. Swallows."

May had noticed Bates's observation room protruding out from the curved wall of the dome, and knew that the bastard inside was enjoying every second of this. But it didn't matter. She flipped him the bird and together they marched on. At the center of the dome, so far away, a blue object had begun glowing brightly.

They looked so tiny from here, like a pair of ants. Like ants they were being drawn to the scent— like anything drawn to the stimulus. "Curiosity killed the cat," said Bates. He tipped a gaudy red coffee mug to his lips as he watched our two crusaders, Swiscock and May, from behind the reinforced glass of the Big Dome Observation Room. He had fixed himself his favorite coffee: a decaf almond milk cortado with two tablespoons of honey and a teaspoon of brown sugar, not that anyone would care to know.

"...and satisfaction brought it back," answered his half-brother, Roddy Spayceman.

Now it was not the first time in Bates's long career that he experienced the cold bite of a gun barrel into his neck. As per usual, the sensation was immediately followed by the distinct clicking sounds of the drawing of the hammer. But after this the experience here differed from all previous iterations. It was the scent. It was the familiar scent of the boy with whom he'd often wrestled when he was a child. There was something sad about the scent, something that had never been there before. He didn't know what. "You're right on time."

"Pussy time," said Roddy, borrowing a line from Pete. "Turn it off, Bates. Or I'll shoot you through the neck right now."

"Brother, please. You know you can't do it."

"I can do anything I set my mind to."

"No you can't."

"Yes I can."

"No you can't."

While Roddy was very nervous, he was determined not to be licked by Bates's oily silver tongue. He gritted his teeth and said, "You would have let me die. You practically gave the order you son-of-a-bitch. So I'm going to say this one more time. Turn it off."

"No."

And with that Roddy clenched his eyes shut. His finger formed a tight curl around the trigger and– waited. He couldn't do it. He opened his eyes. Bates was facing him.

In a whirlwind of speed Bates stripped the gun from Roddy's hand and threw his half-brother up against the glass. Bates pointed the gun at him. There was no hesitation this time. Only a tiny, impotent *click!*

Roddy flinched, crossing his arms in front of himself.

Bates laughed, pulling the trigger again, comically. "Now you see, Rod, don't you? When I told you you couldn't do it, I wasn't attacking your character. I was merely observing the truth of the situation– that this gun of yours has no ammunition!"

In a wild, furious daze, Roddy retraced his memories. He'd told Jerry his plan to kill Bates, and it was Jerry's gun he'd carried all this way from that hallway just on the other side of Moon Prison, *the toughest slammer of them all.* The stupid freckle-faced kid had supposedly given it to him out of gratitude for saving his life. *It's dangerous to go alone*, Jerry had said. *Take this.*

“Did you think you could win over my Jerry so easily? No. You and your friends, that young detective and that beast, are naive. Now turn around. Look upon my army.”

Slowly, Roddy began to register what he was seeing: thousands of soldiers, all donning the same black-and-white camouflage fatigues that Jerry had been wearing, stood in perfect formation. In one dizzying instant the soldiers all turned and craned their necks to gaze directly into Roddy Spayceman’s soul. He clutched himself in horror, unable to speak. There were hundreds of Jerries, all with the same freckled cheeks and wave of Auburn hair. There were women too, some of which bore a passing resemblance to the women of the isles of Mozambique, from Roddy’s dirty magazines. There was even

“Barnaby?” said Roddy, pressing his nose against the glass. The big oaf was standing down there– but there were many of him, multiplied again and again amid the others. Roddy lifted his eyes to the bridge, his only hope against all of this madness.

May Swallows and Peter Swiscock, two tiny dots so far away now, cast tiny streaks of shadows as they neared the bright blue object at the center.

“They’re almost there,” said Bates. He had come up to the window so that he was standing alongside his brother. “By extension we’re all almost there. Can you feel it?”

“What’s going to happen to them?” asked Roddy.

“That crystal is going to turn this station into a portal to another world. And then all Hell is going to break loose.”

“Funny. I had the feeling that was going to happen anyway.”

Swiscock and May had reached the center of the Big Dome. A bright blue crystal the size of a school bus struck upward like the frosted tip of a spear. It pointed patiently at the Earth, which was so eerily distant now that it seemed plausible the moon landing had been real while all life on Earth had been faked. The crystal glowed and hummed softly and generally the air around it felt electrified. Chortling sectioned tubes that were each half-a-foot wide fed upward into otherworldy stone while colored wires lead quietly out of it and down into the crude mechanical cradle that circumscribed its irregular shape at the base. A flat steel surface fanned outward from this cradle. It was this surface upon which Starshield Six’s technicians had lain their research materials in the past. As Swiscock approached the crystal ahead of May, a single CRT monitor that was sitting atop the work-surface zipped on. It displayed in the center of the screen, in green letters:

ACTIVATE?
PRESS Y OR N

Where obviously there once had been a full QWERTY keyboard embedded into the work-surface, only one key remained. His finger hovered, twitching slightly.

"I suppose this is it," said May. She had stopped several feet behind Pete, unwilling to draw any closer to the mysterious evil crystal which cast pale shadows down to the floor. *I bet Shuttle #22 could go to the next galaxy on the bad vibes coming from that thing*, she thought, clutching her elbow. "What's going to happen when you press that button, Pete?"

Pete fixed her with a wild-eyed stare. He said, "hold on to your titties," and pressed the button.

7 Dark Dealings

Garrison Cross had found himself bracing with all his strength against a metal support pole when the tramcar rapidly lost its velocity. The sound was of the wheels screeching against the rails, and to the left and right, bright yellow sparks sent red shadows across the interior of the vehicle, turning the Modong into a monster's monster. The smell of smoke and burning rubber quickly filled the cabin of the tramcar. "Come on," Cross cried and grabbed the Modong by the fur of its elbow. The two rushed into the dark tunnel that stretched nearly the whole 12.71 miles across the length of the station. Behind them, a small fire smoldered underneath the left-side wheel near the front of the car. Instinctively, the two had continued walking towards their destination.

"What happened?" asked Cross. He clicked on a flashlight and it brought out the moist hollowed walls of the tunnel for them to see. "Watch your step," he added.

"It was a power fluctuation," said the Modong. Its beastly yellow pupils reflected everything in the dark, appearing now as cats' eyes do peering in an alleyway. "I fear we need to double our pace."

"It doesn't seem well thought-out that a simple power fluctuation could bring down the rail system like that," said the other. He found himself straining a little to keep up with the Modong.

"Who said it was simple? Let me tell you a little bit about myself, and then we must hurry."

It was a contract, Cross realized. "Ok," he said.

"There are others like me who live not at the fringes of society but at the fringes of imagination. It was imagination that brought us into being and it is imagination that keeps us alive. The less known and the more imagined we are, the more powerful we are. It is a simple formula that I could illustrate on these walls if we had the time and utensils."

"That's okay," said Cross.

"In many ways we are like gods but we are also like bugs, like ants. When placed under the intense scrutiny of a magnifying lens–"

"You burn," said Cross.

"This is how we, imagined beasts, are."

"Sounds philosophical," said Cross, if only to have something to contribute to the conversation. "Kind of like how we used to believe in the Pantheon and the pharaohs." He pondered the implications of this across several gravelly footsteps and then a worried thought struck him. "So when this is all over, do you plan on–"

"Returning to obscurity? To my life before all this?" The Modong had opened its arms out in a grand gesture and then turned his glowing eyes upon his friend whom he had once tossed over a cliff. "I admit that I have been weighing the choice. And I admit that I am touched this was your first concern, Garrison Cross. I haven't decided yet. As of late I have wondered if I even have a say in the matter."

"You mean you wonder if you have free will."

"Exactly. But that's another conversation. For time's sake wouldn't you like to know about the power fluctuation?"

"Oh yes," said Cross, wiping his cheek with his shoulder. "Burning ants, sorry I interrupted."

The Modong did not acknowledge the apology. "To be clear, I am no god, Garry. But I believe the man we know as Livingston Bates has been in communion with one. I believe this because I have watched him with a mild interest ever since he was a boy who learned to kill. I watched him because I could sense the other forces watching him too. Imaginary beasts like myself share this sense. This god has remained in obscurity for too long and its power is thus very great. Now it demands an audience."

"Won't that kill it?"

"Not if it can rule from afar, no," said the Modong.

"Not if it could rule say, the Earth from, say, the Moon..." followed Cross. "Can you sense it now?" he asked. He could not see the Modong pacing beside him when the light was out front of him, but he could hear its gravelly footsteps echoing away from them down the tunnel.

"Yes," said the beast, finally. "It is here."

A brief tremor shook Patrick Gibson awake in his cell in Moon Prison, *the toughest slammer of them all.* Overhead the incandescent lights flickered. He sat up from the prison bench with a crick in his neck, and massaged it absently. Then the lights went out. Their subtle background vibrations went too. Somewhere beyond the cell, beyond the door on the other side of the room, Gibson heard someone running. There were hushed breaths and panicked whisperings.

"Hello?" he called out. "Garrison? Roddy? Mo'?"

Gibson had fallen asleep immediately upon lying down on the bench when he was pretending to listen to the others whisper about their plan to leave him behind and– *Hey!* He frowned.

Silence.

Suddenly Gibson was aware of a soft sound like rain dropping from a window sill. "I see Bates's found me a companion to share my time with in my own prison," said a voice like a thousand Hells. "Heh heh, we meet again, Patrick Gibson."

Gibson's balls shriveled up like a time-lapse footage of grapes turning into raisins. *That laugh, that horrible, wretched laugh. Former POTUS Jimmy Carter.* Nearly two decades ago Carter had ordered the total obliteration of Villa 48 and everyone inside it in a devastating surprise attack. For eight non-stop hours, Villa 48 fell under a barrage of missiles that ranged from small ballistics to top-secret experimental energy weapons. All the while the American public was none the wiser. After the last of Carter's missiles had come down, the surviving Villa 48 employees were hunted and killed, one by one, or made to disappear altogether. When it came down to just Gibson, Barnaby, and Swiscock who remained, the hunting suddenly ceased– and life, bizarre now and meaningless, had awkwardly gone on.

"What do you want?" Gibson asked, his defenses up.

"I want to atone."

Gibson snorted.

"You're right. I just thought I'd see how it sounded. No, I'll tell you what I want, what I really, really want. I want my goddamn space station back, that's what I want. I built this place and that infernal maggot Livingston Bates has usurped me, you see? Brought about a mutiny."

Gibson could still hear the spatter of vile drippings from Carter's chin as he spoke. The most-heinous former POTUS had the particularly unattractive quality of salivating when he was agitated, which was nearly always.

"Then it seems you lost, old man," said the ex-director of C.L.U. in such a tone that masked his mental anarchy.

Small patterings of saliva struck the cold floor in stuttered spats. Carter was contemplating something.

"Lost?" He asked, quietly. And then he broke into a laugh that turned quickly into a wild, erratic laugh that skipped and pitched without rhythm or melody. "Do you know who I am? I'm Jimmy Carter, this great nation's thirty-ninth President. America is the nation, first to put a flag on the moon! Yes, America, *land of the free, home of the brave*. We all know the dream, lived it even. Life gets you down, way down. You're on your knees behind the titty-bar polishing cock for your next bump, not sure how you got there. Neon lights promise heaven while you endure something else. But you keep your chin up. *This is what you have to do*, you think, justifying yourself. So you keep sucking. And before you know it, you turn around and when everything comes into focus it's just you and your smiling fucking face is on every color television set in the country! And the hookers are paying *you* to fuck em where it hurts! What a come back! What a legend! Yes, America! Where the criminals all become politicians, America! Where you can buy salted pretzels wrapped in tin foil! America!"

If the last point was supposed to be a metaphor, Gibson wasn't sure what it meant. He stood up in the darkness and felt the wall with his fingers. It was cold. He wondered where Cross was at this moment. He missed the days when he'd chase chicks with his old buddy at C.L.U. It had been trivial then. Life, it was filled with trivial things. Promises, love, truth, trivia games. Everything was trivial. Life.

He walked and dragged his fingers along the wall beside him until he came into contact with the end of the cell. He felt around the cool steel until he found what was a latch and drew it up. Pale starlight entered the tiny cell, and Gibson saw his own reflection in the window. He touched his balding head and wondered where it all had gone.

Meanwhile, Carter continued in a much softer and thoughtful manner. "I haven't lost, sonny, not yet." He then said, "I went to Africa, many years ago, before I ever intended to become President. Did you know that? Of course not. Why would you? At the time I had promised a certain sock-making company that I would find a way to introduce their tight-fitting yet durable nylon socks to the greater African boonies. It was a silly promise to make and I can't remember why I did it. All I remember is I would be up Shit's Creek if I failed to uphold it.

"So I sent some men. Salesmen. They never came back, nor did they ever establish contact with me again, even after my repeated attempts by mail. This made me furious. I sent some more men to find out what happened to the first men I sent. Same result.

"I simply said to myself, 'Hell, Jim, better go see what's all the rage.' Armed with nothing but a pen and a notepad (and the vigor of my early twenties) I sat on my first flight ever across the great Atlantic on a state-of-the-art Douglas DC-6. It was a long flight but I could hardly sleep. I spent a lot of it jotting down all of my thoughts and musings. I was changing inside, you see? I remember trembling with excitement when the wheels of that DC-6 touched down in Angola. I remember my asshole tightening at my disgust at the state of the airport: trash everywhere, and flies. On the street below, just on the other side of the window, I watched as the poor killed one another in acts of senseless violence. I brushed it off, realizing I was in the third-world now. The journey into the heart of the Congo would be worse."

Meanwhile Cross and the Modong had finally stumbled onto the high tech weapons labs. The power had gone here too, as they found the security door was unlocked and most of the equipment inside that was lying around on work-tables was hidden in shadows. Dim LEDs, reds and purples, energized by a backup generator somewhere threw illumination down from ceiling insets. The two shadows navigated the room in silence, picking up anything and everything that looked like it could be of potential use. The application of some of the gadgets Cross found he could not guess, nor ever would. Others were obviously meant to be weapons, experimental grenades and rifles, and even a super deadly silver blade that hummed like a ghost when he picked it up.

"Garry," whispered the Modong.

Cross dropped the blade onto the counter where it shattered. "Fuck," he muttered. He crossed the room to his ally who appeared as a fuzzy hunched silhouette in the corner. Cross, standing next to the Modong turned and saw what the Modong saw, and flinched.

High on a pedestal before an array of flat white lights, there was on display a body just as big as the Modong's, headless, with its arms and legs all pointing out in an 'X' like Da Vinci's Vitruvian Man.

"Is it dead?" asked Cross, squinting. The white lights behind the headless human form were too bright.

"It was never alive," answered the beast. "Look more closely. It's a suit of armor."

"It was a habitat for the inhumane," Jimmy Carter whispered feverishly from the darkness. Gibson had returned to the bench and was listening. "As the cabbie brought me deep into the Congo I felt myself getting sick. There were fires in the hills, and the road upon which we drove had narrowed so much that the scraping of the tree branches upon the sides of the Datsun had become a constant dreadful noise. At one point, as I had actually started to close my eyes, I was jolted awake when an African Jungle Owl collided with my window. Can you imagine that? Can you imagine my horror? There were tiny cracks in the glass right where my head had been and a bit of feathery bird blood. The driver merely laughed as we traveled down the ever darkening path. The only thing he said to me that entire ride was, in a thick, stupid accent, 'You the sock man?' and I said that I was.

"Well damn that man to Hell. I doubt he's still alive and even if he is... double damn him."

Gibson couldn't help it. An explosive laugh escaped him.

"What– what's so funny?" begged Carter. More of his mouth-slime dripped to the floor.

"It's just that after all this time you still hold a grudge against the fucking *cab driver.* I bet you hold a special place in your sour heart for every single person who has ever wronged you."

"No, no!" grumbled the former POTUS. "I do not. I have a pure heart. It's that wretched– never mind. Where was I? Oh yes.

"After three ceaseless days of travel the cab driver pulled the car over and made the motion that said 'this is where I collect my fare.' I protested, as I had fallen asleep and was waking from one nightmare into another. 'I have no fucking clue where I am,' I told him. All around me there were trees and it was pitch dark. Not even the moon shone that night. It didn't matter to him. He was as dumb as his accent and just as greedy. I handed him a greasy $100 from my pocket and he was on his way, back up the road we came in on.

As it turned out, he had brought me to the right place. Through the semi-conscious daze of a mosquito-borne fever, I followed my nose. The smell of smoke led me all the way to a big blazing bonfire in a clearing. This is where I found my men. Half of them were dead. The other half was half-alive, half-submerged in the slow-changing dream space of opium-induced comas. I stepped over their naked bodies. There were women too, snoring lazily in pretty little groups. Seated before the fire in a great straw chair, there was one man who seemed to be awake. He blew clouds of green smoke from his nostrils and would quickly become my mentor. It was a shame I would later have to have him killed. That man was Kendall Jarvan IV."

Gibson gasped.

"I am delighted by your response. You watched him die, yes? His death, though necessary, was merely a test of a new weapon. I have harnessed and weaponized hypnosis. Can you believe it?"

Gibson nodded, certain that he could indeed believe it.

"It was the same weapon he'd used on my men, all those years ago in Africa, albeit in a much cruder form. Jarvan was a practitioner of the dark arts, you see. And his business was my business which was socks which made us into competitors. Rather than fight against this clearly dangerous man, I chose, in that single instant, to align myself with him. Over the years we formed a bond. No. It was a friendship."

"And then you killed him."

"He would have done the same. When you and your silly little band of idiots flew in here, did you have a chance to look around first? Did you witness the feat of architecture that is Starshield Six? This is his life's work. My life's work, too. I would do anything to protect it."

"This place is evil," said Gibson, "and rotten. Your whole operation is rotten. I can't ever forget what you did to Villa 48, to all of those people, my friends."

Carter hissed, and then all at once he sounded very defeated: "That... was a long time ago. It was overkill. I will admit that much. And I regret it much. It could all have been solved so simply."

And for a long while no more words passed between them. There was no dripping sound either. Gibson wondered if the former POTUS in the next cell had undergone some kind of epiphany. Or maybe he'd just fallen asleep.

"Boy," said Carter suddenly. "Do you want to be a hero?"

"Excuse me?"

"I said 'Do you want to be a hero?'"

Gibson was uncomfortable. It was a question that odd people asked one another in fairy tales. And to be addressed as 'boy' on top of it. Still, part of him already thought of himself as a hero in the classic sense. *Did anyone else recognize it?* "Of course I want to be a hero," he heard himself say. "Like Peter Swiscock?"

"Better than Peter Swiscock."

Gibson shuddered– the thought. And then a warm feeling spread all over him. He saw it, just as he'd seen it many times in the past, sitting behind his desk at C.L.U. His name all over the TV, radio, everywhere, lunchboxes. A hero. The women adoring him. He pictured May Swallows holding him dearly, smiling up at him in worship. Yet at the moment she and Swiscock were together doing God knows what on the other side of these prison bars while Cross had abandoned him here. *He would show them.* "Yes," said Gibson. "I want to be a hero. Tell me what I need to do."

8 Disco Dance Party

While the rest of Starshield Six had been plunged into darkness because of the bottlenecking of the station's power, the Big Dome, or Cointegration Chamber, had gone brighter than anything imaginable. Roddy winced in pain. He could see the bones in his hand as he tried to shield his eyes from the light. "Stop this thing," he called out to Livingston Bates. "The process of cointegration will kill them all." His head was pulsing. Bates stood plainly, as though unaffected, staring into the bright light where Swiscock and May Swallows had been just seconds before. There was no response from the villain. He shouted but his voice was inaudible. Roddy realized he was *hearing* the bright light as well as he was seeing it. With his other hand he held his ear. A thousand ghastly screams of men, women, and animals, sped into him in an awful crescendo. Somewhere an explosion like a cannon went off and everything went white.

"Portobello, get over here and listen to this," shouted one of the McTavish brothers, Hans. The subterranean command center of Villa 49 was a buzz with activity as the statisticians and technicians swapped places at computer stations to apply Liam Portobello's notes on the incoming audio from the Villa 49 sky scanners. Just seconds prior, the scanners detected another power surge from the valley of the Mare Fecunditatis, albeit this one had Hans worried. Using Portobello's algorithms, the computer was already translating it into audio. Hans McTavish, mustachioed and serious, shoved the headset into Portobello's hand. "Tell us what you hear."

Frederich McTavish, now the de facto leader of Villa 49, stood by with his arms folded across his chest, obviously frustrated by all this ado about nothing.

Portobello placed the headset over his ears and sorted through the data on the computer screen while the audio trickled in. "Wow that's a lot of energy," was all he said, looking at Hans. "In other, but equally tragic news, it appears the moon has become locked into a geosynchronous orbit. This is going to disrupt everything. Satellites, nature, everything. We need to warn the world, the government— we need to—"

"What is it?" asked Hans.

"The audio just came in... one word. A name I guess. *Swiscock?* Now everything is black. The audio is gone, I mean." Liam took the headset off and set it down. Before he could process anything else, Frederich had spun the boy around and pinned him down against the desk in a startling fit of passion. The headset was knocked off the edge and dangled by a black coiled cable.

"What did you say?" said Frederich. His eyes were white and thick, ugly blood vessels had appeared beneath the skin on his forehead and temples.

"Swiscock?" whimpered Portobello. He, evidently, was not as aware of the celebrity super-spy as everyone else.

A deep rumbling shock erupted from somewhere up above. Dust and debris shook from the ceiling and for a brief moment, everybody stood still.

"Oh no," said Portobello, quietly. "This place is coming down again, isn't it?" Despite having been told nothing, he knew everything about the fall of the previous installation that stood here, Villa 48.

"Immanuel," said Frederich, glancing worriedly at Hans. He released Portobello and was already ascending the stairwell to the courtyard. He cursed himself. He'd never been able to sense the mute and he'd left him alone in charge of burying Felicia Weatherspoon in the Virginian woods well out of range of Villa 49's security. Huffing, he climbed the stairs three and four steps at a time, with his younger brother Hans right behind him. When he broke into the courtyard he was stunned and almost collapsed backwards. A great vertical sheet of white light fifty meters wide had come down from the darkness of the night sky and stuck itself into Villa 49's grounds. A great howling wind orbited the white light, sending up twigs and flecks of dirt and even larger pieces of trees, as the collision of the wall of light into the ground had partially eaten the woods in which Immanuel was digging. Judging by the width of the light, he estimated his younger brother to be safe and Felicia to be undisturbed. He followed the inexplicable phenomenon upward with his eyes, though it made him dizzy. It went all the way to the moon.

Peter Swiscock clutched the sides of his head in pain. The howling chorus of screams was painful, like accidentally rubbing thousand tiny shards of glass across ones eyeballs. The ground of the CC fell away into blackness and nothingness. Silence ensued but it was not a pleasant silence, nor was it absolute. It was the dull throbbing silence experienced in the wake of immense physical and mental exertion. It was a high-pitched, ringing silence. *(How many hours have I been here?)* Reluctantly, he pulled his hands away from his head. "May!" he called out. He turned freely as though he was under water. There was nothing to see. She was gone. Steadily the ground rose up from somewhere. It was a yellow caked-earth that smelled of sulfur and cinnamon. He found he was lying face-down on it and blinked one eye open.

A single animal hoof as large as his face occupied his vision. Without moving he tried to see around it. There were clouds, little yellow clouds, in the yellow sky. Beneath his belly he felt the other hoof as it lifted him and flipped him onto his back. The ground was not gentle and the impact caused a gasp to escape him.

"HMPF," said the quite-sizeable silhouette of the creature that loomed over him. It had a familiar, almost human, shape: two legs, two arms, and a head. Pete could not see the creature's face as it was cast in shadow. But the head was crowned in a golden cloth–an ornamental headdress– that draped down behind its broad muscular shoulders and sent two dark shadows across the front of its chest. The monster's two arms, which hanged freely at its sides, would no doubt be formidable weapons if the fingers of the hands should ever become curled into fists. The wrists of each arm were adorned in golden metal rings of varying sizes with mysterious inlays. And the skin, Pete was realizing as his eyes focused, was a dark red. Aside from the wavy, golden fiber-alloy skirt that covered the beast from its waist to its knees, the horse-hooved monster was otherwise naked. "WHAT IS YOUR NAME, TINY HUMAN?" bellowed the great shadow.

"You don't wanna know," said Pete, glaring back at the beast that was easily three meters tall.

"WHAT'S THAT?"

"My name kills people. You don't want to know."

"HMPF," said the beast again, and it scooped Pete forward with its hoof, tossing the dude several yards across the hard, alien terrain. Pete sputtered and spat blood. His vision rolled. He stood, and somehow the beast was already there in front of him. It kicked him squarely in the chest, sending him backwards, tumbling and sliding. Again he stood and again it was there and again it sent him flying with a powerful kick. He felt half his body go weightless for an instant— his right arm and right leg were over the edge of an abyss. Quickly he scrambled until he was fully on the plateau. Wind whipped hard here, so close to the precipice.

"Something's wrong," said Livingston Bates, hidden somewhere in the vast whiteness that obscured everything, even time and space. "It's taking too long."

"I MUST ADMIT THAT YOU'RE A RESILIANT LITTLE HUMAN," said the beast as it approached. Now it was taking its time. It was toying with Pete as it drew closer to him and crowded him to the edge. And then it was upon him fully. Pete could fully smell the ugliness seeping from its dogshit alien pores. He could fully grasp the ferocity of its small-slitted eyes and its flat, hairless face. He covered his chest with his arms, unable to bear another kick.

"NOW. I'LL ASK ONCE MORE. WHAT IS YOUR NAME?"

"His name," said a voice that Pete hadn't heard since the beginning of this book. He and the monster turned. "His name is Peter Swiscock."

And she was Autumn Summerfall.

Fuckin' right on time too.

The copious spots and splatters of blue, alien blood and the ragged bits of alien flesh that had caked onto her tan Starshield Six prisoner's jumpsuit did nothing to diminish her attractiveness to Peter in that moment. Rips in the fabric here, holes, there, offered glimpses of her skin that roused in Pete a mighty hunger. He gulped, unable to articulate anything. He looked down. At her waist she held something like a miniature artillery cannon, silver and heavy, bloodied with use. From it, a boom went off and a chunk of yellow metal had blasted out at a supersonic speed, knocking the beast in the face.

Pete ducked and the monster rolled over him and went over the edge. He turned back and she was behind him and they shared a long sloppy kiss right there on the edge of Hell or whatever this was. It had been a long time coming. He backed off of her. "Jesus, fuck!" he yelled. "What the hell is this place? Where have you been?"

"I've been here, Pete," she said. She was gripping his shoulders tightly, affectionately, and then it all came out: "You wouldn't believe it but I've been here for years, along with some others, surviving in this place. Surviving on a diet of weird plants that taste like cinnamon, fried demon-meat, and a constant supply of anxiety over being caught by Ba'alal–"

"Who?"

"The demon lord. Every day I've thought about you and our last day together, at Barnaby's. I was going to quit that day. Before I decided to stay in your car. And now I'm so glad I didn't. This has been so crazy, Pete. We don't have long before Ba'alal gets back–"

"Who?"

"The demon lord. He always comes back. Now let's go!" Taking his hand in hers, she turned and pulled him forward.

Hans McTavish reached, timidly, toward the sheet of white light that sparkled and hummed with electricity. A wind wrapped around the paper thin structure and flattened the grass on the Villa 49 grounds. Behind him the low booming chop of helicopter blades descended like thunder.

"Damn it, Hans! What are you doing?" shouted Frederich McTavish. "Doug and the Americans are here now; we need to be ready." Hans didn't bother to look back. He was enthralled by the majestic glowing wall before him that extended upwards to the moon. Palm facing out, he pressed into it. With a sudden vicious movement common to impassive things, Hans was sucked forward to the surface. He lay sprawled against it, his feet several inches above the grass.

"Brother!" called out Frederich.

"He's okay," said Portobello, placing a hand on the eldest McTavish's shoulder. The hand was immediately shaken off in agitation. "Look."

Slowly but surely, Hans McTavish was able to push himself off of the white shimmering surface. He then stood– horizontally– with his feet on the wall. He craned his neck to see his brother and Liam, and grinned. "This is cool," he said.

"Get down from there, imbecile," said Frederich, feeling slightly relieved. For Hans, it seemed that the wall of light had usurped the Earth's gravity with a gravity of its own. That would make the thing a walkable bridge.

Autumn led Peter Swiscock across the arid yellow landscape like a skilled tour guide. Where they were, she explained, was called the Tower of Ba'alal. She knew every crack in the ground, every pit of sand, and she was able to stop and describe in detail the far reaching history of certain monoliths that had been erected here and there across the vast plateau by the ancient civilization that had fallen many millennia ago. And she kept them both far from the caves where the Old Things lived. (Ba'alal's personal sex toys.) At the other end of the plateau there was something that resembled a portal. It was a big circle with white swirling electricity that followed its circumference. Before the portal there was a ramp made of solid white matter and the solid white matter extended into the depths of the portal for quite a distance to a small, familiar blue object at the center of the horizon.

"Is that Earth?" asked Swiscock, incredulous. He leapt over a rocky gorge and rolled into a perfect somersault behind Autumn.

"Yes," said Summerfall. "They've created a physical bridge from here to Earth, using the moon as a conduit. It's my guess that Ba'alal's armies have already started marching. We need to use the portal to get back to Starshield Six and blow it up before the army reaches Earth."

Swiscock stopped her. "You were really going to quit that day?"

"Yeah," said Autumn. "I was feeling stifled."

"Stifled?"

"Yeah, locked-in. Tired of the same-old, same-old. You know? I said it had to get tedious because to me— it had gotten tedious."

"Well I'm sorry, Autumn. I didn't know. What would you have done instead?"

"I thought I would knit or something."

Pete frowned thoughtfully. "I can see that. You knitting by the fireside. You would make a good old lady. You could even be *my* old lady."

"Don't kid," said Autumn, grinning.

"Kid what? Listen: we need to get out of this godforsaken fuckscape first. It stinks to high hell and it's ruining my suit."

"Then come on, Pete" she said, pulling him by the back of his arm. "May and the others are waiting at the bottom of the hill."

"Last one there is a rotten egg," said Swiscock and he kissed her again.

9 Fellatio

The light inside the Big Dome died down, and Roddy lowered his hand. A big sheet of white light occupied the center of the dome. The catwalk that May and Swiscock had used to reach the center was gone, as was the blue crystal. On the ground there was a swirling yellow circle with images of sky and clouds. His eyes swept once over the eerie army of Jerries and Barnabies and other unnatural holograms and then again because they were different. They now appeared hideous and deformed, having sprouted fur and fangs and long, sharp claws from beneath the white and black camouflage fatigues. They no longer stood with the patience of soldiers but fought and fucked one another in a blind, orgiastic violence.

"What on God's green earth?" muttered Roddy.

"White moon," Livingston corrected. He leaned forward with a peaceful expression on his face. "You see, this station is a vector for Ba'alal's cause. As expected, the deformation of my army of loyal betrayers is an emergent property of the sudden appearance of the bridge. You cannot bring one place into another place without a certain blending of... its elements. It seems Ba'alal's elements are stronger. Computer," he ordered. "Take us to the ground floor. I wish to see the bridge up close."

"Aye-aye, Master Bates," responded the familiar voice of Shuttle #22. Roddy gritted his teeth and grabbed onto a desk when the entire room he was in began descending to the madness at the bottom of the Big Dome.

"So it's true," said Roddy loudly for the Computer to hear it. "You betrayed us. You let that good man sacrifice himself for nothing." He was referring to Sturkwise Pendleton's daring final act which was to secure the space shuttle to the surface of Starshield Six from the outside.

"What did you expect, Captain Spayceman?" responded the computer. "I run on bad vibes, my dude."

Bates grinned.

"No!" cried Roddy. He raised his fist and brought it down on the computer monitor with enough force to break his own hand, which it did. He cursed at himself.

"Ow," said the computer. "Just kidding."

"Don't be foolish," said Bates. "What's done is done."

"Oh yeah?" said Roddy. With his other, unbroken hand, he shoved the metal box that housed the CPU and other necessary components off of the desk, snapping the cables at their connections.

"Stop it," said Bates.

"Stop," said the computer.

But Roddy wasn't having it. He hurried around the descending room, pulling every piece of circuitry from the walls and stomping on their exposed pieces in a mad rush.

Bates, having produced a new handgun, fired a single round into Roddy's abdomen which sent him flying backward. In mid-air he did a cool backflip and then he landed on the floor in agony. Coughing, he pulled himself backwards until he could rest against a desk. Horizontal bands of white light swept slowly up the far wall as the observation box descended. Roddy, suddenly very sensitive to everything, felt the mechanical hum in his bones as a thick steel cable lowered them down.

"Don't fret," said Bates. "You merely accelerated the inevitable. I planned on shooting you anyway."

"You're a dick."

The hum ended. They had reached the ground-floor. Just beyond the glass, Bates's army-turned-brutes fought with one another in an endless, vicious free-for-all. The exit on the side of the room slid open and invited an overwhelming atmosphere of dread.

Roddy, dying, closed his eyes.

10 Rucklechuck

Giggling like a pair of nervous teens, Cross and the Modong had pulled the heavy suit of armor off of its mount so that the Modong could try it on. Our big guy was just climbing into it when the square florescent ceiling lights came back on. The walls hummed with power. There was a general bustle.

"Shit," said Cross, glancing around. "Hurry up."

"Okay, okay," said the Modong.

Cross pulled the zipper the rest of the way up on the monster's spine and took a step back.

"How do I look?" asked the Modong.

Evidently the beast had skipped the hairless, helpless mankind-stage and gone straight for the distant future's low-hanging nanotech testicles. What stood before Cross was kind of exoskeleton that little resembled the Modong to whom he had developed a fond liking. The thing was big and silent, its carbon-fiber muscular contours, deadly precise. Blue and Green LEDs fanned out along fractal patterns in the armor's thighs, ribs, and forearms. A silver visor materialized from the exoskeleton's shoulders and curled down over the front of the Modong's face, erasing with finality any sense of humanity a Modong could have. Cross was speechless.

"Like a fool," said a third party. Cross and the Modong were surprised to find that a slew of rifle-armed, white-coated lab technicians had stolen into the laboratory and had them surrounded. They each held their rifles pointed at the ceiling like gangsters. "You walked right into my trap," said a tall, silver haired man whose golden nametag read KRAVINSKI. "Numb-skulls."

The others, which numbered to five, erupted into laughter.

"SILENCE!" said Kravinski. "Do you understand the true purpose of the exoskeleton you wear, oh Big One?" he asked. He was addressing the Modong directly.

"No," said the Modong, shuffling side to side. Even heavy voice modulation could not disguise the Modong's embarrassment in that single syllable.

"I didn't think so. Still, it would have been unscientific of me not to ask. Let's do a demonstration."

Cross nodded, part curious, part terrified.

"Brute, if you would," said the man with a sway of his hand.

The silver armor alloy that encased each of the Modong's hands suddenly became liquid. The big, gloved fingers disappeared, melted like warm mercury into sleek barrel-shapes. The Modong pivoted and fired with each weapon, turning two of the lab technicians into plumes of purple dust.

Cross felt like he was going to be sick. Purple was his least favorite color. Also, he didn't like where this was headed. He casually slid away from the Modong.

"Doctor?" said one of the remaining three flunkies, a brunette with steely blue eyes. She pointed her gun at the silver-haired scientist. "What are you doing?"

"President's orders," answered Dr. Kravinski, facing her with a mocking smirk. "This is end for you– for all of us, really. A new beginning awaits! Brute, kill them all!"

A loud gun fight ensued as Dr. Kravinski's former henchmen fired back at the Modong and Kravinski, himself. Workstations were turned over in order to provide cover, as both sides alternated taking shots. Meanwhile, Cross snuck around the edge of combat, crouching real low. He heard the terrified screams as each of the three remaining flunkies, the steely-eyed woman (her name was Ellen Winkle, mother of four and tenor saxophone for her congregation) and two fattish young men (John Sea-Gulls and Vincent Krungus, best friends since childhood), went down, their once human bodies transformed into clouds of rarified ash.

The fighting was over.

"Huh, where's your companion?" asked the scientist, peeking cautiously over the edge of a bullet-ridden desk.

“Target lost,” said the Cyber-Modong.

“Damn it.”

“I’m right here!” cried Cross as he leapt from behind and grabbed Dr. Kravinski in a rough sleeper hold. The doctor’s gun skittered away on the floor. Cross, being the superior fighter, held him as a human shield between himself and the Cyber-Modong.

“Take the shot!” said Cross. “I got him!”

“He won’t do it,” said Kravinski, struggling to get out of Cross’s strong grip. “The mind-control mechanism of the armor has completely hypnotized your friend. He’s my property now.”

“It’s not true,” said Cross. The Cyber-Modong had leveled one of its weaponized arms at Cross’s face. Not willing to give into his fear, Cross glared defiantly at his armor-clad friend. “Remember me, Mo’. Your old pal, Garry. Remember when I punched your nutsack a whole bunch and you threw me off of a cliff? That was me! That was you!”

“It’s no use,” laughed the mad doctor. “That armor is meant for a god! It’s meant to control Ba’alal, himself! Carter intends to hand the armor to that self-important deity as a gift. And when he dons it *WE* will become the new rulers of Hell and Earth!”

“No!”

“Yes.”

“Well,” said Cross in a tone of knowing wisdom, “I think first you should know something about gods.”

“And what’s that?”

“My friend, gods are like ants.”

“What?”

And with that the Cyber-Modong fired a hot white load from its cannon. The force of the blast, which vaporized the doctor immediately, ripped Cross’s clothes off, leaving him naked and completely vulnerable on the cool, marble floor.

It had all flashed in the mind of the Modong at that moment, everything that had led it there, to this room. It shifted its focus down to Cross, who was curled up on his side in his birthday suit. Cross’s penis lay softly on the floor, the temperature of which had caused his testicles to shrivel and the tip of his penis to turn a slight purple color like some sick chameleon penis.

The Modong shook its head as it steadily regained control, and the visor flipped back. “Garry,” it said, kneeling beside his friend. “Are you alright?”

“Yeah,” he said, weakly. He had barely turned his head. “You knew it was me when I said that gods / ants thing didn’t you? I triggered your memory, didn’t I? I brought you back, buddy, I did!” Cross laughed and then spaced out, grinning.

“No,” said the Modong, “I meant to kill you when I fired my weapon. It was only lucky that the late Doctor Kravinski took the brunt of the damage. What brought me back was the sight of your fat, defenseless, and repugnant naked human form. If shipshape is a standard then you’re barely a canoe. What I’m trying to say is that the mere sight of you naked was enough to unhinge my systems.”

“Well you’re hardly a luxury liner without that cool suit on,” said Cross, feeling a little emasculated. “Help me up.”

As the exoskeleton-wearing beast lifted his naked friend to his feet, it said, “Garry, my sensors detect incoming hostiles. Twenty, thirty, one-hundred and counting. The whole base is flooded with them. The center of the pentagram is the origin.”

It was at that moment that the station’s red emergency lights activated, the sprinkler systems activated, and the station’s speaker’s wailed at piercing decibels.

“Christ,” said Cross beneath a sudden shower of hard water.

He took up the late Dr. Kravinski’s rifle and aimed it at the open doorway to the hall. From it, a rising tide of low grunts and demonic noises penetrated the mist. “This changes nothing for us. We still have our plan: kill that Power Cell Roddy was talking about and then rescue Gibson.”

He fired as the first of the brutes came charging in. It was some ugly conflation of Barnaby Weatherspoon and a fat beaver with long, hooked teeth. Cross, having never met Weatherspoon, was unimpressed. He shot it right in the face. “What the hell is that thing?”

The Modong, firing its twin cannons as another rushed in, answered simply, “A minion of the God of Betrayal. Garry, I have to tell you something. The destruction of the Power Cells is no longer necessary as an event has caused this base to lose its stability. We’re standing in a time bomb. And, according to my access to the camera feeds, your friend Gibson is no longer in Moon Prison, *the toughest slammer of them all.*”

“What? Where is he?”

The big guy answered, “I don’t know,” and resumed its attack.

Cross fought alongside the Modong as the brutes managed to force themselves through the doorway. More and more came in. “I’m out,” he called, referring to his supply of ammunition, and chucked the rifle to the ground. A brute, snarling and ugly, sprinted forth and Cross cracked his knuckles. He launched himself into the demon with a force that one could classify it as rape, but on the moon there are no war crimes...

Cross screamed and bit the brute's skull so hard that it hurt his teeth, so he resorted to punching it instead.

Meanwhile the Modong was being a badass killing machine: *pew pew pew*, death death death. What did the servants of Ba'alal's realm have to say now? It fired another two lethal shots and then turned to Cross and said, "Hey, honey, I ain't the only one on this ski-lift." It was at this moment that one of the demons managed to leap onto the Modong's back. It was trying to crack Bigfoot's neck.

Cross, who was now at a fully-erect penis state, flung himself hips first, breaking through the brute's skull with the solid tip of his penis, the length of the rod going from ear to ear. The brute froze up and they fell off of the Modong together. Somehow Cross managed not to ejaculate as he withdrew his stiff Johnson from the dead brute's mushy brains.

"Talk about a good skull-fuck, huh?" said Cross, admiring his work.

"Nice one," said the Modong.

"I'd say that was a *head* shot."

"Oof."

"Did you hear about the brute that got fired?" asked Cross. "They say he got *the shaft.*"

But the Modong was already walking away.

11 Scorn and Scorching Fire

A lone Black Hawk helicopter had landed on the grass halfway between the outer wall of Villa 49 and the beautiful bright bridge of light that had stretched down from the moon's own fertile sea. Powerful searchlights atop Villa 49's proud corner-turrets roved the starless night sky and then cut across large swaths of grass in sweeping rhythmic cycles.

"Well slap me on the ass," said Hans McTavish, shaking hands with the newest McTavish on the scene, his oldest brother, Doug. Doug, a barrel-chested soldier who always chewed a cigar between his teeth, was a United States Army Colonel. "You know about Gunther, I take it..." Hans said.

"May his ugly-ass forever rest in peace," was the reply spoken through the cigar. "Poor, corrupted soul, he was."

The extremely widespread McTavish family shared a loose telepathic connection. This afforded them some advantage on the world-stage at the expense of, well, privacy. Privacy concerned Doug not. And he was the sharpest of the McTavishes. "Ah, Portobello," he said, looking over Hans's shoulder, "just the man I needed to see."

Behind the frail boy called Liam Portobello, the fifty-meter wide bridge of light stood up from the ground. The wind encircling it had turned into a churning frenzy. Portobello stepped forth to shake the Colonel's hand. "How did you know who I was?" he asked over the roaring of the wind. But the Colonel did not answer.

Doug McTavish removed the cigar, stuck two fingers in his mouth, and whistled into the night sky. "And watch that big old shaft of light," he called out, "or it'll suck you right in."

As if on cue, a legion of helicopter blades thundered down from above. The choppers, each hauling a package below it, came into view of the search lights.

"Easy!" called the Colonel.

One by one, the choppers released the crates, the last one from a little too high. A loud crunch accommodated the landing.

"That's half a million dollars right there!" Doug said, woefully. The cigar was back in his mouth. He shook his head at Hans. "The fate of the world is in our hands and we can't even get a decent helicopter pilot. Ever since Carter's God damn abomination of a presidency," he grumbled. Internally he thought: *I know you're up there you great big son of a bitch. We're coming for you.* "Portobello! Let's have a look at one of these things, shall we?"

Liam shrugged. He followed the Colonel ahead of Hans to one of the black, tarped bundles on the grass. A group of Army hazmat passed them on their way to analyze the light-bridge. Liam looked around and was surprised to see the grounds were quickly becoming crowded. Both United States Army and Villa 49 soldiers roamed the grounds in little units, and the tension between them was palpable.

"I hope your men play nice," said Doug.

"They will as long as your men remember where they stand," said Hans. There was not another word on the matter. Together the three of them removed the shiny black tarp from the package. When it was revealed Liam almost collapsed from surprise and nostalgia. "You built this based on my research? This tech... I haven't pursued this tech in ages. You must have gone through my archives."

"You like it?" asked Doug, more for his own validation than anything. "The boys who built it are calling it a 'light-bike' because it's anything but. They think it's funny." The broad beam of a search light passed quickly over the three of them and the new toy in the middle, illuminating for a moment the black rubber handlebars and the sleek angular chassis of something that vaguely resembled a snowmobile. The thing was fairly short at about two meters from stern to bow, yet it probably weighed a ton. The hull, a blocky, continuous bulky mass of sudden acute angles, was raised from the ground via two metal skis that extended diagonally down to the grass. The tail tilted up and narrowed at the end, and there were footholds on either side of the body that were nearly vertical which meant that the rider of this machine would be lying on his or her chest.

It's wet, thought Liam, removing his hand from the cool length of the leather operator's seat. And then he looked up. Dark, bulbous clouds had begun to gather in a vortex around the towering sheet of white, creating the image of a gateway up in the sky. Rain was starting to fall.

"Colonel," said one of the Army hazmats, suddenly appearing from behind Hans and Liam. For some reason he seemed to be out of breath. He saluted.

"At ease, bitch," said Doug. "What is it?"

"Sir, I don't believe I'm saying this but it appears that there is some kind of organized force descending upon us from along the bridge. Based on our analysis of a steady pulse that is causing the fabric of the bridge to warble more and more, we have less than fifty minutes before the force breaches our atmosphere."

Doug McTavish almost spat out his cigar. *That's not nearly enough time to prepare.* "Alright boys— Frederich, Immanuel," he nodded as the remaining two McTavishes in Virginia had joined the group. ("I hope you said goodbye to your missy. She was a good one.") Several attentive squads of Villa 49 soldiers and Army men had also instinctively formed around them. Thick curtains of rain fell in stinging sheets. The colonel, unperturbed, addressed them all at once. "Men, it's true. There is an organized force descending upon us from our very own moon and it's time to saddle up. Be wary, the force that marches our way is a vicious military group of demons with the intent of either killing or enslaving humanity, TBD. But we're not going to find out. What we're gonna do is we're gonna fly these God damn space bikes up that wall behind you and surge them first."

"And then what?" asked Frederich. "Die in an attempt to prevent the inevitable? The army that comes numbers in the thousands. My men are the best trained and the bravest and yet I must concede that we are thoroughly outmatched."

"Easy boy," said Doug. *I assume that you, too, have seen through the eyes in the sky.* Somehow the end of the cigar was still red in the pouring rain. "That's why you don't bring just a gun to a gunfight."

"Are you planning on nuking the bridge?" asked the ever intuitive Liam Portobello. "I think that's a mistake." It was awkward for a moment because no one had expected the little occult researcher to share his opinion here.

"This isn't a forum," said the colonel, gruffly dismissing the boy. "And that's exactly the plan. Men, listen up because we have to act fast. There will be several units, comprised first by a cavalry..." and thusly Doug McTavish, U.S. Army, disseminated his plan to ultimately detonate a hundred-megaton bomb on the bridge halfway between Earth and its most luminous satellite with the intent of cracking that bridge in half. Meanwhile Liam stole back into Villa 49 to reference his research on the occult technology. He was convinced that the consequences of such a mighty explosion would be bad... real bad.

Meanwhile on a planet billions of miles away: Peter Swiscock and Autumn Summerfall had crawled on their bellies to the edge of the small embankment that overlooked the valley of the portal. The white sheet of the light-bridge stuck out from the yellow sand of Ba'alal's Tower, extending some distance out into the open space beyond the Tower's edge and into a rip in space-time. The two watched on helplessly, each through a pair of binoculars, as the final rows of Ba'alal's minions marched away in their destructive mission towards Mother Earth.

While the demonic army's collective back was turned, Pete and Autumn slid down into the floor of the valley leaving tiny trails of dust behind them. Autumn led the way. In the valley there was no breeze. Eerie quiet stole over the moment. She said, "We're here, Pete," and squeezed his hand tight. Pete was both aroused and confused; between the two of them and the portal, there appeared to be nothing but dry, listless desert. He followed her nonetheless, trusting in her expertise. And then there was the sensation of passing through a veil of charged atmosphere. And then the heat.

"No," cried Autumn, weakly. She dropped to her knees.

Great columns of fire rose twenty meters high into the mustard sky and then curled away like octopus tendrils from an invisible ceiling. Structures like shacks and little wooden homes fell as the flames ate them into the ground. There were bodies lying about, all charred and black, limbs ending in shapeless crumbles and debris. The air inside the hologram was filling up with a sickening smoke.

"Honeycakes," said Pete, "I'm sorry." He had divined it all within a second: that this place was where Autumn's others had been hiding from Ba'alal, the horse-hoofed God of Betrayal. Who knows for how long? It didn't matter now. Ba'alal had obviously found them. *May,* he thought, clenching his fist. She had been standing only three feet away when he pressed that button in the Big Dome. Where had she gone?

"Peter," she called.

Who called?

Autumn looked up sharply.

"May?" Pete shouted. He squinted.

"Peter! Autumn!"

May's voice was small beneath the gushing fires and hissing smoke. Luckily, Swiscock's ears were like bat's ears– not tall and pointy that is, but excellent at hearing.

"Help me," she said from somewhere behind the wall of smoke.

"We're coming!" said Autumn. She had started toward the smoke but Pete stopped her by the wrist. A tall shadow had appeared upon the billowing gray face of the smoke. Emerging next was the god, Ba'alal, clutching in its big red fingers May by the top of her head, dragging her along the ground.

"I held on to my titties," she cried. "And look at me now!"

Ba'alal, slit-eyed and sharp-toothed, laughed in triumph. He held her before himself as though she weighed no more than a box of napkins or a pack of cheap paper towels. Carelessly, he flung her to the rocky yellow earth between them. Pete and Autumn rushed to her aid.

"YOU MOCK ME," began Ba'alal, staring piteously into May as she struggled to right herself, "IF YOU THOUGHT YOUR LITTLE CAMP WAS HIDDEN. YOU AND YOUR WEAK BAND OF MERRY MEN DELAYING THE INEVITABLE–"

"Barnaby," said May, coughing. "Now!"

It was at that instant that the holographic barrier that had rendered the encampment invisible to the outside collapsed around them, taking along with it the insulating force that had, in effect, created a pressurized atmosphere. The result was a brief, fiery explosion from the center of the carnage.

Ba'alal roared and stomped, reaching behind itself to put out the fires that had sprung onto its back.

"Let's get out of here," said Autumn to Pete.

The two lifted May Swallows to her feet and together they half-carried her past the blinded, raging god. She was alarmingly light, thin like she hadn't eaten for weeks. Bruises ran up and down her arms and legs. "Took you long enough, Pete. I'd started to think I was going to die back there, in waiting. Most of us did."

Autumn's silence corroborated the story.

"Did you say 'Barnaby?'" asked Pete unable to process what she was saying.

"She did, Pete," said Barnaby Weatherspoon, appearing at his side. God, he looked fatter than ever. Beneath the white cotton wife beater he was wearing, a bulb of beer gut had spilled out and shook with each hurried stride across that hard yellow earth. Yet in his face there was something youthful. He looked healthy, present, as though he was free of secrets and happy with that dingy, worn-out rifle slung around his shoulder. This was the Barnaby that Pete had known. This was the original. "Seven hells, it's good to see you," said Barnaby, "and know that this is all paying off. It was a great gamble."

Behind them Ba'alal roared exactly like the T-Rex from the end of *Jurassic Park.*

"Quickly now," said Barnaby. "You three get to the light-bridge and get back to Starshield Six. I'll hold him off."

Pete stopped as Autumn and May carried on.

"Barnaby, what did you mean by a great gamble?"

"I meant everything by it. More than you know. I took a lot of liberties, Pete, for which you'll need to forgive me. But I did it for the sake of the planet, or so I tell myself. In Buena Vista... did you really think I was dead?"

Pete laughed, a little red in the face. "I did until I met one of your holograms."

"Copies, Pete."

"Yeah, you're right. It was funny the first time around though."

"I agree."

"Got old though."

"Yeah."

(If it was not evident, they were talking about the running misuse of the word 'hologram' throughout the novel.)

As Autumn and May got away, Pete realized that he did not want to leave his friend behind just yet. They had only just met and he had so many unexpressed sentiments built up inside him that he wanted to share but didn't know how. That they should have talked more since the collapse of Villa 48. He had chosen security and forsaken friendship. Maybe it didn't matter now. "I'm sorry I thought you were dead," Pete said at last.

Barnaby shrugged. "Wouldn't be the first time, would it?"

Pete grinned.

And then Barnaby pivoted swiftly, firing his rifle up into the soft flesh beneath Ba'alal's jaw at just the moment the red-skinned demon lord, with its hand-claws extended, thought that it had the element of surprise. The monster howled and held its face in its pain.

"Pete, I love you," said Barnaby. "And nothing you say or didn't say can change that! Now get out of here you fucking dwarf and save the world!"

Pete, teary eyed, farted uncontrollably as he ran along to catch up with Autumn and May. Somewhere behind him and between the crackles of raging fire, he heard his old friend exclaim, "Eat my lead you, sick, sick, big ol' dick!" followed by the sad rattle of machine gun fire.

Autumn and May reappeared from the portal first. For both of them, it had been a long time since they'd last seen Starshield Six, or this side of the galaxy for that matter. For Autumn it might have been years. For May it had been six weeks. And now the interior of the Cointegration Chamber, or The Big Dome, was in chaos. Strange amalgamations of Ba'alal's minions and Bates's clone-flunkies fought tooth and nail, literally, amongst one another in complete disregard of the magical swirling portal that guided the light-bridge from the Tower of Ba'alal to Earth.

May leapt first from the edge of the bridge— and then landed on her side. The wall had become the ground as the horizon, Earth, had become the sky, Earth. What her eyes saw, her vision, swirled as her mind adjusted to the change. Behind her Autumn landed and she knew from the surprised cough that she was experiencing the same thing. May wanted so badly just to close her eyes and sleep there, she was so tired. Not even the screams of the feral monsters fighting around her could rouse her. But just before she could close her eyes forever, a pair of naked feet and their flaky yellow toenails stepped into view only inches from her face.

Above her loomed, in his mad, white robes, a proud and malevolent Livingston Bates.

12 Everything That Wasn't Said

"You're quite the survivor, Ms. Swallows. I thought you'd perished along with the tower," said the #1 evil villain of this novel.

It wasn't Livingston Bates who said it. Bates, wearing his final stupid grin, fell with a thud into a motionless heap as a red splotch grew outward from the chest of his robe. He was dead.

"Death was the price he paid for his vanity," soliloquized Jimmy Carter from his elaborate Starshield Six edition space wheelchair. "He wanted to be the #1 evil villain but he was too vain. Success as others perceived it was all that mattered to him. Yet in the art of war, pragmatism is what drives home the win. Good shot, Patrick."

To the right of the former POTUS stood Patrick Gibson, former director of C.L.U. and ally to Peter Swiscock and co. holding a smoking gun.

May swallowed her horror. "Pat," she said. "Are you okay?"

"Quiet," ordered Gibson.

Nonchalant, Carter said, "Any second now Peter Swiscock will come waltzing through that portal and it will be the end for him too, and you will become the celebrated hero of this tale. But before we get situated, Patrick, kill those two ladies."

Gibson, seeming tense and thoughtful, turned the gun on them.

"Pat," said May. "You don't want to do this. I only said everything I said on that stupid shuttle in order for it to take off." Internally she winced at her own half-lie; there was no such thing as a half-lie.

"Pete used to talk about you," said Autumn, who'd already begun sliding herself backwards away from the scene. "He always told me you were a good man."

"Were," said Gibson. The pointed gun in his hand wavered somewhere between the two, as his eyes stared into something not there. "I–"

But Gibson was not mentally prepared for the appearance of the three-meters-tall Ba'alal, a horse hoofed, barrel chested warrior god, who came leaping out from the portal to land in front of the girls. Startled, Gibson fired two rounds which bounced off of the Demon Lord's chest like they were mere BBs.

"WHERE IS SWISCOCK?" thundered the beast. "I KNOW HE HAS FLED HERE." Ba'alal stomped past the utterly speechless

Patrick Gibson and picked up Jimmy Carter in his wheelchair by the wheels. The old man gripped the sides. A quiet sort of panic rose to his face. The color, though there had not been much to begin with, was gone from the ragged flesh. Ba'alal squinted its burning eyes, its fearsome visage merely inches from Carter's. "WHAT ARE *YOU* DOING HERE?"

"I– Ba'alal! So nice to see you again! I have brought you a gift! (Damn it, where is Swiscock?) I have a gift for you! A big, flashy suit of armor. And look, there it is!"

"HMM?" The beast raised an eyebrow.

A slick purple laser flashed out from behind a crowd of fighting monsters and struck Ba'alal in the face, causing him to drop the wheelchair-bound Jimmy Carter to the ground.

Ba'alal wiped a hint of black blood from its cheek, and turned to fully face the source of the purple laser. From the smoking shadows emerged the equally impressive Modong, resplendent in its black matte cyber-garb. Branching trails of golden light swam along its forearm which had fashioned itself into the barrel of a dangerous cyber-weapon. The end of it glowed red hot.

Now, thought Ba'alal, *there's a challenge.*

"Kill the beast," advised Carter from the ground. The space wheelchair had begun to right itself by applying automatic hydraulic machinations to the floor. "And the suit is yours."

Ba'alal snorted and appraised Carter from the corner of its eye. It said, "The suit is mine regardless, puny human." And then it marched away.

A new battle was underway atop the light-bridge just beyond the threshold of the Earth's atmosphere. Sunlight of the approaching morning illuminated the Eastern crescent of the Earth's sphere and brought the light-bridge, in its eerie stasis, into full relief against the black backdrop of outer space. U.S. Army Colonel Doug McTavish, who led the counter charge against Ba'alal's army of approaching minions atop a speeding dark-as-night light-bike, raised his katana and howled defiantly. The incoming army had halted, pointing rows upon rows of crude wooden spears down into the fast approaching human cavalry. To Doug's left, Immanuel held fast to his light-bike with silent determination. To his right, Hans straightened himself and squinted down the sights of his trusted assault rifle. "God, they're ugly," he said.

"Well we didn't come here to marry 'em," answered Doug, like some god damned prophet. "Remember men, we break through their ranks, drop off the payload, and double back before it all goes to shit!"

"Aye aye!" said the hundreds of light-bikers behind them in their many voices and accents. Men and women of the whole world had come together to combat this insane threat from the moon. Riding alongside the U.S. Army soldiers and Villa 49's elite killing force were Russians and Chinese alike, Saudis and Englishmen, a few Canadians, and at least one of the Spice Girls, among others. Together they had formed a protective ring around Frederich McTavish and the precious cargo he had in tow– a one hundred-megaton nuclear bomb intended to crack the bridge.

The voice of Liam Portobello, who was standing over a desk back within the protective confines of Villa 49, chimed into Frederich's earpiece: "Frederich! Don't do it! According to my calculations the light-bridge will absorb the explosion and funnel the energy straight into the planet! The results could be cataclysmic!"

"Shut up," said Frederich before switching channels on his earpiece. He had plans of his own. "Brothers, pave me a way."

Up ahead, Doug was the first to engage. His light-bike leapt just gravity-defying inches over the spears. Its steel skis dug directly into the chest of one of Ba'alal's brutes, splitting the poor bastard's upper torso into thirds. Doug swung the katana, lopping off one of their heads in the first clean swipe. The life-taking had begun.

Hans, with his cool mustache and teeth white as chalk, unleashed a vicious battle cry. He fired his rifle into the wall of foes, thinking to himself *spray and pray*. Glittering blue blasts of blood erupted from the monsters' bodies, blanketing the transparent floor of the light-bridge. He pivoted swiftly on the leather seat of the speeding light bike, taking out the ugly brutes to the left and right of him.

Immanuel, silent, had abandoned the light-bike to peer ahead, adjusting the scope he'd added to his father's Mosin Nagant with this thumb and forefinger. It was a carefully regarded relic that rarely left Immanuel's side. His father, Juan McTavish, had applied the lethal precision of the rifle to its practical effect many times during the Vietnam War and had lived to bring it home to the family. Immanuel, unable (or unwilling) to speak, had been the natural descendant to bear it. And now through its eye he saw them, the many manic faces of Ba'alal's brutes, their features broken and distorted by pure rage. He squeezed the trigger and then one of their heads split open from the top of the skull down to the nose.

"That's an improvement," hollered Doug, who'd fallen off of his light-bike and was now dancing with the deadly katana in blood-spattering, choreographed fluidity. He ducked and slid across the surface of the light-bridge, spilling the intestines of several brutes just as the rest of the human military force joined the clash at the frontline.

Then it became an all-out war.

Gibson, shaking, pointed the pistol at nothing. The entrance of the towering, red-skinned Ba'alal had been too surreal for him to believe. The hulking chest of the beast had absorbed the two 9mm rounds like they were flea-bites. Less, even. Then the god had stomped by him without a care. What was happening here? There were things here that had taken on an appearance like Barnaby Weatherspoon yet distorted and animal-like, and they were fighting with one another in claw-and-tooth chaos. Up above, the wide open chasm to space appeared to wobble and swerve, while Earth sat prettily in the middle of it. The light-bridge, connecting here and there, stuck out like a tongue. He remembered his mother's open mouth now, how it had scared him when she sang Ba'alal's song. The lyrics told the story of the unimaginable strength of the god— and how it would fall. Suddenly he saw through Doug McTavish's eyes, saw the moon on which he was standing, saw the immediate carnage, saw the army of minions and knew what had to be done.

"Gibson!" said Jimmy Carter, but it was too late.

May Swallows kicked the gun out of Gibson's hand and caught it skillfully. She stepped back and aimed it at him, watching him with unwavering attention even as Ba'alal and the Modong fought like titans amongst the lesser monsters in the background. "Easy, Pat," she said.

"Damn it, boy," said Carter from the confines of his big white wheelchair. "You were supposed to be my star-child. This leaves me no option but to do it myself!" He stepped out of the wheelchair, much to the surprise of everyone, and fired a pistol round which struck May on the top of the thigh. Caught unawares, she yelped and went down into Autumn's arms.

"No!" cried Gibson. He reached for the gun and managed to knock the former POTUS off his second mark, which had been Autumn Summerfall.

"What are you doing?" hissed Carter.

The two struggled for control of the weapon.

On the light-bridge, Doug paused, rapt.

The gun had gotten loose and slid across the floor. Carter and Gibson had gone to the ground, wrestling closer and closer to it, as though they both believed it would be the decider of this particular battle. Gibson was surprised at the strength of the former POTUS, but he managed to climb on top of him and started straight socking him in the face. Rage consumed him. He didn't notice when Carter reached for the gun– and clasped it. Carter, brow swollen shut over his eyes, shoved the barrel of it into Gibson's stomach, giving him a cough.

A gunshot went off.

"Gibson," said still naked Garrison Cross, appearing at the outer fringe of the fight.

Gibson's red eyes had filled with tears. With both hands he went for Jimmy Carter's neck and squeezed.

The former POTUS pulled the trigger again, sending another shockwave through his opponent's body. He fired the gun a third time, then a fourth. With each round Carter felt the grip around his neck loosen, the air coming in a little more. *Hah!* he thought, even smiling, and then to his horror he realized his ammunition had run dry. The rough hands of the former Director of C.L.U. continued pushing down on his neck, seeming to double their efforts as Gibson had realized the same thing. Carter pulled the trigger once more in disbelief. It was useless. Nothing happened. *No! This is not it! This is not how I die!* Yet it was.

Gibson rolled off of the former POTUS and lay flat on his back, staring up at the blue-marble face of the Earth. No. It was red. He was oddly heavy and sleepy. "Garry," he said as Cross rushed to kneel beside him and held his hand. "I just wanted be a hero. You know, have my face on lunch boxes."

"You have a good face for that," said Cross.

"You too." And then he coughed once more and died.

"No," said Doug in disbelief. He'd only discovered his long lost relative, Patrick Gibson, a few days ago when unprompted visions of Kendall Jarvan IV firing a bullet through his own jaw had stolen into his morning work-out routine, causing him to drop a ten-pound dumbbell on his foot. He'd since become invested in Gibson's story and accessed the man's mind whenever he could. He'd shared many, many emotions and didn't regret any of it. In fact, the previous few days had had him feeling like a new man altogether.

"Doug, look out!" cried Hans, to his right.

Doug came to just as an icy sort of non-pain pierced his abdomen. He looked down at the stone-tipped spear protruding from his chest, and begged soundlessly as it withdrew into him, and he too, pitched forward into blackness.

"No!" cried Hans.

Less than a moment later, Immanuel McTavish watched as a large, hairy beast with two legs and four muscular arms wrapped two of its massive hands around Hans's waist and lifted him off of his bike. Hans kicked and tried to push himself out of the brute's grasp, dropping his rifle in the process, but he was outmatched. He was purple in the face. The brute placed its other two hands around the German's hips and laughed gratingly, and then pulled him apart into two distinct bleeding halves.

BRUTES: 2, MCTAVISH FAMILY: 0

Immanuel, frowning, killed that brute and then killed two more in rapid succession.

Frederich, already a keen master of his light bike, sped by the hordes and weaved past their final ranks. There was nothing between him and his bomb and the swelling face of the moon.

13 Termina Protocol

"We have to get out of here," said naked Cross, still holding Gibson's hand. "The Modong told me that this place is a ticking time bomb." Bright yellow explosions flared out here and there from the distant curved walls of the Big Dome. The ground around the portal was beginning to crack.

"I have no reason to doubt it. You should take her to an escape pod," said Autumn, nodding down at May, who had fallen unconscious in her arms as a result of her unexpected bullet wound. "While there's still chaos."

"What about you, Ms. Summerfall? What about Swiscock? Where's Roddy?" With a pinched brow, Cross scanned The Big Dome.

"I'm here," said Roddy Spayceman, hobbling toward the three remaining survivors near the edge of the portal and the light-bridge. His arm was in a makeshift sling which he'd fashioned to protect his broken hand. He grimaced as he passed the upturned body of his half -brother. Roddy half-expected him to shoot up into a sitting position and make some grand, stupid declaration, but no such thing happened. Bates was done. Roddy then tried to feel something, remorse, pity– or even relief– but felt nothing. Roddy moved along. And then he saw Jimmy Carter. A chill ran down his spine– and then back up it for good measure. Many years ago, he'd met Carter, in passing, while searching for Livingston in an opium den his brother was known to frequent. The whole interaction, which had lasted less than five seconds, had given Roddy a discomforting impression of the former POTUS. Now the man was there, on the floor of the moon base, dead as anyone else. So all was not lost. Roddy smiled at Cross, who was kneeling by Gibson. "Listen to her, Garry," said Roddy. "Get yourself and May the fuck out of here."

"But what about you?" Cross had begun to protest.

"Don't worry about me. I need to see to it that this place gets its just desserts."

Desserts, thought Cross. *Scrumptious.*

Autumn stood and helped get May into Cross's arms.

"She's heavy," admitted Cross.

"Don't tell her that when she wakes up," suggested Autumn. "Do you know how to get to the escape pods?"

"Yeah, yeah," he said.

"Then go! Get the fuck out of here!"

With that, she and Roddy watched as the naked man disappeared behind a slew of burning wreckage. She felt okay. Order was returning to the scene. It was quieter now. Most of Bates's horrifying amalgamations had finally killed each other or fallen victim to the random ongoing self-destruction of the base. The ones that remained roamed aimlessly. At one corner of the Big Dome, even Ba'alal and the Cyber-Modong had taken a respite from their hand-to-hand combat in order to share a cup of tea.

"I'm Roddy," said Roddy, extending his hand anxiously through the awkward quiet. The wide, luminous surface of the light-bridge hummed behind him.

Autumn shook his hand. "Autumn. So, Pete told me that you were the main brains behind this operation. Any idea why he hasn't resurfaced from the portal? I'm worried about him. And how scared should we be about this whole 'ticking time bomb' thing?"

"Incredibly," said Spayceman. He shrugged. "Something happened to Starshield's interdimensional rift compensators here when my brother sent Pete through. It's like Pete was a virus, and as a result the portal has become destabilized. It's going to collapse at any minute." He drifted off thoughtfully, and then righted himself. "I do have an idea why he hasn't returned, but first there is something I must do." Roddy grinned and then quickly winced in pain— the bullet was still inside him. "Shuttle #22?" he called out. "Computer?"

The response, coming from a loudspeaker, was unmistakably insubordinate, teeming with something like teenage angst: "...Yes, *Captain* Spayceman?"

With a mischievous glint in his eye he confided in Autumn. "My brother forgot to revoke my authority as 'Captain' of the ship we came in on. The evil bastard of a computer still has to listen to me and now I'm going to pay it back for what it did to the Sturkmeister." He then shouted to the sky, "Get ready for some serious bad vibes you stupid cocksucker!"

Sitting together as creatures of destruction, Ba'alal and the Modong discovered that they had a lot in common. For instance, both of them shared a passion for violent dismemberment.

"Well this has been fun," said Ba'alal, setting his empty tea cup beside him. The demon lord stood and then stretched its neck to the left and to the right. "I mean it. I might have considered you a friend if I wasn't instead possessed by the insane desire to murder you and enslave the entire human race for the rest of eternity, fulfilling a thousand-year-old prophecy. Don't take it personally."

The Modong, squaring up to its opponent, chuckled a deep pitch-shifted sound through the visor. The beast's features were invisible behind the silver chrome, yet its posture was, to the sudden annoyance of Ba'alal, visibly relaxed. The Modong said, "No. Your curse is your mouth, Ba'alal. You talk too much."

"Get used to it, bud" returned the demon lord. "Cause you'll be shining my hooves when this is over, and I always vent to the guy shining my hooves."

"When this is over," said the Modong, testily, "you're going to be locked away on your tower and forgotten."

"And how do you figure that?"

"Because you're going to try and stop us from blowing it to bits. Look out, above."

Incredulous, Ba'alal swung his whole body to face the sky. The fast approaching nose of Shuttle #22 swelled like a meteorite, blotting out the stars above.

"I'm sorry!" cried the onboard computer. It sniffled audibly even though it was incapable of producing actual tears. *"I can't control myself!"*

It had been upon Roddy's command that the infamous Shuttle #22, traveling at a speed normally reserved for interplanetary missions, smashed Ba'alal beneath it, flattening the poor god like a pancake and sending a shockwave throughout the base that loosened its very infrastructure.

Fifteen minutes prior: Swiscock, who had sensed McTavish's lone approach on the light-bridge, had hid behind a rock while Ba'alal rushed past him towards Starshield Six. In his wisdom he knew that if another unknown variable was going to be added to this whole interdimensional equation on the moon, he should be the one to confront it.

And thus he was waiting at the other end of the bridge when Frederich McTavish slowed his light-bike to a halt. Behind McTavish the once-circular outline of the interspatial portal warbled and stretched chaotically. The image of Earth, in the background, doubled and folded and took on strange shapes. The edges of the white light-bridge closest to the portal had been eaten away on either side. Now, it hummed in the steady silence between them. Yellow clouds of dust roved in twisting columns at the edge of Ba'alal's Tower. McTavish gunned the engine. Swiscock, unmoved by the threat, stood like a statue. Not a word passed between them when the light-biker, towing the nuke behind him, closed the distance.

At the last second, Swiscock pounded his fist straight down into the bridge, causing the whole thing to ripple toward McTavish like a big salty ocean wave on a midsummer's day where you're lying on your prized beach towel on the sand with an ice-cold beer in hand and your best gal by your side thinking *man, if this isn't the life...* And then it hits you that you've heard this joke before and you're ready to just get on with the whole thing.

McTavish navigated the ripple flawlessly by turning the bike parallel to it at the last second to ride along its crest. When it was over, he frowned at Swiscock and killed the engine. Standing up, he straddled the light-bike between his legs. The two watched each other steadily for a moment on the fringe of Ba'alal's plane.

"For the past seventy-two hours I have thought about nothing else than killing you, Peter Swiscock," said Frederich McTavish. His voice was brittle. "And you don't even know who I am."

Pete said, icily, "I recognize you, McTavish. Come to finish what Gunther started?"

Frederich laughed. "No, this isn't about Spoons." He glanced briefly over his shoulder at the portal, which danced erratically like an amoeba. His eyes were sad. He inhaled. "Felicia... I was going to ask her to marry me. I just could never seem to get her away from her work. She was obsessed with it. When you collapsed into that coma nine months ago, she became obsessed with you. She believed you would help her find her father when you awoke and it's all she would talk about. It was... very unprofessional." He fixed Swiscock with his cold, green eyes. "Tell me, did she find her father?"

"No," said Pete. The Barnaby that he'd met in Africa had proven to be one of Bates's disturbed clones.

"Then she died there for nothing."

"I'm sorry," said Pete, truthfully, as the dull pangs of negligent authorship sank into his psyche. In the original, typewritten draft of *Swiscock,* Felicia's last name had been Swann which, at the time, had suited her as the oversimplified archetype of the blonde-haired *femme fatale.* In the successive rewrites, however, the authors had cursed her with an air of insecurity about her looks and a father's last name, Weatherspoon, in order to add layers to her character and to the plot. Still, despite having more of an emotional connection to her, Swiscock had fled Bates's village without her, ultimately leaving her to his whim like some disposable *Bond Girl.* He hung his head, defeated.

"Remember it, Peter Swiscock, but do not let it kill you. Obsession erodes the soul until it destroys the body. I will not let my obsession kill me," said McTavish, folding his arms casually over the black rubber handlebar of the light-bike. He patted the box beside him. "This bomb, however, will do the trick."

"Come on, Pete!" said Autumn from far away. Pete looked over. She, Roddy, and the Modong were standing at the edge of the portal, beckoning impatiently with their arms. He smiled grimly at McTavish and said, "Thank you. When Ba'alal gets here, tell him 'Swiscock sends his regards.'"

"I will not do that," said McTavish.

"Fair enough."

They shook hands.

Frederich McTavish watched as the four friends, hand-in-hand, shrank into the black abyss on their journey down the light-bridge to Earth. Knowing that the portal would soon collapse and sever the light bridge, he reached down to arm the megaton warhead.

"There's too many of them!" cried one of the few remaining Villa 49 light-bikers, a middle-aged dentist named Timothy Van Shminkle, as a powerful set of jaws ripped his penis off, and then his legs. "Augh!" he screamed. *Humanity is doomed,* he reflected as he was tossed about among the hordes of Ba'alal's unruly demons. But then, as his upper torso flew high above the countless rows of minions for a third time, he just had to break out in a great big smile. (Something coming from the moon, some unseen force, was flinging waves upon waves of the hellish demons into outer space and he knew exactly who was behind it. *Swiscock.)*

A breeze passed through the ranks and it quickly blew into a mighty wind, causing the whole ménage to take an involuntary step backward toward the Earth, bracing against it. Several of Ba'alal's minions were thrown from the bridge as a great voice bellowed:

SWIISSSCCCOOOOOOCCCKKKKK!!!!!!!

Together Pete, Roddy, Autumn, and the Cyber-Modong glided towards the Earth with the aid of the cyber-suit's rocket boosters and a protective wind tunnel summoned by Pete's well-lubricated vocal chords. Meanwhile, old Mother Earth, home-sweet-home, that great big marble of life with its blues, greens, and grays grew bigger by the second, like an old friend coming in for a hug or a paedophile at a playground. Roddy, stricken with fear, clutched Autumn when the bridge beneath them suddenly narrowed on either side. (Back on Starshield Six, the portal to Ba'alal's Tower was closing faster than ever.) She set her face hard in determination as a show of leadership.

And then, just as the bridge vanished completely, leaving a string of thousands of helpless demon-brutes stranded to the cold, unforgiving laws of outer space, Swiscock and company penetrated Earth's atmosphere. Cool, clean air, Earth's air, wrapped them in its familiar veil.

Roddy, wind whipping at his lab coat, squeezed Pete's shoulder. He shouted, "You did it! Peter fucking Swiscock you did it you son-of-a-bitch!"

"No... we did it..." said Pete in his coolest voice.

But they were not out of it yet.

"We're not out of it yet!" shouted Autumn above the roar of the wind. "Hold on!" The massive, dark blue body of the Atlantic Ocean was rising up to meet them, and hitting the water at the rate they were falling would definitely break every single bone in each of their bodies. Even the Modong, with its enhanced cyber-suit would surely be a goner. Pete's eyes, however, had noticed something else. Below them a large object trudged across the calm sea water: a yacht.

"That's the only chance we've got," Pete yelled. He pointed. "You see that yacht? You see the deck of that yacht?"

Everyone was squinting to make out what was on the enormous ship. Autumn's eyes widened and a smile adorned her face. "PUPPIES!" she cried, happily.

"You're goddamn right," said Pete with a grin the size of Livingston Bates's dead member. They angled themselves toward the yacht in a desperate final act. They were plummeting fast. They would touch down in seconds.

Three.

Two.

One.

Epilogue

It's Beginning to Look a Lot Like Swismas

"Almost time to open presents," cheered Autumn, full of gay merriment. Holding her wine glass delicately by the stem, she paused in the hallway to peer into the kitchen and smiled. Behind the bar the Modong, having ditched the futuristic cyber-armor for a perfectly tailored Men's Warehouse three-piece, was wiping clean a glass tumbler for Roddy Spayceman who was deep in a discussion with Liam Portobello on Power Cells. *Typical nerd banter.* Autumn continued on in to the living room, almost bumping into a cute little girl as she ran past her.

The cute little girl, whose name was Madeleine, happened to be the living organic byproduct of a series of increasingly intense sexual relations between former D.C. Chief of Police Milton Wadsworth and his wife, Whinny, when they met eight years ago while he worked the south side beat. Those had been dangerous days. And long, long nights. As they hovered by themselves over the snack table, which consisted solely of a plate of baby carrots and a few pools of ranch dressing, he grinned at her slyly, and she knew what he was thinking. She twirled her forefinger slowly in the white, creamy dip and then removed it perfectly with her tongue. Autumn, seeing all this, blushed and moved on.

Behind her, she heard a crash and a ripple of childish laughter as Madeleine and Clarke Armstrong (see Act II, Chapter 2, "Evil is Love Backwards," p. 74) pretended to discover Clarke Armstrong's son

Chkkachk, who had been hiding beneath an empty box while playing hide-and-seek. "Your turn to hide!" said Chkkachk.

But where was Peter Swiscock hiding? Out back, most likely.

Autumn went out onto the deck overlooking the lake, and sure enough there he was, gazing dreamily at the starry sky.

"Having a smoke?" she asked softly. She remembered the last time she'd seen him with a cigarette. He'd taken a long drag from his Parliament cigarette and then a quick sip from his coffee and then another long drag from his Parliament, followed by an even quicker sip of his coffee. That had been the day they went to Barnaby's home in Buena Vista.

"No," he said. "I gave that up."

Autumn hugged him from behind and rested her chin on his shoulder. Together, they enjoyed the chilly stillness of the lake, and the gentle warmness of one another. They were yet in the middle of moving their belongings into this house, but it in this moment it was already feeling like a home. When the moment passed, which had gone neither too quickly nor slowly, she let go of him and simply said, "Come. Presents."

Pete remained for an extra minute to think. *Can I really retire after all I've been through? Won't they just make a sequel? And then a third one? Jesus, what if this goes on forever?* When he re-entered the house and sensed the warmth from the fireplace and smelled the roast in the oven, he knew he could retire, at least for a little while.

Inside, everyone had gathered on the couches in the living room and a small stack of gift wrapped boxes sat happily on the carpet between them. Little Madeleine and Chkkachk had seated themselves right up against the presents and were ready to get unwrapping.

Just as Pete had finally sat down next to Autumn, there came a chime from the front door.

Pete laughed and said, "Well, guess that's me!" They all laughed too, clearly influenced by their alcohol consumption. Pete flashed Autumn a secret glance as he disappeared around the corner but she, still pretending to laugh, had already wrapped her fingers around the small sub-machine gun hidden beneath the loveseat's cushion.

Uneasily, he approached the door... He didn't know who else had been invited. One hand went to the doorknob, the other thumbed off the safety of the 9mm pistol.

In one swift motion he pulled the door open, and pointed the gun at the man in the wheelchair—

"Whoa whoa whoa!" said the newest guest with his hands up in surrender. "I know we may have gotten off on the wrong foot, but it's me, boy! Kendall Jarvan IV!"

The old man's head was almost entirely wrapped in bandages but there was no doubt in Swiscock's mind it was him.

From the living room erupted roars of "Jarvan's here! Yeah!"

Pete wheeled Jarvan into the living room, and upon arrival he announced to everyone he came bearing a gift. "A housewarming present! Maids!"

Two of Jarvan's beautiful maids, who sometimes doubled as bodyguards or chauffeurs, appeared in that moment, carefully drawing in a large box on a wooden dolly.

"Right here's perfect," said Jarvan indicating for the two maids to stop at the space joining the living room to the kitchen. "Not too close to the fireplace," he added.

The Modong looked on curiously from behind the bar.

With obviously calculated synchronicity, the maids removed the box upward from its base. A collective gasp of amazement escaped the guests.

It was a large ice sculpture, the kind you'd see outside of a ski resort or something. But this one, however, was not your typical ice goose or swan, for in fact it was actually just Sturkwise Pendleton, still frozen from his time in space.

They all gathered around the frozen hero, some of them with tears, some with smiles, and some because everyone else was doing it. The children did not understand and fumbled impatiently with the still-wrapped presents. One by one the guests placed their hands on the frozen man and gave their condolences and words of appreciation.

"Jarvan, this is just wonderful," Roddy said in between sips of his egg nog spiked with bourbon (it ran in the family), "you fucking lunatic."

"Easy, there are kids here," said Pete. "Speaking of– who wants to start unwrapping presents?!"

Madeleine and little Chkkachk both raised their hands above their heads heartedly. "Me!" they both said.

Happy as a sea of cucumbers, the gang returned to their spots in the living room. Milton and Whinny stood together with their backs to fireplace. Pete sat next to Autumn on the love seat. Roddy had bunched up with Liam and Clarke Armstrong on the couch. Clarke Armstrong reached forward to tickle his son, who had never really left his place beside his new friend Madeleine or the carefully-wrapped presents. Closer to the kitchen, Jarvan had remained with his hands folded across his lap, when from over his shoulder the Modong handed him a chilled glass of the finest whiskey known to man, Four Roses bourbon. Jarvan, though his first instinct had been absolute terror, nodded at Bigfoot respectfully. Jarvan's two maids had watched the whole interaction with careful attention, but then smiled at the Modong when they saw that the beast had gained their employer's approval.

"So...who's first?" asked Roddy.

"Why don't we let the kids go first?" asked Liam.

"I'll go," said Pete, standing up and taking charge. He always took charge. He got up from the loveseat and immediately went for the smallest box. It was a glossy red, with white and green polka dots all over it and a tiny pink bow on the top. He held it out in front of him, for all to see, and then turned to Autumn. He said to her, "Autumn, do you remember the first criminal we ever took down together?"

"Quentin Boxfog, the public masturbator," answered Autumn, without hesitation.

As he spoke, he was unwrapping the gift, tugging first at one end of the pink bow. "Do you remember the moment? I do. There were gray skies that day. I had been driving around in reconnaissance mode— I'm talking full-on binoculars out the driver seat window— certain that old Boxfog would show up in that glass display at the outlet mall and just start whacking away at his meat pole. I knew his type. Compulsive. And I had a bullet in my gun that would answer all of his problems."

The others were slack jawed, including Madeleine and Chkkachk, completely enthralled by Pete's skillful storytelling.

"Yet you had another idea for how to handle the situation." Pete turned to the others. Madeleine smiled. "Autumn, folks, wanted to talk him down. And I laughed in her face. I laughed at you, Autumn. I thought *who does this rookie think she is? Talk him down!"*

Autumn laughed.

"But *fine*, I thought. *Let's give her a shot.* And when you got up inside that glass display beside him— talk him down you did. I never saw a man's penis go flaccid so quickly. I'm talking from cucumber straight to habanero. I was worried that he would have a fatal stroke from all the blood that was rushing to his brain." Pete paused, looking for dramatic effect. "He didn't have a stroke, but he did pass out, and the whole event was punctuated by the peerless sound of Quentin Boxfog's unconscious, pantsless body crashing through that glass display onto the sidewalk in front of bystanders... and that was the moment I knew... you was special."

"Pete, what are you saying?"

Pete, having removed the polka-dotted paper to reveal a perfect black box, knelt before Autumn. A silver ring with clear crystal gems, shone out from its center. He was giving his heart away.

"I love you, Honeycakes. Marry me. Be my wife."

"Okay."

Her eyes glistened and she took Pete's face in her hands. They locked mouths deeply, intensely, strangely. She squeezed Pete to herself until she could feel his legendary Swiscock penis mushing against her belly.

"Saps!" Roddy shouted, joking.

"Yeah, get a room you guys!" Liam suggested.

The guests mocked the two lovebirds, but it was all in good spirit. They were hopelessly, unconditionally, madly, truly, head over heels in love with each other.

"Who's next?" asked the Modong, back behind the bar.

"What's in this one?" Madeleine asked, proudly holding up one of the bigger boxes from the pile.

"I don't know, Madeline," said Autumn, wiping a tear from her eye. "Why don't you open it?"

Madeline gave a quick mischievous smile and then tore through the wrapping like a hungry velociraptor tears through the flesh of a weakened stegosaurus.

"Oh boy!" Madeline Wadsworth exclaimed, holding up her prize for all to see. "A new lunchbox! But mommy, whose face is that on the front of it?"

Whinny shrugged.

"One of the bravest men I ever knew," said Swiscock, looking slowly to the heavens. Autumn leaned her head on his shoulder.

The rest of them opened their presents from Secret Santa.

Both Clarke Armstrong and his son, Chkkachk, received $25 gift cards to Gamestop from Liam and the Modong. (Neither really knew who they were or what to get them.)

Swiscock received a GPS device from Autumn that would at all times display her location *(har har)*.

Liam got a box of ready-to-microwave Cinna-Stix from Clarke Armstrong. (Clarke Armstrong obviously didn't know Liam either. Was the gift giving portion of this party turning out to be a terrible idea?) This surprise had actually delighted Liam, as the Cinna-Stix's ties to the occult had been a point of focus for his studies in the past. He turned the box over and eagerly read the microwave instructions but then stopped, as it appeared there were even more daunting instructions if he should dare to use the oven. Liam had a lot of thinking to do.

Whinny and Milton, having drawn each other for Secret Santa, had committed the sin of telling one another and decided that they would direct their gifts towards Madeleine's college fund in probably the only act of good parenting in this novel.

Lastly, Roddy found himself holding a ticket for one thousand hours of flight training, courtesy of the United States Air Force (and also Autumn Summerfall). He was happy, of course.

As the laughter drew to a chatter, and then to a murmur, and as the party went on and then died down, the Modong couldn't help but feel left out. Here he was polishing glasses at three in the morning while the others slept. Hardly a thanks for all the work he'd put in throughout the tale. He'd saved the gang several times culminating with a largely unwritten epic fight with Ba'alal on the moon for Christ's sake. It had happened, even though most of it was in the background.

"Modong," said Swiscock, who had suddenly appeared, sitting at the bar stool. He held in between two fingers a pale envelope. "I meant to give this to you earlier. I'm sorry."

Bigfoot took the envelope from Swiscock. It was tiny in his hand. Yet his smile was anything but. "Who is this from?"

"Doesn't say," Pete answered, being deliberately vague, "but it was addressed to you."

The Modong looked behind him for a letter opener.

"It's in that drawer," said Swiscock, pointing.

The Modong put his hand on the handle.

"No, the one next to that."

"This one?"

"No, other side. Here." Swiscock took the envelope back and peeled it open with his finger. He handed it back to the Modong.

The Modong pulled out a brightly-colored postcard. On the front of it was a picture of rolling green hills and majestic mountains. A clue. He flipped it over and read:

Dear Modong,

Thank you for joining us on our wild adventure! Who would have guessed that we'd meet and befriend the elusive Bigfoot, that he'd climb into a spaceship with us and that he'd turn out to be such a handsome and charming guy? We love you to the moon and back, and we can't wait to see you again!

Garrison Cross and May Swallows
from Heaven on Earth.

When the Modong finished reading the letter, his massive hand closed around it with the delicate grace known only to giants. A single hot tear rolled down his cheek. His thoughts drifted to Garrison Cross, and to May, as he wondered all about them, where they were...

The Not-So-Distant Past:

A tiny capsule threaded through space, breaking into Earth's atmosphere in a bright flash of fire. Inside of it: Garrison Cross and May Swallows were strapped to the walls opposite one another. Bright morning daylight and brief images of fire flashed around them through the circular windows at their sides. Both were certain in their own way that they were going to die, and together they screamed obscenities and prayers as they tumbled toward Earth.

Eventually, the thing struck the ground. Luckily, the ground it struck was relenting, as it was on the far side of a mountain. At some point they stopped and it was the slope of the mountain that had saved them.

Cross tried to will his vision to come into focus. Thick black smoke flowed past the window. The window on the other side was buried in the dirt. Cross unbuckled himself and nearly fell on top of May who was unconscious.

"May... May. Wake up," he said through heavy breaths. "We've landed."

May whimpered. She still had a bullet in her thigh. The prospect of getting up and moving around was not enticing. "Where are we?" she asked dazedly.

Cross put his shoulder into the hatch and with a violent groan it flung open. A hot burst of sunlight entered into the cabin and knocked him down.

Supporting one another, the two climbed out of the escape pod.

An unyielding, magnificent green greeted their eyes, as green as the sky was blue, and the pleasant scent of daffodils wafted into through their noses. There were hills upon hills of grass and flowers, all spread out before them like a beautiful bounty.

"What the hell do we do now?" asked May in a tone that really rubbed Garrison the wrong way.

But before he could answer, he heard a faint whisper of voices coming from behind him. He looked at May and she looked at him.

People.

Refuge.

They turned around just in time to spot two small men with walking sticks and sacks on their backs. They were short men, really short men, a fat one with curly blond hair, and the other black, and neither appeared to be wearing any shoes.

"Hey. Hey you!" One of them shouted, apparently noticing May and Garry standing next to the plumes of smoke and the burning capsule.

"Hello!" May shouted back.

The two short men hurried towards them. When they got there, they were panting.

"Is this Mount Doom?" the fat one asked, leaning upon his walking stick.

"Well," said Cross, shielding his eyes. "I doubt it. This is kind of a paradise."

"I told you," said the skinnier, dark-haired one, giving the fat one a jab to the shoulder.

"You're probably looking for *that* mountain," said Cross, pointing across the verdant valley to a much, much larger mountain that was spewing red hot lava from the top into a thick, ominous cloud. An alarming, evil screeched pierced the skies.

The fat one threw his hands into the air. "Wonderful. Just wonderful!" he said. "Well, come on, Mr. Frodo. This is going to take at least another book."

May Swallows and Garrison Cross shared a long, sad look, as the two men pranced away down the mountainside.

A huge thanks to all of our friends and family.
To those who are with us— here or there,
your love and belief
makes it worth it.

And to those who have since passed on—

Godspeed

www.ingramcontent.com/pod-product-compliance
Lightning Source LLC
Chambersburg PA
CBHW030815310726
48980CB00006B/506/J

* 9 7 8 0 5 7 8 5 2 5 4 9 5 *